MW01491521

FOURTH AND VICTORY

A NOVEL

RUTH BYRN

BRIGHT FRIENDS PRODUCTIONS

Fourth and Victory/Ruth Byrn.—1st ed.

Paperback: ISBN 978-1-943634-11-8

E-book: ISBN 978-1-943634-10-1

Library of Congress Control Number: 2021915127

Bright Friends Productions

1818 N. Taylor Street, Suite 8, #327

Little Rock, Arkansas 72207

www.brightfriendsproductions.com

CONTENTS

AUTHOR'S NOTE

This is a fiction novel. No character is meant to resemble any actual person, living or dead, nor are the events real, or the settings. There exists a Fourth Street at Victory Street in Little Rock, Arkansas, and I liked the sound of that, but none of this story happened there or in any other actual location.

Cast your bread upon the waters,
for you will find it after many days.
Give a portion to seven, or even to eight,
for you know not what disaster may happen on earth.

Ecclesiastes 11

FOREWORD

This is the story of the time, place, and people of my early life. All of that has gone on now, I'm what's left of it. Much of this story I witnessed firsthand. Other parts I know because one or another person told me or left the tracks behind. The lost pieces, I filled in as I think they must have happened.

M. M. Lewis

1

DADDY TOLD MOTHER HE WOULD NOT BE DRAFTED INTO THE military. This was early one night in January 1941. We three had eaten supper downstairs in my grandmother's boarding house, and then full of good food we climbed the stairs while the two of them had a sort of conversation about the draft. They were side by side on the worn wooden steps and each took one of my hands and lifted me up the stairs while I tucked my legs. Because I liked it. When we entered our two-room apartment it was snug in there because we were between the first floor and the third. Our little gas heater turned low was enough. Daddy thought it was too hot, and opened our one window an inch and told Mother to leave it that way. Which she might do for ten minutes.

"Cesarine," he said, "For God's sake will you stop worrying about the draft. I told you you don't need to. Could you for once just take my word for it and let it be."

He took off his shirt and tie and draped them over the back of the sofa. Down to his sleeveless undershirt and trousers, he dropped himself sideways into our easy chair, with his legs and feet dangling. He pulled his shoelaces untied and pushed one shiny brown shoe off and then the other, letting them clunk to the floor of the little room. He wiggled his toes inside his brown silk socks and moaned. He reached behind his head without looking, feeling for the radio knob.

Mother went to him and caught his hand. She looked down into his face, and said, "I won't stop worrying. You say you know you won't be selected, but you don't know. They could take you away from us any day, Patrick. And then what would I do? What would we do? And you could get killed."

He said, "All right, there's something I'm going to tell you. But you can't tell anybody else. Especially not your bridge friends. Or your mother. I have it taken care of. Here's how it is. Our local draft board has the final say-so on who gets taken. Curtis Haskell knows important men on the draft board. And it's in his interest not to have to replace me at work. Besides which, he's my friend. If my number does come up, and odds are it won't, he'll see to it that my information would get counted the way it should. First, I'm head of a family where the wife has a serious health problem. Second, I'm the only son to take care of a widowed mother."

Mother stood quiet, still holding his hand, thinking.

I was kneeling on the sofa with his shirt pulled like a tent over my head, smelling his nice male smell. I tried to guess the meaning of what he said, but I was just past my fifth birthday. I said through the shirt, "What serious health problem does Mother have?"

"Good God," Daddy said to Mother. Then to me he said, "That's not for little girls to bother with, Sugar. We'll tell you when you get older. It's nothing bad."

I knew that was the end of that part. From them, anyway.

So I stuck my face out from under the shirt and went on to Item Two, and said, "Mama Linnet's not a widow, she's a separated."

He looked at Mother and said, "How could she know any of that?"

I said, "Mama Linnet told me. And in the Bible it says we're supposed to take care of the widows and orphans and other kinds that can't do for theirselves, but she's not a widow. Her husband is not dead. He's My Granddaddy. Someday I'm going to get to see him. He's your daddy, Daddy," I explained, "And she's one of the ones that does the taking care. She takes care of us, too."

"The way it is, is, she might as well be a widow," Mother said to me, walking over to sit beside me and gather me up on her lap. "She's the same as a widow because her husband ran off and left her and your daddy. Your grandfather ran off and left them, and they were about to starve and in debt without a penny in the world. Your daddy was just a little boy."

Daddy stood straight up out of his chair in his sock feet and said, "It wasn't his fault. He couldn't get work. He left because he needed to go look for work."

"Did he find it?" I said.

"Eventually, yes," he said.

Before I thought, I had said, "He wants her to take him back."

"Who told you that?" Daddy said, quick as a whip.

And just as quickly I told what I think was my first lie to my parents. I said, "I don't know. I forgot."

MISS SAVORY WAS the one who had told it, days before, about Granddaddy wanting Mama Linnet to take him back. Miss Savory and Miss Claire had been talking while they worked in the kitchen, which was big and equipped for large-scale meal preparation. There were three deep zinc sinks, three iceboxes, a wooden chopping block, cabinets, worktables, and oversized pots and pans hanging on the walls. Breakfast was over and the two women had done the cleanup for that. They were now into their next task which was slicing a bushel of potatoes and one of onions into white pans for the lunch menu. I was on the other side of the swinging doors, in the dining room, doing nothing in particular. I had too much of that to do.

"He's been angling for Miz Lewis to take him back," Miss Savory had said. "She won't, though, long as he's drinking. At least I hope she won't. I hope she don't believe he's quit drinking. Everybody knows he ain't quit. But the very one who ought to know might not. It's all I can do to keep my mouth shut. You think I ought to tell her?"

"Can you find out if she knows?" Miss Claire said.

"If she did know, she ain't letting on. Never says a word about him, good or bad."

"Does Pat know?" Miss Claire said.

"Wouldn't matter if he did. Mister Patrick's partial to his daddy." Miss Savory shook her head. "He will not see one bit of it, what his daddy's done and still doing. Nor see he's using him, trying to get Miz Lewis to take him back."

"How long have they been separated?" Miss Claire said.

"About ten years, I figure. I been with her five years. Mister Lewis Senior is a master steam shovel operator and one time they had a lot of money. She never worked a day after she married him as a young girl, except in their own house, until they hit the skids. She told me they had so much money saved—and she was the one who saved it, you can bet—the two of them would get out their hundred-dollar bills and just for fun see how much of their bed they could cover with them.

"But then when everybody else got out of work, he did too. He couldn't get work he would take, because he was too proud to do just anything, and after awhile they used up their savings and were down to nothing. He could have worked for the WPA, they been all around here, but no, he was too proud.

"He was so proud, that Mister Hampton Lewis, he wouldn't work for the government, no, nor do common labor to put food on the table for his wife and them two little boys, nor take them to a doctor when they was sick. Nor take any public help. Of course he managed to get enough money somewhere to drink.

"He was so proud, his own child died of it. They had two boys, not just the one. The other one, Mr. Pat's little brother, that little child died of the whooping cough in Miz Lewis' arms because they didn't have money for the doctor and the hospital."

"No," Miss Claire said, stopping her knife.

"Yes. After that child died I believe it took a long time for Miz Lewis to pull herself together. But then she realized it had to be her to do something to keep them alive. And she had to do it against his will, which is against her religion. She likes to stick to what she believes, I don't have to tell you. He didn't want his wife being the breadwinner. And he didn't want charity or borrowing. But she borrowed a hundred dollars from somebody and rented Fourth and Victory and started this business. And then he was too proud to have a wife that supported him, and to boot, she did it by serving meals and washing and cleaning for people outside the family. He told her she had to stop it. But she wouldn't submit to him. I don't know if she threw him out or if he just left.

"Anyway he took his bottle and went off to Tennessee. Now here it is ten years later and he's had good work again up there that he ain't too proud to do, and he wants Miss Lewis to give up this boarding house and go back to him."

MISS SAVORY WAS mouthy and Miss Claire was quiet. Miss Savory was little and Miss Claire was tall. If they had been plants, Miss Savory would have been the wild rose vine in the hedgerow and Miss Claire would have been the willow tree. But they got along like the peas in the pod.

Neither one told enough about herself that you could pin down where she came from or how she ended up in Little Rock, Arkansas.

No, that's not quite right. At the beginning Miss Claire had told Mama Linnet the facts about herself and her absent husband, the father of her twelve-year-old boy Roger/Tian. But telling Mama Linnet anything was like putting it in a lockbox.

Probably Mama Linnet, listening to what Miss Claire said, was already thinking of a way to shelter and feed them, especially since she herself had had the experience of being woman alone trying to provide for a young son.

So Miss Claire and Roger/Tian had room and board at Fourth and Victory in exchange for her work in the dining room and kitchen. They had been there about a year.

Everyone except Mama Linnet was left to imagine whatever they wanted about this mother and son pair, except for the matter of Roger/Tian's race. He was half Chinese and he and his mother both made that clear whenever it came up. Which it did at first. During the time when they were still near-strangers to everyone, people typically referred to Roger/Tian as something like, "That big little half-Jap boy."

And if Roger/Tian heard or even guessed that he was being thought of as Japanese he would lock eyes with the offender and say, loud enough for the world to hear, "I am not Japanese. The Japanese are our enemy. I am Chinese." Miss Claire did a quieter version of that, but she was firm. Whereafter the speaker might call him, "That big little half-China boy," for a while. After they were used to him they called him what his mother said his name was, Roger.

He fascinated me, but I was nothing to him. I complained to Mama Linnet that he wouldn't play with me or even talk to me and told me not to follow him around. She said I would have to accept that because he had the right to be left alone. And she explained that almost no boys his age want to play with little girls.

FROM LATE SPRING to late fall usually one or more of the boarders, and sometimes their visitors, sat out on the porch that stretched across the front of the house. It was on the west side, so they waited until the sun went down enough to be blocked by the houses and big trees across the street.

Near one end of the porch a three-person wooden swing hung by thin chains from the ceiling. At right angles to the swing, against the house wall, there was a four-person red metal glider with no cushions. I learned that grown people only liked to sit two at the most to either the swing or the glider. And they might like to drift gently back and forth but they did not like to really swing or glide fast, even if I offered to push. Also sitting around were a couple of painted-white metal lawn chairs that would bounce you if you worked at it.

Each year as soon as the danger of frost was past Mama Linnet put some of her bigger plants on the porch, in their pots that were whatever she had on hand to use for pots. The plants liked to be near the white wall of the house where they got a lot of light but not the direct sun. People said, "Look at that angel wing begonia. Leaves big as my hand, and just covered with blooms," or, "This here mother-in-law's tongue is almost as tall as I am. She could get a corn stalk to grow in a glass of water."

Except for the seating and the plants, the porch was clean and bare. Mama Linnet said she would not tolerate a trashy front of the house. She directed that someone clean out there at two o'clock every day: sweep the porch and the concrete walk between the hedges from the porch to the sidewalk, pick up any dropped pieces of paper or cigarette butts, and then hose down the swing and glider and chairs and porch floor and the two windows and the two steps, and even the walkway in case men had spat there, but not get water in the flowerpots. Mama Linnet liked to water her plants herself.

Mr. Tony was one of the boarders who sat on the porch that year, starting in late March, which was unusually warm. He was there about half the sittable evenings. His half were the times when other men weren't there except maybe Daddy. Daddy got along with nearly everyone, and if you were one of the few he didn't like, you probably wouldn't know it. He said private sideways things to Mama Linnet or Mother about this or that person once in a while, but otherwise even a good guesser would not suspect his real feelings. Mr. Tony had no idea that the reason Daddy was out there on the porch, chewing the fat with him, was partly to keep on top of what he was up to. He thought Daddy believed every word he said.

Miss Sara Ann did believe Mr. Tony, or at least appeared to.

Daddy said to Mama Linnet one night in the kitchen where she was finally getting to eat her supper, "Sara Ann thinks that fishy Tony Bishop hung the moon."

Mama Linnet said, "Oh well, that's all right, she's just a late bloomer in judgment. She thinks the same thing about one man and then another."

That was one of the harshest things he had ever heard his mother say about anyone, she had forgotten herself, and it encouraged him to go on.

"You're right. She thinks it about men she sees as likely prospects. Not about me, though. Since I'm not a prospect, I might as well be a fly speck," he said.

Miss Savory was just before leaving to go home. She had opened the icebox door to put in the next day's roll dough, and she was stooping and squinting in there, making sure the trays were stacked and balanced. She said into the dark of it, "Jesus send us a blessing and let all fly specks leave well enough alone."

Miss Sara Ann's hair was the envy of other women, or the jealousy, depending who. It was peroxide blonde and she had a talent for fixing it in movie star ways. Up in a roll like Joan Fontaine. Down so it could fall over one eye like Veronica Lake. Neat with a band around it like June Allyson

or Judy Garland. Women complimented Miss Sara Ann but
most of the men didn't know how to say things like that, or
since she was so eager-acting some were afraid she would
think they wanted to go with her. Mr. Tony, though, made
fun of her hair-dos and other things about her after she
started dating him, when he thought it was just the two of
them and no one else to hear. She would cry, and the next
day run after him the more. I heard him call her a leech.

Miss Sara Ann was a school teacher. So was Miss Lucy.
They both said, and it was the truth, that they were lucky to
get other jobs for the summer months when school was out.
Anybody was lucky to get any job anytime.

Miss Lucy worked summers at The Home where her
husband was a vegetable. Mother told me what that really
means.

Miss Sara Ann worked that summer at Walgreens. Afternoons, when she got off work, she went to see her mother
and her little dog who had to live with her mother, she said,
because Fourth and Victory couldn't allow pets. From her
mother's in the late afternoon she came to the boarding
house in time to eat supper, and then re-do her hair and
makeup, and change clothes, before going out with men or
her girlfriends. Miss Savory once said, to anyone and
everyone in the kitchen, that the going with the girlfriends
was so she could be seen where she could meet more men.

Miss Sara Ann had been going out three or four nights a
week until she started dating Mr. Tony. Then she went out
only with him, and that wasn't as much. He may or may not
have had a job. At first everyone thought he did because he
was always gone all day, and sometimes overnight. But he
never referred to it, and dodged questions about it. He did
get money from somewhere, maybe or maybe not from his

family, which is where he hinted it came from. Miss Sara Ann gave him money, Mother found that out. He always paid his full bill to Mama Linnet on time. He paid cash in advance like most of the boarders.

Mr. Tony and Miss Sara Ann made a good-looking couple. He saw to his looks as much as she did to hers. His hair was almost as light as hers and looked more natural. He was medium tall for a man, and she was for a woman. They both had blue eyes. His were normal and looked the same whether he was telling the truth or not. Her blue eyes were big and round and wide open, and so pretty it was a jolt every time she looked directly at you. But he and she were different about their clothes. His were presents from his mother, he said, and they were the kind of clothes men movie stars wore. Mother said he dressed beautifully and Daddy said that was exactly the right word for it. Mother said Miss Sara Ann's clothes looked as cheap as they were, that she should buy less and pay more, or else sew her own clothes. Daddy said Miss Sara Ann's clothes looked all right and Mother let that go, maybe because I happened to be there.

———

ONE NIGHT my parents and I had come downstairs to the sitting room, to sit on the soft upholstered furniture and listen to *Mr. District Attorney Champion of the People* on the radio. Even though we had our own small radio upstairs, it was nice to get out from being cooped up. Unless Miss Claire was giving a music lesson in the sitting room, that's where all the borders went when they wanted to listen to the big radio, and sometimes it was almost as good as going to a movie.

Roger/Tian was there a lot, but not this night. The Lawyer
Cato was there, having already smoked his cigar outside on
the porch. He liked *Mr. District Attorney* as much as
Daddy did.

It was not my favorite program. I wandered to the
window and peered out at the almost-dark of the porch.
When I put my forehead to the glass and cupped my hands
beside my eyes I could make out Miss Sara Ann and Mr.
Tony in the glider with their backs to me. I could barely hear
their voices and couldn't tell what they said. But she kept
touching her face and I realized she was crying.

Daddy was lost in the radio. I whispered in Mother's ear,
"Mr. Tony is making Miss Sara Ann cry again." She thought
a second and then whispered back, "You stay here." She
slipped out in front of Daddy and he didn't even know. She
had on a white dress and I could see her go out there and sit
in the swing. She was trying to pretend she was only passing
the time. Mother was not good at pretending. When she had
something in her craw the sound of her voice was like a
piece of broken glass. Before long Mr. Tony came inside to
go upstairs. He passed under the hall light looking happy, so
stuck on himself he didn't know Mother had run him off. I
returned to watching Mother and Miss Sara Ann, but they
were just sitting there talking and I lost interest. Daddy
remained off in radio land and I climbed into his lap. He
stroked my hair but he didn't quite know I was there.

I woke up, at first just a little, when they put me to bed.
Then I went more alert behind my closed eyes.

"So what were they fussing about?" Daddy said.

"They weren't fussing," Mother said, "He was insulting
her for no reason, the way he always does. She's perfectly
sweet to him, and he says every hateful thing he can think of.

If she won't break up with him, next thing he'll be beating her."

"Well then, the silly thing, why doesn't she break up with him?" Daddy said."

"I can certainly understand it but I can't explain it," Mother said.

Something in her tone struck Daddy wrong. He said, "What do you mean, you can certainly understand? Who insults you? If ever I was to insult you one time, I'd pay for it forever."

"You have insulted me. Not like him, you're not like him. But if you want to know, you have."

He said, "I beg your pardon. I believe not, missy. Never one time have I ever insulted any woman. I was raised better than that."

Silence from her.

Behind my eyelids I heard our door open and shut hard, but I didn't dare peek to see which one of them had left. Then I heard Mother's steps going across our floor into their bedroom. She began removing the bedspread for the night and turning down the top sheet.

Soon Daddy came back. Maybe he had just been to the bathroom. At first they didn't say anything. Then he said, "It's late and we're tired. We should make it a rule not to talk about touchy things at night."

"Do you want to know when you hurt my feelings?" she said.

"Hell no."

They shut the bedroom door, and I heard no more.

The next morning they were lovey-dovey.

2

MRS. LEWIS' BOARDING HOUSE AND FAMILY STYLE MEALS is what the sign out front said. The family and the help called it by its location, Fourth and Victory.

Mrs. Lewis, Linnet Lewis, was my father's mother. Before I was born she gave Daddy and Mother a place to live there. Daddy was supposed to pay her by helping in his off hours.

He liked to tell it, laughing, that when he was a boy, and on up through the time he was a bachelor, she had sometimes asked him out of his bed downstairs, to rent it. Back then he had a little annex room to himself next to hers. She would wake him, steer him half asleep into her own room, make a pallet of old quilts and cushions for him on the floor, put clean sheets on his bed, and let some lady sleep there temporarily for fifty cents a night or, a few times, for less than that or for free.

She eventually splurged and bought a secondhand cot for him for those times. But he told it that next thing she might sometimes also rent the cot too, moving it out on the screened-in back porch to let some decent man sleep a night or a week of nights. That was how many perfectly nice people were down on their luck and needing a place to sleep and eat during what was supposed to be The Last of The Depression.

Fourth and Victory was a huge house, and it was old even then. Once it had been a mansion with a ballroom. Also it had a dark attic with wonderful abandoned items. I still sometimes dream of being just before finding another treasure in that attic.

Under the house was a basement with a dirt floor. Scary. Spiders and damp boxes. Jars of canned food so old everybody said don't touch them, they might explode. And other things. I have dreamed about that basement too, you can believe.

A red building at the edge of the back yard had once been a stable and carriage house. It was big enough to park two good-sized trucks, and Mama Linnet rented it to a man with a transport business. Her own dear black Buick, she had to park out in the sun or rain on the south side of the house in the parking lot which once had been lawn but was now dirt and rocks.

The property took up a fourth of a city block. The next street up was Broadway. Across the street, in front, sat other big old houses. Most of them, too, had what used to be servants' quarters or carriage houses. Several of those were now made into little apartments or garages. Their yards were lined with black iron fences and giant trees. Likely as not, any back yard had an old pecan tree that shed a bushel or two of small sweet nuts in the fall. The River was twelve blocks east.

The house had a ground floor and then two stories for boarders. Downstairs, Mama Linnet had a two-room apartment with a private bath that only she and I were allowed to use, except sometimes Daddy did without asking.

My parents' apartment was the only other two-room place in the house. The other boarders had one room only. Even Miss Claire and her son Roger/Tian squeezed together in one because that was the best Mama Linnet could do for them. We were at the end of a hall, which was quieter, and we were on the middle floor. She had let us have the heart of the watermelon, just about, for our apartment. That was unusual for her to do. Typically she would save the best to rent or sell.

Mother didn't like having to share a bathroom with the lady boarders, but she didn't say so to Daddy. He would have said that at least the one she shared was on our floor, but the men's boarders' bathroom was up a flight of stairs and clear down a hall.

In our mornings Daddy needed to be first at everything so as to get to work on time. We were proud of his job, and Mother and I helped him dress for it. After he came back from the bathroom Mother handed him a white shirt that she had starched and ironed, and a tie and clean socks, and one of his two suits. I wound his watch. We watched him comb his pretty brown hair and get himself looking right for the day. Manly freshness glowed out of him in the mornings when he hugged us just before he left. I thought no other man compared. He would be on his way to the breakfast Mama Linnet and the help were putting on for the boarders and the general public, downstairs.

Then Mother dressed me, never fast enough to suit me,

so I could follow him. She did not come downstairs with me. She made her personal breakfast in our apartment, usually toast loaded with butter and jelly, and coffee that was half sugar and cream. Since I spent most of my daytimes downstairs in the interesting company of Mama Linnet and the help, Mother took the first part of the morning by herself and called it her time, although plenty of other time was also hers.

Usually I could make it to the dining room (once a ballroom) before Daddy finished eating. If luck was with me I could eat sitting in his lap. If he had eggs and I got there in time he would leave me a part and let me eat from his plate. I have never been able to get my eggs to taste like his.

I begged every day to go to work with him because once he had taken me. But he said, "Not today honey, Daddy has a lot of work."

With Daddy gone, there were still as many people left in the dining room as anybody could want to talk to. And sometimes one or two you might not. Mostly men, maybe one in five a woman. Three long tables of folks dressed every way from business suits to overalls, coming and going. What they had in common was that they were clean.

If a dirty person came in, whoever was working the cash bowl at the dining room door said we were full and turning customers away. But if the dirty person asked for a handout, or plainly needed one, they were told to go around the house to the kitchen door, where they got a plate of food for free, to eat on the back steps. It was Mama Linnet's rule that anyone who asked for food at her house was to be fed. Further, they were to be told they could have as many refills as they wanted of everything except the meat. Only one serving of meat.

But in the dining room would be, sooner or later, the ten-or-so of us who lived in the house, and then more who were meal customers from outside. There were drivers for two trucking companies, plus men and women from the stores on Main Street which was three blocks away, men from the Post Office who came in two shifts, and other people who worked farther away and came by car or streetcar. A few more customers, nobody knew where they came from because they were so close-mouthed. Even Mama Linnet and Daddy, who were both good at getting people to talk, didn't know much about them.

Some customers came once a day, some twice, and a few for all three meals. At the start of a mealtime there were more customers than seats. Those who had to wait, did. The cooking was that good, the bowls and platters that full, the price that low. Admission was twenty-five cents plus a penny. Usually that was the price, I should have said. There was one fat lady who started coming and she came three times a day and took second helpings and then thirds on nearly every-thing. I can still hear her voice, which was very demanding, saying, "Pass the bread puddin' please!" After a week Mama Linnet told her she would have to charge her double because she was eating for two, and the woman paid it without a word of fuss.

Breakfast, lunch, or supper, it might be the only meal some of those people would have that day.

Two big identical signs were fixed to opposite walls of the dining room, high up. You couldn't miss them. Mama Linnet had them made at a discount at the hardware store where Daddy worked.

Take All You Want
But Eat All You Take
No Carry Outs

Miss Savory and the other help, and their kids and nieces and nephews who weren't in school, ate free after the public mealtimes, at a plank table on the screened-in back porch. Or the kids, if the weather was nice, ate sitting on the back steps with their plates in their laps.

———

AT SUPPER one night that spring, one of the mystery customers wrapped four biscuits in his napkin, put them in the pocket of his jacket, and left with them. Another customer saw him, and told on him to Mama Linnet.

The next night he tried it again, but this time she was watching. She went directly to him and asked him into the hallway to talk.

He scraped his chair back from the table, got up, and followed her out there, no expression on his face. His hands were in his back pants pockets.

She had her apron on, and still had a serving towel in her hand. She was smiling at him. She said, "I'm Mrs. Lewis, the proprietress here. Would you want to tell me your name?"

"What's it to you?" he said.

"It's always nice if you know each other's names when you're having a friendly talk."

"None of your business," he said.

By this time, Miss Savory had got wind of what was

happening and had slipped out of the kitchen into the hall. She was standing thin in the shadow against the wall.

Mama Linnet hung her towel from her apron pocket and began pulling a string to untie the apron. But she was still smiling. "Well then I'll get right to it. I noticed you put a napkin with some biscuits in it in your pocket?"

"And?" he said.

"Probably you didn't see my signs that say no carry-outs. I want to explain why that is. It's because I can't afford it. If I let people take more food than they eat, I'd need to raise my prices to stay in business. I don't want to do that. My customers can't afford it. Some of them can't always pay what I charge now. That's the reason for my policy." And she added, "And good cloth napkins are expensive to replace."

"And?" he said.

Mama Linnet depended a lot on the fact that most men went weak when she smiled at them. But she also knew some went weak and then, because of that, went mad. She stopped smiling, and said, "I'm asking you to give me my napkin, and the biscuits."

He pulled the white bundle out of his jacket, dropped it on the floor, and stepped on it gently with his boot. "There you go, bitch," he said.

Miss Savory instantly and silently came to stand at Mama Linnet's left side. We family and the rest of the help knew Savory was never without her five-inch switchblade.

Mama Linnet said to Miss Savory, "It's all right." She and the man looked into each other's eyes, but she didn't let it go on long enough to be a staredown. She pointed to the mess on the floor and said to him, "Is that satisfaction enough for you?"

He turned toward the front door.

"Let him go," Mama Linnet whispered to Savory.

As soon as the door slammed behind him, Mama Linnet turned back into the dining room, walked on through the green swinging door into the kitchen, and stayed there. Miss Savory and Miss Claire did all the rest of the serving that night, and Miss Claire also tried to be available to take the money and make change when she could. Because they were a person short and Miss Savory wasn't used to serving, the work in the dining room was slowed down considerably.

I knew we were supposed to have fresh-peach cobbler and when it didn't come I slid down from my chair and ducked under the door to see what Mama Linnet was doing. She was bent over the deep double sink, up to her elbows in hot dishwater. Miss Savory usually washed most of the dishes.

Mama Linnet saw me and said, "Is your daddy home yet?" I said, "No Ma'am" and she said, "I need you to go up and ask your mother to please come down here. Tell her I need to ask a favor."

Mother was still sitting by the window in the breeze of the electric fan, sewing my latest dress in the last of the daylight. The sewing machine's cabinet was unfolded with its drawers open and half-open, and our living room was a mess of scraps, spools of thread, pieces of material pinned to their patterns, scissors, pincushions, tape measures, gauges, chalks, and gadgets that I never knew what they were.

I said, "Mama Linnet said please will you come down to the kitchen so she can ask you something."

"What is it, do you know?" she said.

I thought about it. "No Ma'am."

She looked at me a second. The handwork she had on her lap, she laid across the arm of the couch. "All right then.

I need to stop anyway. I can hardly see." We went out into the hall and she locked the door. "Did you eat?" she said.

"Not fresh-peach cobbler yet." I said.

"Oh," she said, brightening, "Fresh-peach cobbler. I thought it was supposed to be that fruit cocktail cake."

"It was, but one of the truckers had some peaches from Texas for dirt cheap except they had to be used right away."

Downstairs at the kitchen she pushed aside the swinging door and stopped just inside it and said to Mama Linnet, "Mary Mavis said you wanted to ask me something."

Mama Linnet looked up from the sink and said, "We're shorthanded tonight and I wonder if you could work the cash box until Pat gets here."

"Why are you in here and Savory's out there?" Mother said.

"It's a long story."

I said, "She feels bad because a man tried to steal some biscuits."

Mother looked from Mama Linnet to me and back. Mama Linnet kept washing dishes silently. Finally Mother said, "I don't understand, not that that would make any difference to anybody, but anyway I can't make change."

Mama Linnet took a slow deep breath and let it out. She said, "Then could you ask Claire if she can work the cash bowl, and would you help serve. Mostly there's only dessert left."

"I don't think my husband would like having his wife be a servant to strangers," Mother said.

Mama Linnet straightened up from the sink and said, "What about your husband's mother?" She looked Mother in the eye. Then she remembered I was there. She picked up a dish towel and dried her arms and hands, and used her apron to wipe the perspiration off her face and neck. "I'm sorry to have bothered you," she said to Mother. She took a clean apron off a shelf and put it on. Then plainly she meant to go back through the swinging door into the dining room no matter that Mother and I were standing there in the way. Mother put a hand down across my chest and drew me to herself, squeezing back against the doorframe and making us small, and Mama Linnet marched by.

Next thing I knew, Mother had me by the arm, pulling me fast through the dining room toward upstairs.

I screamed.

"Be quiet!" she said. "What's the matter?"

"I didn't get my fresh-peach cobbler," I yelled.

Some of the customers ate on and pretended they weren't hearing anybody having a fit. Others stopped eating to watch it. Across the dining room Mama Linnet froze with a pan of cobbler in each hand, and stared at us.

"Hush. Hush!" Mother shook my body a little, by my arm. "You can have it, hush." And she let go of me.

Mr. Tony was eating in the dining room during all this. When he finished his meal he went into the kitchen to Mama Linnet and offered to handle the cash bowl duty, and she let him. After all the customers had left Miss Savory checked the amount of the money and volunteered a report to Mama Linnet. "He didn't steal none of it."

Mama Linnet said, "I have no reason to think he would."

EVERY NIGHT MAMA LINNET counted the day's income when all else was done. She did it in her bedroom, pulling down the slanted front of a little antique bureau desk that had waited abandoned in the attic of the house when she rented it. She had said she wanted to buy the house to own the desk. She sat at it under the harsh light of a dented metal floor lamp that Daddy had salvaged somewhere when he was a boy, to light his homework.

She could all but tell just by looking at a bowl of coins and bills how much a total would be, and she already knew in her head approximately what it ought to be. She was good with figures, especially those with a dollar sign. She liked making this nightly reckoning. It took the rough edges off the day, and gave her a sense of having accomplished something. At the finish she wrote the sum of her earnings smartly into a ledger, in blue ink, and took a second or two to look at it in satisfaction. Then she would go on to finish the ritual.

In her desk were two secret drawers. She would open one, get out a long heavy iron key, and take that and the day's money into the clean silent dining room. There she would go to a huge wooden armoire that stood against a wall like a brown mountain in front of a white sky. She would unlock the chest's doors and spread them wide, reach in deep to a metal cash box, open its lid, and add her day's income to the week's money. She would close the box, lock the armoire, return to her little apartment to put the key back in its secret drawer, fold up the writing flap to her desk, and when the clasp clicked she would take a deep breath and gratify her lungs.

Her last self-indulgence in the nightly ceremony was that she would go into her bathroom, run hot water in her tub—she turned off the faucet when the depth was just before sumptuous—and get in.

But three nights after the biscuit-stealing episode, when

Mama Linnet started her final close-up, she found the secret desk drawer empty. The key to the armoire was gone. She knew she had put it there the night before, but anyway she made a half-hour unsuccessful search.

Then she climbed the stairs and knocked on our door. Because my bed was also our sofa in our living room, and near the door, I was the first to hear her. I knew who it was because she was quietly calling, "Hello?" And even though I had been forbidden to open the door to anyone, I would have, except I couldn't reach the chain lock. I knocked on the door to my parents' room—I was never supposed to open that door either—and woke Mother. Who woke Daddy.

Mama Linnet said to him, "Please get dressed and come down and help me get into the armoire. The key is gone. Hopefully we can break into it without ruining it. We'll have to pry the doors open, or saw through that little flat bolt. It's almost a whole week's money and I'll need part of it first thing tomorrow for Farmers' Market."

"Then let's do it in the morning," he said.

"Patrick. Wake up and think please. I need to know if the money is in there."

"Oh. Well. Mama if it's not, there's nothing you can do about it tonight anyway."

"Are you going to help me? If you're not, I'll have to wake up Willard Cato."

"All right, Mama, for God's sake. For gosh sake," he said.

The money was gone. Mama Linnet stood in front of the wrecked armoire, and looked at the cash box which was empty even of the tax pennies. She still wore her day's work dress and second-best black shoes, and she stood in the light of the dining room's grand crystal chandelier.

"Lord Jesus let me know who did this and help me get that money back," she said.

"I know who I think it was," Daddy said. "Mother, don't cry. Money isn't everything in this world."

"Then you don't live in the same world I do," she said.

———

THE NEXT MORNING, instead of driving her Buick to the Farmers' Market at dawn as she did every Saturday, she stayed in the kitchen until a polite eight o'clock, and then she knocked on the door of each of her five boarders and asked them to meet with her in the dining room. It being the weekend, they were all still at home, and they came obediently, dressed as if for a workday: The Lawyer Cato in a business suit that was a bit too tight, Mr. Tony in a creamy V-neck sweater over a baby blue shirt and silk tie, Miss Sara Ann in a tight fitted skirt and low-cut blouse, Miss Lucy in a print dress of intense pattern, and Miss Claire in one of her plain but elegant dresses. And Daddy was there, looking rumpled. He had on his yesterday's trousers and shirt open at the neck, with the sleeves rolled up. He had earlier been with Mama Linnet in the kitchen acting hungry until she made bacon and eggs and toast for him.

She sat them all together at the table nearest the hall door, and shut the door and joined them.

"I have had a setback. I want to tell you about it because I'll have to ask your understanding," she said.

Most of them sat up straighter.

Miss Lucy said instantly, "What is it?"

Mama Linnet said, "A week of my income is gone missing. Apparently someone borrowed it, and I'm sorry to say that has to be someone who lives here. I'm asking whoever it is to please give it back right away because I need it to run the house. If the money is returned today there will be no questions asked, and no penalty of any kind. I'll treat it like it never happened."

She gave them a minute to digest the information, then went on. "If I don't get the money back, I'll have to ask you to meet with me again tomorrow, because for a while I won't have enough to meet some of the conditions of my rent agreement with you."

There was another silence, then The Lawyer Cato said, "'Scuse me Miss Lewis, for possibly complicating this, but something came to mind a while back in what you were recounting. I believe my thought has merit, and I would like to introduce it to the body here, in that we are one and all influenced, or at least likely to be influenced, in the proceedings at hand and what caused them to come into effect at this time . . ."

"What are you trying to say?" Miss Lucy said.

The Lawyer Cato said, "Has not something been overlooked?"

Miss Lucy said, "What?"

"The help," he said. "Is it not as logical to assume one of the help is the . . . ah, temporary possessor of the money, as to assume it is one of the present company? I say this because . . ."

Mama Linnet broke in, putting a hand down flat on the table, saying, "No, it couldn't be Savory, or any of the part-time help. That's because of the time period when the key disappeared to where the money was. I know between when and when that had to be, and they weren't here then." She stopped, and then finished. "Well. I'll be here all day, available to anybody who wants to talk about it."

She stood, and they stood. She said, "The Saturday breakfast spread will be as usual, except a few minutes late getting started."

On the way into the hall, each of the boarders said a version of how sorry they were, and she said thank you.

3

THE NEXT MONDAY, THE DINING ROOM'S BREAKFAST customers, who were used to eggs with bacon or ham plus optional pancakes, got pancakes only. And that, with not much butter or syrup, and only water or coffee to drink, no milk. Lunch and dinner customers had to make do with various concoctions of potatoes, macaroni, and bread, plus small amounts of odds-and-ends vegetables that were home-canned, such as pickled beets or tomato chow chow. No platters of gravy-smothered pounded steak, no pork chops, no fried or roasted chicken. And for dessert, pale-looking, pale-tasting pudding heavy on the cornstarch and light on everything else, or cake that barely held together, topped with thin icing.

Mama Linnet was embarrassed to put this food in front of her customers, and she said almost as much to them, one by one. "I hope you'll understand this is just a temporary setback, and we'll be up to our usual standard soon," she said. "We had a break-in, in the middle of the night, over the weekend, and I haven't had time to make adjustments."

On Tuesday she was saying, "I hope you'd keep bearing with me another day or two, about my reduced menu. I'm still making arrangements. It won't be long before I'll be feeding you right again."

The full truth was, neither of our city's two banks would give her an unsecured loan.

The meal customers began to fall away as the week turned into another week, because they were repeatedly disappointed and still slightly hungry after eating. In Mama Linnet's cash system, two weeks of income from meals had paid the monthly rent on the house. Now it would take three weeks of meals, with the number of customers getting smaller every day.

She said, talking to herself and the divine together, "Dear Jesus, you know it's almost impossible to get past a bad public opinion. Please don't let my reputation go to stingy meals."

And day by day she was forced to spend a greater part of the income from the meals to buy at least something to cook the next day. And buy it from the grocery store, where much of it was more expensive than from the Saturday Farmers' Market.

Although some of the meal customers left, all of the boarders stayed, despite that they didn't get clean bath towels or bed linens for nearly a month. And not one complained about the poor quality and scantness of the meals which were included in their thirty dollars per month rent.

In fact, The Lawyer Cato knocked on Mama Linnet's door and quietly offered to pay two months' rent in advance. She took him up on the latter. But the advance of the sixty dollars only gave her more elbowroom in robbing Peter to pay Paul.

Cato was secretly adding to his diet elsewhere, and she suspected it, but neither of them mentioned that.

Miss Savory took a temporary cut to half-pay, and worked overtime for nothing. The meals for her children were down to almost scraps.

The part-time help suffered the most. There was no money to pay the two women who helped with the laundry twice a week. It was impossible for Mama Linnet to get in touch with them, and so Miss Savory had to give them the bad news. Their unexpected loss of the money, plus the loss of the meals for themselves and their children, was a crisis for them. Mama Linnet cried when they came to work and she told them they had no work because she had no money to pay them. Then she went to her apartment and shut the door. Miss Savory knocked and called to her, "Miz Lewis, let me come in and be some comfort to you. I don't pray much, but we could pray." Mama Linnet opened the door and said, "I've prayed all I can. I'll thank you to add to it, though."

The punishing work of the laundry—bedsheets, cotton blankets, bedspreads, pillow cases, bath towels—Mama Linnet reduced to only table linens and kitchen towels, and she did the work herself along with Miss Claire, and Miss Savory, whenever they could make time.

MAMA LINNET SAID to Daddy one night in her bedroom, in the soft light of her reading lamp, sitting on the edge of her bed because he had taken the chair, "Both of the banks said they'd loan me the fifty dollars if I let them hold the title to my Buick. I told them I'd think about it. But I paid three hundred dollars cash for that car, and it has gone 'way up in value since then. The paper said last week that pretty soon there may not be any new cars made at all. I don't want to let them have that title, even temporarily. Fifty dollars for a car that'll be worth no telling how much as time goes on. What if something else happened and I couldn't make the loan payments? If worst came to worst I could sell the car, but not unless I hold the title. Son, would you please not lean so far back in that chair. It's an antique and you'll break it."

He brought the chair's front feet to the floor. "You always say that, but it's just a plain good old chair, it's not gonna break. Mama . . . "

"What?" she said.

"Ahm . . . Daddy has some money. He said he does, anyway."

"What do you mean, 'He said'?"

"Ma'am?" he said.

"What was the occasion, that he told you that?"

"You did know he's back here now? Working highway construction? He's making good money. He's thinking of buying some property," he said.

"No, I thought he was in Tennessee. But you've been talking to him?"

"Is that a crime?" he said.

She pulled a Kleenex from its new pop-up box on her night table, removed her wire-rimmed eyeglasses, and wiped her brow and cheeks. Then she put the glasses back on and laid the Kleenex on top of its box for another use.

She said, "Son, I hope there would never be a time when I wouldn't want you and your father to love each other and talk to each other. If I haven't made that plain to you, I'm sorry. Probably you've felt like you had to keep something from me, and I'm sorry about that too. I wouldn't, for anything, want to put you in a position where you couldn't do what your heart tells you to and openly tell me the truth about it."

"Yes'm. If you want, I could ask him for the fifty for you," he said. "That way, you wouldn't have to pay it back. He wouldn't let you."

"That's not something I want to do. Thank you, though. I'll get through this somehow. The Dear Lord won't let us down."

"Oh come on, Mama, don't keep your back up so high about him. He'd do anything for you, you know that," he said.

She opened her lips to say more, but then only shook her head no. Then she said, "I keep some desperation money. For matters of life and death."

"You never told me that!" he said.

"I know," she said.

———

FIVE DAYS after the robbery she showed up at the hardware store where Daddy worked.

Curtis Haskell was in his usual easy chair behind the cash register. "Well hello there Linnet Lewis, what a nice surprise. What can I do for you today?" he said.

Daddy was replenishing a parts drawer, deep in the dim store, and he peered around a floater and called, "Mama? What are you doing here?"

"Hello to you too, son," she said. To both of them she said, "I want to buy a safe."

Curtis Haskell said, "Well now. That's a big decision for a

little lady. Those cost real money, you know. Way more now than used to be, since it's made of metal. And then there's getting them transported. They're heavy, you can see that," he tilted his head toward his own head-high black safe nearby.

"I do know. I want a small safe. One not much bigger than a breadbox. Do you have one of those?"

"Naw, you don't want that. They're too easy to carry off. You put your valuables in a little safe and then the thief just carries off the safe. Surprise! Who'dathunkit! Huhuhuh."

"I'm going to have steel plates recess-bolted to the studs in a wall, and the safe welded to the plates."

"Whoever heard of that," he said.

"Maybe nobody else. But that's what I'm going to do. Curtis, do you stock a small safe like that?"

"Matter of fact, there is one back there, been there a while. Now, it's a good one, understand. The best," he said.

"How much is it?"

"I forget exactly, thirty, forty dollars I think, let me go look," he said, pushing his body out of the chair.

"I'll go too," she said, drawing near.

"Naw, naw, that's all right," he said.

"It's fine," she said.

So they both went into the back room's darker gloom, and bent down squinting, and saw that the price was nine-teen dollars and ninety-nine cents.

Back at the cash register, opening her purse, she said, "Oh, and Curtis, do you still have an employee discount arrangement with Pat, if he were the one to buy it?"

"Aw heck, I guess, yes. Why don't l just give away the rest of the store while I'm at it," he said.

DADDY SPOKE his mind freely to her the night she bought the safe, starting as he was coming through her apartment door. "Mama, what can you be thinking, spending that money on a safe? You haven't got enough to keep the business going and here you go buying something extra."

She was at her desk, writing. She turned to him and said, "Hello to you too, son. I believe getting the safe is the thing to do."

He said, still standing just inside the doorway, tall over her, "I know. You don't need to say it. You studied and prayed on it."

"I would have, except I think The Dear Lord is tired of hearing me whine. I'm tired of it myself. I want the safe, and it's time to make an act of faith."

"Make an act of faith? You still haven't even made a police report. Looks to me like you'd want to let them find out who the thief is, and get our money back. Some of it anyway, maybe," he said.

She sat up straight. "Our family do not call in the Law, nor look to the Court, if we have problems with our neighbors."

"Mama, your family were hillbillies, and, one, this is a city, in civilization. And two, these are modern times. You can't stay stuck in your background."

"My Background. Let me put it this way. We are not going to the police," she said. "Son, are you keeping in mind that whoever took the money has to be somebody I know and trust? That whoever would be able to spy on me close enough to find out I kept the armoire key in an invisible drawer, and then watch for an opportunity to sneak into my apartment and get the key, and then watch for an opportunity to use the key and get the money . . . would be somebody I might not want the police to find out about?"

After a pause he said, "I told you who I think did it."

"Tony Bishop is the one person with the least opportunity. He's gone every day. And except for meals he never sets foot in this part of the house."

After another silence he said, "So who do you think would have the most opportunity?"

She looked at him and said nothing.

"Good God, Mama, do you suspect me?" he said.

"The police might. You might want to think about that. Please stop taking the Lord's name in vain."

THE NEXT NIGHT he said to her, "I can't go on without knowing. It's all I think about. Do you believe I took that money? Because I didn't."

"I don't think of anybody as the one who took it, because I don't know."

"That's not what I mean," he said.

"But the principle of it is something you might want to keep in mind. Everybody's innocent unless they're proven guilty."

"You owe me a straight answer, I'm your son. Do you feel like I took it?" he said.

"No."

"Maybe you really do," he said.

"If you can't take my word for it, then what?" She went on, "But before we leave the subject, you haven't said how you're going to pitch in on the money shortage."

"Pitch in." he said.

"I've been hoping you'd suggest something. But since you're asking, I think it's time you started paying some room and board for the three of you."

"With what? Cesarine spends every dime I make except what I keep for myself, and that's only walking around money that any man should have. I thought we had an understanding," he said.

"What did you think it was?"

"You haven't said a word since I asked you if I got married could we live here," he said.

"Do you remember what I said?"

"That's been six years ago. I don't remember we had any conversation about it."

"We can bring it up to date then. You've had a full-time job for three years and more. You don't have any debts—that I know of. You're steady on your own two feet in life. It's time for you to start paying on food and rent for you and your family."

"How much did you mean?" he said.

"At least half what I'd charge anybody else."

"How much is that?" he said.

"The full price for a month's room and board for two adults and a child is seventy-five dollars."

"Maybe, maybe, I could do fifteen," he said.

"Thirty-seven fifty."

"Mama! Cesarine would have a fit if I asked her to give up that much," he said.

"Thirty-seven fifty if you also pitch in on the work twelve hours a week. That was part of our original agreement too, that you forgot. That's a full day on Saturdays and half a day on Sundays."

"When am I supposed to be with my family and friends?" he said.

"When am I supposed to be with mine?"

"Fourth and Victory is your family for all anybody could tell. You care more about making money than you care about me, that's for sure," he said. He stalked out and slammed her door.

———

TWO DAYS later Curtis Haskell installed the safe himself. It took him half a day. When he finished, he came across the hall to the kitchen where Mama Linnet was, to write out a bill. Miss Savory and Miss Claire were there too, working, and I was outside on the top step, on the other side of the screen door, with my coat on against the mild cold, where I had been talking to Miss Savory's nephew Antoine.

"Linnet," Daddy's boss said, "I hate it I'll have to charge you for the labor too. Pat ought to been able to do it hisself, on his own time, but . . . "

"It's all right Curtis, it's well worth it."

"A hard working pretty lady like you. My goodness. That boy of yours is a born salesman, but when it comes to doing anything with his hands . . . " He shook his head and laughed and said, "Put Pat in a closet with a welding torch, he'll burn the house down."

She didn't say anything.

He raised his eyes from his figuring on the bill and into the look she was giving him. He crossed his arms in front of his chest.

She said, "How much do I owe you?"

"Altogether for the safe and materials and labor, which I

also gave you a employee discount on, in case you was wondering, twenty-eight dollars and twelve cents."

"Just a minute." She left, came back, and handed him the exact amount in bills and coins.

"You ought not to keep so much cash in the house. All these people coming and going." He swept his eyes and head around, starting with Miss Savory and Miss Claire, and indicating also the rest of the world.

She didn't say anything.

"Of course, that's why you got the safe," he said. "Huhuhuh." He sniffed like a dog and looked toward the deep skillets, which for the first time in a week held bubbling lard with fried chicken browning in them, and the vats of mashed potatoes. "Godamighty that smells good! Tell you what. I'll eat some lunches over here and swap you some off this bill."

"We'll just leave it like it is," she said.

He talked more until he realized he was talking to himself and felt off balance, and then he did leave, but from his looks he still thought he was in her good graces.

I came inside. "Why did Mr. Haskell say my Daddy is going to burn the house down?"

Miss Savory took the lid off the potatoes and said into them, "He's a fool is why."

"That's not exactly what he said," Mama Linnet said to me. "He said something else and I don't know why he did. He thought he was making a joke and you don't need to pay any attention to it. I'm going downtown this afternoon, do you want to go?"

I jumped up and down.

Mama Linnet said to Miss Savory, "Apparently he doesn't

know about the robbery. It's nice to know not everybody does. Yet, anyway."

"Mister Pat did a good job keeping his mouth shut," Savory said.

"He's good at that," Mama Linnet said.

THREE DAYS later the mailman brought a special delivery addressed to Mama Linnet. It was an oversize manila envelope, heavy because the contents were shielded by cut-to-size cardboard. In it was a folded letter, typed. The letter held five twenty-dollar bills.

There was no date, just:

Dear Mrs. Lewis,

I am the one who borrowed your money. I return it here with interest. If this has caused any inconvenience you have my regrets.

There was no signature.

MAMA LINNET RECALLED the part-time help. She also paid to have plumbing, hot and cold, run to the screened-in back porch, to ease their job of laundry. The old water hose was laid to rest under its spigot by the back steps.

Daddy waited a few days until one sunny day when she was on her knees doing spring work in a flowerbed out back, which was one of her luxuries, and he ambled out there and made conversation, and eventually asked, roundabout, whether we could go back to living free. She kept weeding and without looking up she said, "Thirty-seven fifty a month and twelve hours' work a week. The end. Unless I decide to make it more."

IT WAS LATE SPRING, and a Thursday, the bigger of the two wash days at Mrs. Lewis' Boarding House and Family Style Meals. I was the only one who enjoyed the washdays: I was still five. The help ranged from bearing with it to hating it. For them, out on the screened-in back porch, processing the items from one big square tub to another, and then out in the back yard hanging out the heavy linens and the clothes on sagging lines propped up with sticks, and bringing them in, always the job was huge and exhausting. In winter it was wet shivering cold. In summer it was wet sweating hot.

For me, the child dawdling around out there, it was pleasant. I loved the smells of water and bleach and Rinso soap. I admired the funny little cobalt bluing bottle with a cork, like a genie's bottle, and if I was there at the right time they let me be the one to dribble the blue-black liquid into the water and watch it become a long, squiggly, slow, ever more intricate moving stain of oddness. I would then plunge my whole arm into the cold water to stir it so that, as Daddy would have said, Eureka!, I had changed the color of all the water in the tub to a pretty light blue. Mama Linnet and the help had made thick wands of cut-off wooden broom handles, now bleached white, to poke the swimming linens and clothes so the dirt would come out in the wash water. And then in the rinse water, poke them again so the soap would come out. In between the wash and the rinse was, now, also the New Motorized Industrial Strength Wringer for which everybody who washed was grateful.

That Wringer was another one of Mama Linnet's well-considered investments, bought at wholesale plus cost at, guess where, the hardware store where Daddy worked. The old wringer had required to be cranked by hand, meaning by the whole body. The New Motorized Wringer eased the work and freed nearly a whole worker. Whoever was washing or rinsing could just turn the switch to On and feed the first washed piece between the thick rollers that turned and squeezed against each other. The rollers would, by themselves, pull even a bed spread right on through if need be. But as the piece traveled, if you saw it wasn't clean after all, the Wringer would not let you pull it back. It was too strong. The only way to remove something from between the rollers was to turn the switch Off and adjust the pressure to Release. Or simply let the piece go on through to the other side and retrieve it from there. I was not allowed to feed pieces through the Wringer. They told me and each other a story about a woman somewhere whose fingers got pulled through, then hand, then whole arm to the armpit, until her arm was nearly skinned and nearly pulled off before anyone could help. It turned black, they said.

Mama Linnet owned only enough bed linens for two sets per bed throughout the house, and barely enough table linens to do with. It was important that nothing stop the flow of the wash work. Nor, at the same time, could the work pertaining to meals be delayed, wash day or no. She hired extra help on wash days.

Miss Abien, whom we thought must be related to Miss Savory, came at first on washdays only. If she couldn't come or if we needed still another help person, Miss Savory got somebody else, a cousin or a sister, so their family would not lose out on the hourly money and the share of food extras.

Mama Linnet directed the cooking so that there was always food for the help and their children. She said it was in the Bible to do that. And she said any hobo who came to the back door was to be given a full plate.

She didn't have full confidence in the washdays' extra help. Their job was none of the kitchen or house cleaning, only the wash. Every washday she said to them about me, "I need you to keep a good eye on her when I can't be out here." She would not say that to the regular help, who watched me as their own and would have had hurt feelings to be told. I wouldn't have been out there that day except Miss Claire had the day off and was gone, and Mama Linnet and Miss Savory were extra busy inside. I knew I was supposed to mind the help, whoever they were, and they were all friendly to me, and my worst behavior was to get in their way occasionally.

Miss Abien screamed just before I knew my hair was caught in the Wringer. She was standing on the other side of the washtub with a strange look, and then my head was being turned so my eyes saw the white painted ceiling boards, and about the time I knew what was happening, it hurt. Then I went unconscious.

The flow of the work stopped that day, I tell you.

It was Miss Savory who saved me. When she reached me I had stopped yelling and gone limp. They said she grabbed a poke stick with one hand and with the other she grabbed the Wringer post, and forced the stick between the rollers. She yelled, "Pull the plug!" But she had me out of the Wringer and in her arms before someone finally got the thing stopped.

"Oh Dear Jesus help my baby," Mama Linnet said. "Savory, is her neck broken?"

"I can't tell. Miss Lewis, open the door. Run start the car. Abien! Get that piece of hair out of that water and wrap it up in a clean towel and bring it. And bring me some clean towels to the car. "

Abien must have looked down into the clean rinse water with only the blood and hair in a piece of scalp in it. She said, "No."

"Woman, you get that," Miss Savory said.

Abien, or someone, did.

4

MOTHER, UPSTAIRS, DIDN'T KNOW ABOUT MY ACCIDENT UNTIL Daddy came home for lunch. He was dumbfounded to see there was no lunch. No tables set, even, and the noon customers beginning to file in. No Mama Linnet. No help. Except for one wash woman in the back yard at the clothes lines.

Daddy said that Abien was standing out there crying, holding on to a clothesline. When he asked her where Mrs. Lewis and Savory were she said, "They done took little Mary Mavis to the doctor."

"What for?" he said.

She shook her head.

"What happened? Do you know? Tell me if you do, I'm her daddy. Did she fall off of something? Did she get burned? Well goddamn it, how long ago was it?"

She only shook her head. He grabbed her by the arms and tried to shake something out of her. But nothing. When he let go she walked away like a zombie across the parking lot, he said.

Daddy thought Mother was with the others, with me. But when he ran back in the house he saw her coming down the stairs, smiling. She was looking for him because he hadn't come upstairs the way he usually did, first thing at noon. They met at the bottom of the stairs, in the middle of the crowd of customers who were trying to decide whether to wait or go.

"What happened?" he yelled at Mother. She looked blank. "Cesarine, stop that and tell me what happened to my daughter!"

At "What happened to my daughter," Mother melted down on the bottom step in a near faint. She said, "Oh Pat, what happened?"

He said to the customers, "Please take care of my wife," and ran out.

HE RAN ALL the way to the doctor's, about a mile. When he arrived the nurse said they had taken me on to the hospital.

"Get the doctor out here," Daddy said.

"Sir. He went to the hospital with them."

"What happened? What's the matter with her?"

She said, "Sir if you would lower your voice please. Dr. Haynes thinks her neck could be broken."

"Oh God no. And he's there with her?"

"Yessir."

"Senior or Junior?"

At that moment Dr. Haynes Junior came into the waiting room to see about the shouting.

"Senior," the nurse said.

"Oh thank God," Daddy said. He ran out the door. A block later he turned around and ran back.

"Which one?" he yelled at the nurse.

"Sir, please. I told you. It was Dr. Haynes Senior."

"No! Which hospital! St. Vincent's or The Baptist?"

"Oh. Sir, I don't know. They never brought her in from the car. He examined her out there, and then got in with them and they left."

———

Dr. Haynes Senior stayed in my hospital room that night with Mama Linnet and Mother and Daddy, in case I would take a turn for the worse. At daylight he woke me up and played a game with me. My part was to close my eyes and guess whether he had or had not touched me on my arms and hands and legs and feet. I didn't know he was actually sticking me with something sharp.

He would say, "Did you feel that?" And I would say, "Yes." Talking felt odd, and it took longer than I was used to.

"Where was it?" he said.

"My big toe."

"What did it feel like?"

"You pushed on it with your finger."

"And . . . did you feel *that*?" he said.

Sometimes it was hard to tell. "No."

And so on.

"She's not fudging," he said to Mama Linnet. "She has sensation in all her extremities. She's stable. She's doing very well, and it's entirely possible she could recover completely."

"Oh, Harry," Mama Linnet said, and started crying.

He put his arms around her. "I have to go now but I'll be

back this afternoon. If anything happens, tell the nurses. I'll tell them to get me." He took Mama Linnet's hand and held it. He said, "Linnet." Then I thought he was going to kiss it, but he didn't.

He said to Mother and Daddy, "Any questions, now, before I go?"

Mother said, "What about her hair?" Underneath a big bandage, half my head had been shaved and about a fourth of my scalp was in stitches.

"That's the least of our worries," he said on the way to the door, "It'll be fine."

With the doctor gone, after a bit Mama Linnet said, "We could take turns being here now."

They all thought on it, then Daddy said, "Mama, you and I could go for the morning. I still have time to bathe and get to work. Curtis probably isn't expecting me but he'd be glad to see me." He said to Mother, "That all right with you, honey? You to take the morning shift?"

Mother said, "I would welcome the chance to take care of my own child."

Mama Linnet said, "Do you want to get some breakfast first? They have a cafeteria now. I have some cash."

Mother said, "My husband gives me money, thank you. And no, I can't eat."

Miss Sara Ann was my first hospital visitor. Her boss at Walgreens let her off to come for a few minutes. She had soft ways. Best of all, she brought a present, a little white duck that could waddle by itself if you put it at the top of a slant and let go. She worked it for me. I smiled, only, because they had told me I didn't have to talk.

She said, "My little girl has one of these and she loves it. We'll put it here where you can see it, and you can play with it when you feel better. I heard a good report on you." She said that as if it were praise. She turned to Mother.

Mother said, "Yes, the doctor said she has sensational extremities and there will be a complete recovery."

"Oh I'm so glad. Since she's doing so well, I could take a turn and sit with her. I could come right after work, and stay a while. I could call Mother on the telephone. My little girl likes to know if I won't be there. My little dog, I mean. I call her my little girl. Isn't it amazing how attached you get to a pet?"

"That's so nice. But I don't want to leave her."

"I kind of thought you wouldn't," Miss Sara Ann said.

THREE DAYS later the doctor said I could go home. I could almost stand then, with someone holding me, but he said I had to stay in bed. At home, one visitor came right after another, even Mother's family who rarely came to Fourth and Victory.

Miss Claire made her son Roger/Tian stop running errands for money, and practicing ball, enough to come every day and play with me one hour, with one of the board games I suddenly had, or read or talk to me. He was twelve, the best-looking boy I had ever seen. He was not thrilled to spend time with me, but he was nice about it.

The second time Roger/Tian came he told me his father

was from Canada and was a special kind of soldier in The War. He said he was in Intelligence.

I said, "I know what that means: he's smart."

He said, "That's not what it means, but he is the smartest man in the world."

"What's his name?"

"Same as mine. He's Tian Lee, Senior. I'm Tian Lee, Junior."

"Huh uh, you're not. Your name is Roger Evans-Lee."

"Not really. When I'm a legal adult I'll have it changed to what it really is." He stared a hole through the wall when he said that, as if his beautiful half Chinese eyes could see through it to somewhere else.

"Do the rolling ball trick," I said.

"If you call me by my real name. Call me Tian when it's just you and me."

"Do the rolling ball trick Tian."

He reached to his baseball glove and got the ball out. As if it were alive it rolled from his fingertips along his arm, across his shoulders, along the other arm, and back again, and stopped at the nape of his neck.

"My Daddy said you're some kind of ball genius," I said.

"I am. I'll be playing with the Cardinals when I'm eighteen. Or nineteen. If I don't go in the Service first. That would delay me, even if I could get in when I'm fifteen."

"I think you're good enough to play with the Cardinals right now, Tian."

"Not big enough. But I will be. The best players are big, most of them."

"My Daddy said you're big for your age."

"I am. I take after my father."

"Is your father a ball genius?" I said.

"A different kind. Mathematics."

I didn't know what that was. "Where is he? Is he where a lot of fighting is?"

"I can't talk about that. It could put his life in danger."

"I wouldn't tell anybody," I said.

"The walls have ears."

The way he said that, I knew he was repeating something from a grown-up, so it was just a senseless thing.

He said, "I don't know *precisely* where he is. I know what country, and what part of that country, but that's all. My mother and I are the only ones who know even that. His own brother doesn't know, so don't get your feelings hurt that I'm not telling. I would never tell anybody, even if they tortured me."

That alarmed me. "Who?"

At first he didn't answer, and I could see he wasn't teasing.

"Who?" I said again.

"The Japanese."

I said, "They're not here where we are, they're where they are."

"Some of them could be hiding here right now. Down the street in a basement somewhere. In this basement, even, why not? Sneaking around at night to find out things. And do sabotage. And if they win the war they're in, they'll fight us in the United States and come by the millions, and if they win that they'll take over everything and kill everybody."

"Well they just better not!" I said.

THAT NIGHT after Mother and Daddy had turned out the light and shut their door, I got scared. Finally a screech came out of me all by itself.

Both of them were beside me in a second, saying, "What is it? What's the matter? Are you hurting? Where does it hurt?"

"I'm scared."

"There's nothing to be scared of, punkin," Daddy said. And Mother said, "My poor baby, there's nothing to be scared of."

"Daddy, see if somebody's under my bed."

"Honey, there's nobody under there. Nobody could get under there, it's not high enough." he said.

"See anyway."

He lay flat on the floor with his face sideways so that he could look into the black inch between the floor and the couch. "Nobody," he said, getting up.

"Put the lock on the door."

"It's locked," Mother said. "We always lock it at night, you know that, darlin'."

"No, the chain."

Daddy stepped to the door and put the safety chain in its slot. "There. Listen here, my girlsie, no ol' booger is ever going to bother you while your Daddy is around. Why, I would just grab him up and spin him around, and throw him right out the window, and that would be the end of him."

Mother said, "It's an aftereffect of your accident, honey, that's what. Your little brain got a shock, and it's making up things. You never were afraid of the dark before, you remember that?"

"Yes Ma'am."

She said, "It'll go away, don't you worry. You want to sleep with me, and let Daddy sleep on the couch this one night?"

"Yes Ma'am."

Neither of them, then or later, thought to ask me what I was afraid of. And I somehow didn't want to tell. And the Japanese, not one of whom I had ever met in person or would meet until I was in my teens, became as much a part of my early life as they were of Tian's.

PEOPLE BROUGHT my meals up on a tray, and Mother's too, for the two weeks I was on complete bed rest. I liked meals in bed at first, but soon I missed being in the mix of people in the dining room and the kitchen. I began to whine about that. And I missed Mama Linnet. Before My Accident I had spent most of my days in her company or near her. Now I could have her only when she came to sit with me for a few minutes that went too fast a couple of times a day. That was all the time she could steal. I didn't care why she had to go, I just wanted her to stay, and I bawled and brayed when she tried to leave. "She's getting spoiled," Mother said.

Mother was at her wits' end from my crying and whining out of the boredom of getting well. Also I couldn't stay in bed. Not wouldn't: couldn't. My body had its own will that was too strong. When Mother got lost in her sewing by the window I began getting up behind her back and walking quietly, steadying myself by holding on to the furniture or touching the wall, all around that part of the room, and then into their room. Usually Mother caught me before I got back in bed, and fussed at me. But then one day I made it all the way out the open door and into the hall without her knowing, and down the hall, and down the stairs by sitting down and easing down on my bottom, a step at a time. All the way down. Then of course I ran out of gas.

Mama Linnet found me sitting on the bottom step about to cry, and her hands went to her heart. After she found out I was all right she asked me kindly what I was doing there. I told her I was coming to find her. She sat down beside me and we were together in silence for a while, holding hands.

"Are you ready to go back upstairs now?" she said then.

"Mother won't like it that I was gone."

"Maybe she'll just be glad to see you. Come on, I'll take you." She stood and picked me up.

Mother looked up as we came in the door, but it took a few seconds for her to put it together. "Mary Mavis!" she said. To Mama Linnet she said, "Where was she?"

"She's getting well fast. I think we could telephone Dr. Haynes and let him know how much better she's doing since just last week. He might change his orders, what she can do."

"Where was she?"

Mama Linnet told her.

"Mary Mavis," Mother said, "What am I going to do with you? What am I going to say to your Daddy? He'll be mad at you and me both." She started crying.

I had seen her cry before, but never because I made her do it. I started crying too.

Mama Linnet put me down on my couch bed and straightened up toward Mother. "Seems like there's no harm done. It might even be good for her."

"What you really think is, I can't even watch over my own sick child," Mother said.

"No, I think you do a fine job. She's the smartest, the prettiest, and the best, child in the world. And the cleanest. And the best dressed."

Mother's tears were stopping but she didn't say anything.

Mama Linnet gave my leg a little rub, and she left.

Mother put aside her sewing and sat and watched me lie on the couch. I pouted and fiddled with my fingers.

Before long Mama Linnet was back, knocking on the frame of the open doorway. She said, "Dr. Haynes said she can walk three times a day until she gets tired, and in the meantime she can sit up in a chair at the table several times a day." She added, "So it turns out we actually didn't break any rules."

"You see?" Mother said, "I can't even talk to her doctor! I never get a chance to. Just because you're paying the bill doesn't mean you get to run the show. We're going to pay you back, you know."

Mama Linnet thought about what to say and decided it should be nothing, and she left again.

Mother said to me, "You can put all this out of your mind and forget it, you're too young to understand it. And don't bother your daddy with it. Do you want to sit up in a chair?"

"Do you mean keep it a secret from Daddy?" I said.

"No I don't mean keep it a secret from Daddy! I just mean don't bother him with it." She got calmer as she talked on. "He's got enough on his mind. Sometimes if there's no reason to tell people the bad part, you can tell them just the good part."

"What's the bad part, and what's the good part?" I said.

"I told you: put the bad part out of your mind. The good part is that the doctor said you can get up and walk, and you did."

THEY LET me eat in the dining room again, starting that evening. Dr. Haynes Senior had come by to be sure he was right in changing his orders, and he accepted Mama Linnet's invitation to supper. We were late getting down there, and lots of my grownup friends were already gone, but I was glad to see everybody who was still there, even Mr. Tony almost. Everybody gathered at one table. On my side were Mother, Daddy, me, Roger/Tian, and Dr. Haynes Senior. Across from us: Miss Sara Ann, who had come in in a rush at the same time we did because she was late getting back from seeing her little dog or girl, and Mr. Tony, The Lawyer Cato, Miss Lucy, and Miss Claire who had served fresh-filled bowls and full platters before sitting down herself. Last of all, Mama Linnet came out of the kitchen and sat to eat at the only place open, beside Dr. Haynes Senior.

The menu was ham steaks, turnips, boiled buttered potatoes, corn bread, red Jell-O salad with apple bits in it, and white cake with yellow icing.

"How's your pitching coming along?" Daddy asked Roger/Tian.

"Fine, sir. I might get a try-out with the Blues. I'm trying to get one. Not to play, though, at first. For ball boy. Then maybe if they see what I can do they might let me play. Some." He was talking about the city's amateur team. The players were men and a few boys a lot older than he was.

"That's pretty ambitious, even for you," Daddy said.

"Yes sir, but I'm going to try."

"You're going to cause yourself to be real disappointed, is what. Wait a couple years."

"There might not be a Blues then. If the war keeps on,

too many of them will have gone into the Service. They say some of the good ones are already going. I thought that would help my chances."

"You got a point there," Daddy said. "So why not wait until more of them are gone? You'd have even a better chance."

"I can try now, and then if I don't make it, try later. Mr. Lewis, would you want to pop some flies after we eat?"

"I'll pass this time," Daddy said.

Roger/Tian looked around to see who else might be available. His eyes passed right across Mr. Tony, hesitated on The Lawyer Cato, and came to rest on the only other man in the room. Dr. Haynes Senior had taken his eyes off Mama Linnet and had turned his head to look at Roger/Tian.

"Good evening, Sir," Roger/Tian said to him. "We haven't met. I am Roger Evans-Lee."

"Good evening to you. I am Dr. Harold Haynes Senior."

"Have you met my mother, Dr. Haynes? Mother, allow me to introduce Dr. Haynes Senior. Dr. Haynes Senior, Mrs. Evans-Lee."

Everybody was staring at Tian by now.

"How do you do, Mrs. Evans-Lee," said Dr. Haynes Senior.

"It's very nice to meet you, Doctor," Miss Claire said.

"I overheard that you play baseball," the doctor said to Tian.

"Yes sir, I do."

"He's a prodigy," said The Lawyer Cato from behind his red mustache. "Willard Cato at your service, Doctor. Very talented boy. Very talented."

"Is that so, Mr. Cato," the doctor said.

" He is."

"And you aspire to the Blues, Roger," said the doctor.

"I aspire to the Cardinals. But the Blues first," said Roger/Tian.

"Do you know any of the Blues?" the doctor said.

"One, Sir. Dave Harding. Shortstop . . . second string."

"Yes," the doctor said.

"Do you know him?" Roger/Tian said.

"I know them all. I'm the Blues' coach and manager," the doctor said. "And sponsor," he added, smiling and shaking his head as if he had two different feelings about that.

"Well *Sir!*" Roger/Tian said.

"Dang you say," Daddy said. "I didn't know that!"

"I can hit some flies with you after we eat," the doctor said to Roger/Tian.

And so just before dusk on that hot summer evening, we on the front porch were treated to a show of skills. The two of them played in the shaded empty street. Dr. Haynes Senior hit the ball again and again so high above the trees that the setting sun made it glow up there, and yet it came down every time for Roger/Tian to catch it in the middle of the street. Roger/Tian caught every one. Then they changed roles, and with Roger/Tian hitting the pop-ups we slowly saw that the doctor had been the better hitter and was now being a better catcher, even without a glove.

They were good to watch. Roger/Tian was, yes, big for his age, but not as big as he seemed. His body was well made, and thick and solid, and his muscles were hidden under his flesh. But even at age thirteen when he lacked some grace because he had to struggle to get the job done, you could see the power that would come. His hair was different from anyone else's I had ever seen. It was shining black and stood straight out, two inches long, all over his head.

I had always thought Dr. Haynes Senior was nice enough looking, but I had never before seen him except indoors where his arms and legs looked too long for the furniture and his feet looked too big even for his own body. That night outside in the coming dark, as he played ball in his dress shoes and trousers with his white shirt unbuttoned at the throat and sticking to him with sweat so that his long strong neck showed, and his sleeves rolled up above his elbows so you could see how heavy the bones were underneath the ropy muscles in his arms, and all his actions done with such graceful power . . . he changed before my eyes from a halfway handsome scarecrow into a moving spectacle of beauty. I realized I held him to be more wonderful than Daddy, and a feeling of guilty confusion came over me about that, like a blush throughout my body that wouldn't go away. To me, my admiration of this other man was a betrayal of Daddy and I was helpless to do anything about it.

All of us on the porch saw that side of Dr. Haynes Senior that evening, and also we saw the promise that was beginning to fulfill itself in Roger/Tian. The two of them made a magic pair, and we all saw that too. Mother did, Daddy, The Lawyer Cato, Miss Sara Ann, Miss Lucy, Miss Claire, who smiled watching her boy. And Mama Linnet, who had postponed the supper clean-up to come out and watch.

Dr. Haynes Senior came around often after that night.

He took Roger/Tian under his wing, and made him a Blues' bat boy, and came by in his car to get him for games and practice, and trained him, and saw to it that he practiced with boys and men as good or better than he was. He gave him paid work sweeping and washing windows and mowing grass at his office and house for an hour every weekday and two hours on Saturdays. Roger/Tian had a lot of happiness that summer.

Dr. Haynes Senior came to see me three times a week for at least a month. After the first week Mother said each time, "It's nice of him to come, but she's practically well." Soon she said to Daddy, "He's running up his bill, that's what. You need to say something to him."

Daddy said, "Cesarine, will you hush about that. Mama is paying the bill, and I'll cross that bridge with her later. Probably he's not charging her anything. I'd be a fool to mess that up."

Miss Sara Ann and Mother had become sort of friends with each other by then. One day Mother said to her about the doctor, "It's nice of him to come, but Mary Mavis is practically well." Miss Sara Ann said, "Oh, I think it's because Somebody is attracted to Somebody, don't you?"

5

A DAY OR TWO LATER MR. TONY SAID HE GOT DRAFTED. MISS Sara Ann told Mother, crying. He was to report soon. Miss Sara Ann wanted Mother to help give him a surprise going-away party. As she talked about her plans her tears stopped and she turned cheery. "We could have roses and candles on the white tablecloths, and gifts," she said. When she saw Mother's look she added, "Little gifts," and went on. "Mrs. Lewis could make a big sheet cake, chocolate is his favorite. And we can make crêpe paper garlands and streamers. Claire could play the piano with the door open to the sitting room, beginning with For He's A Jolly Good Fellow at the surprise, and then transitioning into a quiet serenade so that there would be background music the whole time. Including our song worked into the medley several times."

She paused but Mother didn't ask what their song was. I started to ask but didn't get a chance because she went on telling the plans.

"If I can find out his parents' telephone number, I'm sure they have one, they're rich, we could secretly invite them.

Would you talk to them? I wouldn't want to appear forward. I would pay for the long-distance call."

"Have you asked Mrs. Lewis? About the cake and using the dining room and everything?" Mother said.

"Oh she'll be all for it. One of her own called to the service. I know she'll want to do everything she can."

"Maybe, maybe not," Mother said, "Mrs. Lewis has her own way of thinking about things."

"Could you get Pat to ask her? If it were Pat's idea I know she'd do it."

WHEN MOTHER ASKED Daddy to ask Mama Linnet if we could have a party with a cake for Mr. Tony, he said, "Hell no I won't ask her to have a party for Tony Bishop."

She said, "Do you care if I ask her?"

He said, "Why? You don't like him any better than I do. Nobody does."

"Sara Ann does," she said.

"No, she thinks she does. Underneath that blonde hair is a custard pie," Daddy said.

"Don't you like Sara Ann?"

Daddy was careful of that question. He said, "I like her all right, I guess you could say."

"Don't you remember how good she's been to Mary Mavis and me, after the accident? I've told you. Don't you think she's been a friend to all of us?"

"I guess. Yeah," he said. "But Cesarine, giving her boyfriend a party when nobody really likes him makes no sense."

"When she's your friend, and it will make her really

happy, and it won't hurt anything or anybody, why does it have to make sense?"

Daddy looked at her and after a while said, "You beat anything I ever saw."

THE NEIGHBORHOOD HAD a lot of roses but the blooms had come and gone. In Miss Sara Ann's mind they were still there. It was the morning of the day of the party-to-be, and as I passed her door in the hall, out she came. I was surprised because she usually went Saturdays and Sundays to her mother's. This day she wore a white straw hat with a floppy brim and a blue band that matched her eyes. Her hair was in long curls. Over her dress was a white apron. Hanging on her arm was a basket containing white gloves and a pair of scissors. She looked like a picture in my book of nursery rhymes.

She locked her door and dropped the key in her apron pocket and said, "Mary Mavis! Just the one! How would you like to go to the flower garden with me and gather some roses for tonight?"

"I'd like to," I said. "Where is it?"

She sang her answer as she moved down the hall in a dance step. "Come with me to the garden, the garden. Come with me to the garden, come with me, my girl." She circled back, still singing and dancing, and took my hand. I tried to skip with her but my feet would not. I still had to be careful when I walked. She stopped immediately and said, "I forgot you're still getting well." She kept my hand and led me slowly down the stairs, out the front door, down the porch stairs, and a left turn onto the little brick path in front of the porch. This put us passing The Lawyer Cato, who was about two feet above us, up on the porch, in the swing, with a glass of orange juice in one hand and an unlit cigar in the other. Miss Sara Ann stopped and sang to him, "Good morning to you, Mister Cato."

"Mmhh. Good morning."

"We're after flowers," she said.

"I see. So I see."

"Will you be at the party tonight?"

"Mmhh. That would be hard. Something else on my schedule," he said.

"No! I hope you'll change it. The circle wouldn't be complete without you. I wanted to talk to you earlier, but we're both gone so much." She reached up and briefly patted his knee. Her blue eyes got even bigger. His brown eyes got bigger.

She said, "Will. Is it all right if I call you Will?"

"Certainly. Certainly."

"Promise me you'll try to change your plans and come. No. Promise me you'll *succeed* in changing your plans."

His glass tilted and some of its juice spilled on the nice blue pants leg of his knee. He crammed the cigar into his mouth and with the free hand grabbed around into his pockets. Then he transferred the juice glass and searched the other side of his clothes. Eventually he came up with a white folded square of handkerchief. He tried to shake it out, and spilled more juice. She reached up and took the handkerchief from him and dabbed and blotted his wet knee while he sat still as a rock.

She said, almost like saying a secret, "If it's a date with somebody, you could bring her."

"It's work," he said loudly. "End of the fiscal year."

"They'll just have to do without you." She gave him the handkerchief and looked up into his eyes. "Please tell me I can expect you."

"Do the best I can," he said.

She and I went on around the side of the house without running into anybody else. No one in the parking lot nor walking on Fourth Street. I think she was disappointed.

At the backyard, she looked around as if we were in a new place. The steep wooden steps to the back door. The green paint-peeled lattice that made a skirt for the house. The little wooden door to the cellar. The brick walkway half buried under the creeping grass. The clothesline posts and the lines. A fig bush. A couple of other bushes. And a green mound made of many tangled rose vines covering an old trellis that couldn't support them anymore.

"What happened to the flower garden?" she said.

"Where is it?" I asked again.

MRS. TABOR, the old lady across the street, did have flowers around her house. I pointed this out to Miss Sara Ann and she took me straight over there and turned the doorbell.

I had met Mrs. Tabor only through her front screen door but I knew she was nice. She and Mama Linnet were friendly neighbors although their paths seldom crossed. She lived alone and didn't have much company except for the woman who was her helper and housekeeper, who was almost as old. A man mowed her yard every week and kept up the shrubs and flowers the way she told him. When she answered the door, Miss Sara Ann introduced herself and talked a blue streak. Soon Miss Tabor had been invited to the party and had accepted. Next Miss Sara Ann and I were out in her back yard gathering yellow gladiolus as tall as I was, and zinnias of all colors as big as bread plates, and huge red-orange cannas and giant blue-and-pink balls of hydrangea. After we made the first trip to bring all the flowers across the street and were about to go back for another load, The Lawyer Cato stuck his head out from hiding behind his newspaper and said, "You need help, there."

"Would you, Will? That is so wonderful of you!" Miss Sara Ann said.

He had a gimpy leg. As a young man he'd had his knee shattered when something scared his horse just as he put his foot in the stirrup. He walked with a cane and a limp, and didn't like to be noticed for it. She took him across the street and piled him with flowers for two more trips before we had them all. Mrs. Tabor's garden still had so many blooms it was as if no one had cut any. She said it was a pleasure to know they would be enjoyed.

MAMA LINNET HAD SAID the party could be in the sitting room and dining room both, if Miss Sara Ann would be responsible for the cleanup, ready for the next day, but they could only use one tablecloth. She said she would make a sheet cake with icing but it couldn't be chocolate because of the cost. She said yes, the water pitchers could be used for flower vases but in that case the flowers would have to be thrown out before the next morning and that would be a shame. Miss Claire said she would play For He's A Jolly Good Fellow on the piano at the beginning but after that she would rather enjoy herself with everyone else. The Lawyer Cato halfway promised to be there. Miss Sara Ann still thought she might get the telephone number for Mr. Tony's parents. The crêpe paper was too expensive for Miss Sara Ann but Mother bought one roll of blue. Miss Sara Ann was thrilled with the way things were turning out.

I SAID TO MOTHER, "I know where some big vases are."

"You know where some big vases are," she said back in kind of a sing-song. She was three steps up on a ladder at the dining room doorway, with the crêpe paper and a hammer and some tacks.

"Yes Ma'am," I said. After a while I said, "Do you want to know where?"

"Mmmm," she said. By then she had some tacks in her mouth.

"'Way 'way back in the basement."

"Mmmm."

She kept dropping tacks and I kept picking them up. She wasn't a good hammerer.

"Who could get them?" I said, thinking of the spiders and who knows what else down there with the vases.

"Are you remembering to watch out for somebody not knowing this ladder is here and knocking me off?" she said.

I had long forgotten that. "Yes Ma'am," I said.

But when she had finished and climbed down and had pulled the ladder to its place on the screened back porch I said, "Mother!"

"What!" she said.

"There are some big vases in the basement. I saw them."

"What were you doing in there? Haven't I told you not to get in there?

"No Ma'am."

"Well, you know better. You stay out of there. Next thing, you'll be snakebit."

Snakes in there had not occurred to me exactly. After a while I said, "Someone could go in there and get them. Daddy could."

"I don't want him snakebit either," she said. She was thinking it over. "What do they look like?" She could see I thought she meant snakes, and she said, "The vases."

"I think they're different colors. It's dark in there. They have gold on them. They're big." I showed her, about as tall as my waist.

"How many?"

I couldn't remember. "Eleven or eight," I said.

DADDY WAS SITTING in Mother's sewing chair by our window, reading a magazine, when she started in on him about the vases. "Aw, Cesarine," he said, "There's no gold-decorated antique 'vahzez' in that cellar. Who would do that! It's not even a cellar, it's just a place under the house."

"Maybe they hid them from the Yankees," she said.

"It wasn't like *Gone With The Wind* here, honey. Don't you know any history at all?"

She said, "You don't know what's under there and what's not. Probably nobody does. From what Mary Mavis saw, there just might be some very valuable pieces. Whatever they are, I want to know," she said

"Whatever they are, they're not ours."

"Finders keepers," she said.

"Now you're wanting me to steal from my own mother. Not that there's anything to steal. No. Period. Get some other sucker to go on a wild goose chase for your antiques."

"I'll go myself," she said.

He laughed and said, "No you won't," and went back to reading the paper.

———

BUT SHE DID, soon as he left for work the next day, and took me with her. It was a bright day. We stood outside in the hot morning and looked at the wooden door behind which I knew were six rock steps leading down into blackness. I said, "Are we waiting for something?" She had Daddy's flashlight and turned it on before we folded the door back. The sun lit up the top steps. Beyond that we were looking at a dark hole. She went down first, and then held me so I couldn't fall as I came down. When we were both at the bottom she grabbed the shoulder of my dress and held it. She directed the pale flashlight toward just about every different place down there, making the light jump around.

"Listen to me," she said. She was whispering. "Don't touch anything. And don't let anything touch you. That's the way spiders get on you. Watch every step before you take it, in case of a snake. Phew this musty smell. Which way are the vases?"

"They're on the other side of that big thing over there," I said, pointing to what I knew was a set of shelves in the black depth. All we could really see, though, was something huge and looming.

We shuffled and inched along on the dirt that nearly

covered the concrete floor, stepping also on a lot of forgotten old stuff. Some of it was soft. Maybe snakelike. Whenever Mother's foot touched something that scared her she gasped and jerked my dress. Once she thought something had fallen or jumped onto her hair, and she slapped her head in a fit, making the flashlight crazy. We finally got to our destination but the precious daylight from the stairway was blocked there. We could hardly make out anything, even directly in the flashlight.

Mother whispered, "All right. Where are they?"

I had begun to dread this part. I didn't quite remember where the vases were.

My voice sounded little and far away, even to me. I said, "Over that way?"

She stood stone still a while and then whispered, "Mary Mavis, just exactly how could you have seen any vases in this pitch black? Tell me the truth."

I said, "I did too see them. I borrowed Mama Linnet's flashlight. It's better than Daddy's. I put it back!"

She turned the flashlight toward the stairs and pulled my dress shoulder in that direction.

I said, "Aren't we going to get the vases?"

She said, "Not right now."

EARLY THAT AFTERNOON after the last of the lunch customers had gone, Miss Savory did what she always did and locked the front door. No sooner did she head back toward the kitchen than somebody started turning the doorbell like a fire alarm. Miss Savory opened the door and a big man came right in without being asked. He wore a blue suit and a tan cowboy hat.

He took the hat off and said, "Mrs. Lewis home?"

Miss Savory said, "Have a seat. I'll tell her you want to see her." She tilted her head toward the hall bench with the long flat cushion and started away.

"Who is it you're going to tell her wants to see her?" he said to her back.

She turned around. "Her ex-husband," she said. She might as well have said The Devil.

"You didn't get that right," the big man said, "maybe I better find her myself." He walked past Miss Savory, who didn't make it easy, toward Mama Linnet's apartment and the kitchen, which were both in the same direction. I was there at that end of the hall.

When he got to me he stopped and looked at me and squatted down and put his hat back on, and tilted it, and smiled, and I smiled back. Everything about him made me want to hug his neck.

He said, "I know who you are. I can tell by looking."

I said, "I know who you are, too."

He said, "How do you know?"

I thought about it, and said, "I just do."

He said, "Are you too big to be picked up?" He was grinning and teasing me.

"No!" I said and threw myself at him.

He stood up with me. I was squeezing him.

"What's this?" he said. "Looky here, what in the world is this?" His hand went behind my growing-out hair to my ear, and pulled out a quarter.

He let me pry it out of his fingers. "What you gonna buy with that?" he said.

I told him about my piggy bank and saving to buy a little brother or sister. We were sitting on the bench discussing that when Mama Linnet came into the hall.

She stood looking down at the two of us before she spoke. Then she said, "Hampton."

"Good afternoon, Mrs. Lewis," said Granddaddy. They looked at each other for a pause, and then he jiggled me and said, "She's a keeper."

"She is," said Mama Linnet.

"This is our girl. She looks like you and me both, pet. This is the girl we never got." Then he started growling and put both his big arms around me, pretending he was squeezing me too hard. "But now we got her," he said. I was laughing and squealing, up against him, pretending I was trying to get away, and the two of us knocked his hat off.

Mama Linnet picked it up and brushed it with her fingertips, and kept it for him while we played. When we settled down she said to him, "You're looking well."

"And you are looking more beautiful even than the last time I saw you," he said. "How is that possible?"

"What brings you?" she said.

"You do."

For an answer, same as she always asked everybody, she asked him, "Would you like some ice water? or a cup of coffee?"

He said coffee.

She said, "I'll get it. Have a seat in the dining room."

He said, "How about somewhere more private?"

"The dining room will be fine," she said, and left us.

HE LOOKED AROUND and saw the closed double doors to the dining room. He nodded toward them and asked me, "That still the dining room?"

"Yep," I said. I had never said less than 'Yes sir' to any grown man, but I was playful and sassy with him. I had my hands on his hair by that time. His head was covered with short crispy waves of brown with silver mixed in. I stroked it, then patted it. "Your hair is nice," I said.

In the dining room he pulled a chair out from a table in the dining room and sat down with me in his lap.

"It runs in our family," he said. "I have hair like my mama's. And you have hair like mine, what do you think about that?"

"I do not. My hair's not really as short as yours, it's all cut off because I had a accident. And I'm almost a blonde."

"Well," he said, "Your hair will be long again pretty soon. Hair grows fast in our family. My hair used to be long. One time I let it grow just to see what would happen. Next thing, I looked just like my mama. Even my daddy couldn't tell us apart. And then to see what would happen, I let it keep growing, and left off my hat. My hair was down to the ground. I had to be careful not to step on it. Long curls. The sun bleached it out to pure shining gold. People I'd known all my life would say, 'Who is that beautiful woman? I think I've seen her in a famous painting.' My hair was so long I couldn't lose anything. If I dropped something, my hair would catch it and carry it along home. If I was short of rope or string I could cut off a curl of hair and use that. Very handy. But I kept having to get in fights because one man after another wanted me to be his girlfriend."

Mama Linnet had come in. She said, "Hampton."

"It's all right, Missus Lewis. This story has two endings," he said.

I didn't get to hear either ending. Miss Claire came to the doorway and said she was going to the zoo and did I want to go.

"Is Roger going with us?" I said.

"No," she said. It didn't occur to me that it was odd for her to be going to the zoo on a workday by herself. I begged Granddaddy to go with us, but he said Next Time.

———

THAT NIGHT MOTHER told Daddy about My Granddaddy's visit. She was going to tell him all that she had been able to find out about it, but Daddy acted some way that made her suspicious on the front end. She stopped talking and then said, "Did you already know he came here?"

"Did I know it?"

"Did you know it."

"No, I didn't, Cesarine, not for a fact," he said.

"I don't keep secrets from you," she said.

"Like heck you don't, but that's another one I'll let go by. There can't be anything secret about a man talking to his own father."

"He told you he was coming? Or he told you after he'd been here?"

"What difference could it make?" he said.

"If you're bound and determined to talk to him, what you should tell him is to stay away," she said.

"Cesarine, none of this is your business," he said.

"I'm not a member of your family?" she said. "I thought I was, for some reason."

6

SOMEHOW DR. HAYNES SENIOR AND GRANDDADDY BOTH GOT invited to Mr. Tony's going-away party. Mama Linnet had had no idea either one of them would be there.

I was glad to see the doctor, and then, next, thrilled to see My Granddaddy, who was one of the last to come. My hero-worship for Dr. Haynes Senior had melted to just admiration when I met Granddaddy. What I felt for Granddaddy wasn't worship, it was too cozy for that. Now I crossed the dining room and threw myself at his legs, and he picked me up and walked around holding me in his left arm while he made acquaintance with everyone. He already knew a few of them. Soon he came to Mama Linnet and Dr. Haynes Senior standing together, and he smiled and patted her arm while he said hello. Then he stopped smiling while he said his name to the doctor, and the doctor said his own name. There was no handshake. Granddaddy and I continued around the room full of people.

Miss Sara Ann came from the hallway and appeared in the frame of the door, arm in arm with Mr. Tony. He was a half-step behind her, and they pretended she had to pull him in. Everybody yelled, "Surprise!" and "Speech!" Mr. Tony pretended to be embarrassed, and shook his head and put up a hand, No No. Miss Claire interrupted by playing loud chords on the piano in the sitting room. Double doors that slid on tracks back into the walls made the two rooms open to each other. Miss Claire sat at the antique square piano and played "For He's a Jolly Good Fellow," and everybody sang and then clapped.

Miss Sara Ann got The Lawyer Cato started at the record player. She had sweet-talked him earlier into saying he would keep the music going, and he seemed more comfortable having the job. The music was a true variety, from a collection of random big black records in paper jackets. They lived inside a cabinet in the sitting room. A hodgepodge of people over the years had donated or forgotten them. Chopin, Roy Acuff, Kate Smith, and more. One, though, was new. Miss Sara Ann handed it to The Lawyer Cato and he read its name out loud. He was trying to be playful and modern. But the way he said it, I almost didn't recognize it. "The Boogahwoogah Bugal Boyah Frum Compahneh B." But then I knew what he had said, and got excited. I had heard it on the radio, and knew it was to jitterbug to. I was dying to see someone jitterbug. I wanted to know how, for the time when I would be able to dance again. But then he chose a different record to play.

With the flowers in the water pitchers, and the crêpe paper garlands, and the cake and punch laid out on the one table cloth, and about twenty people all in such a good mood—or I thought, all—it seemed to me a wonderful party.

Mama Linnet caught up to Granddaddy and me. She

said low, so that only we could hear, "Hampton, why are you here?"

"I was invited," he said. "It would have been rude not to come."

"Hampton. Just please . . . "

"May I have this dance?" he said to her. It was the Missouri Waltz. He winked at me and said, "I knew her before I knew you," and carefully put me down.

He took her hand, then turned toward The Lawyer Cato and said, "Start that one over again, would you buddy."

She danced with him.

They were so good at it everybody began to watch and give them room. They had turned into movie stars. I almost couldn't believe that one of them was my Mama Linnet. Roger/Tian came up to me. He kept his eyes on them and said, "That man can dance. So can your grandmother . . . how could she be anybody's grandmother? She's not old enough."

They ended it close to me and came back to me. He bowed and said to her, "Thank you, Most Beautiful Lady In The World, for the next-best dance I ever had." The way he said it, and the way she took it, made you know his very-best dance had also been with her.

She nodded.

He said, "I'll be going, soon as it won't call attention."

She nodded.

To me, he said, "Guess who this is for?", and reached in his pocket and pulled out a little white box tied with white silk ribbon. I grabbed for it. He wouldn't let go. He said, "You have to promise to wait 'til tomorrow to open it."

"I promise."

But still he pretended he would put it back in his pocket. He said, "Naw, I bet you can't keep a promise."

"I can too!"

He let me take it from his fingers. To Mama Linnet he said, "You might want to help her not lose that."

She nodded.

Then he slipped out the door and got his hat off the rack in the hall, and was gone.

Mama Linnet said, "Why don't you let me keep your present until in the morning." I gave it to her and she tried to put it in her apron pocket before she realized she had no apron. With her empty hand she picked up some used punch glasses and backed through the swinging door into the kitchen. She did not return.

———————

MRS. TABOR from across the street, soon after she came to the party, had taken a seat near The Lawyer Cato. She wore a garnet red dress with a gold pin with garnets, and she had put her silver hair into a refined style. I was surprised, and I looked her up and down. I had known her only as a shape with an agreeable voice in the gloom behind her screen door. She and The Lawyer were having a nice talk, in between his changing the records. She was doing most of the talking, and The Lawyer looked at ease.

She said. "My son was an attorney. I lost him nineteen years ago. Do you take new clients?"

"I'm with the state. I don't have a practice."

"But you could. Ethically. Have a practice." she said.

"Oh . . . yes . . . ethically. Theoretically. There would be no conflict unless I'd do private work on state time."

"And you would never do that, we know. Surely people ask you? To help them with their legal matters?"

"Oh . . . no . . . just a few relatives needing their wills done, or bills of sale. Deeds. Like that. "

"Would you be interested in helping me along those lines? On your off time? I don't need much, just to change my will. A bit of direction to make sure it's right." she said.

"Hm, I possibly would. Now, I don't have an office."

"My son sometimes made house calls. Would you be in a position to do that, just across the street?"

MISS LUCY HAD the day off from her extra job at the nursing home. She kept terribly busy at the party. She traveled fast from one couple or cluster to another but her worried brown eyes never really looked at anyone. Each time, she listened just long enough to latch on to whatever they might have been talking about, then butted in to add something herself, and waited barely long enough to be civil, then moved on again. She laughed a lot, with a fretting sound. She got around to everybody at least twice.

Mother and Daddy slipped out into the hall for a few seconds when they thought I wouldn't notice, and spiked their punch from a flask he had brought downstairs and hidden behind a curtain. I knew without being told that they wanted to keep it secret from Mama Linnet that they sometimes drank whiskey. A little later they came back in and picked out two records and danced. They weren't as good as Mama Linnet and My Granddaddy. Then Daddy held my hands and I put my feet on top of his feet, and he danced with me once, slowly. Miss Sara Ann got Mr. Tony to dance with her for part of a dreamy song, but he didn't want to. Until yet, until yet, until yet, no one had jitterbugged.

But then Omar Phelps, the trucker who leased our garages and slept on the back porch twice a month, asked if there wasn't any faster music. The Lawyer Cato put on The Boogie Woogie Bugle Boy.

Omar Phelps had found a partner, one of four girlfriends Miss Sara Ann invited. He danced with her and then asked for a repeat of the record, and then later asked for it again. He was a heavy, wild rough dancer and jerked her around a lot, and everybody else got out of their way. His longish straight dark hair fell down across his sweaty face. Either his partner didn't know how to do the dance at all or didn't know how with him, I couldn't tell, and I was disappointed about the jitterbug.

But the two of them liked each other and stayed closer and closer together for the rest of the party. Omar Phelps too had brought some alcohol to secretly drink. Mama Linnet would have sent him on his way if she had still been there. Mother and Daddy talked about it on the sly.

"He's drunk. Are you going to do something about him?" Mother said.

Daddy shrugged. "None of my business."

"I will, then. That poor girl. I'll tell Sara Ann to tell her to get away from him."

Which Mother did, but Miss Sara Ann only glanced around at her girlfriend and Mr. Phelps in the corner and said she'd see what she could do, and never did anything but keep on being the hostess and partner of the guest of honor.

Mr. Tony's parents were not there.

Roger/Tian could jitterbug! And of all things, so could his mother. He went to her where she was sitting in a corner talking quietly with a couple of other people, asked her to dance, took her hand, led her to the record player, asked for the music, and they danced a fast and sophisticated swing that revved up to jitterbug steps.

Their feet flew and miraculously their heads didn't move. I recognized the real thing when I saw it, and was not disappointed anymore. Also I started planning how to get Roger/Tian to teach me when I got well. I was easing in his direction even before their dance was over. "How did you know how to do that?" I said. He told me his mother taught him, that she was a professional dancer as well as musician. I asked him what professional meant and he explained she used to make her living dancing—all kinds of dancing, he said—and playing music. In New York and Europe. He said Europe was where his parents met and married.

THE OTHER THREE of Miss Sara Ann's girlfriends stayed bunched together for a long time. I heard one of them tell the other two who Dr. Haynes Senior was, and they glanced his way a lot, whispering. Finally one said, "Here I go," and headed toward him, pretending to be wandering the room.

The doctor and Roger/Tian were talking baseball. Soon after the young woman reached the doctor he excused himself and went into the kitchen. He went from there to the hall, knocking lightly on Mama Linnet's apartment door.

"Linnet? It's Harry."

She said something I couldn't make out.

"If it's that bad let me get you something. My bag's in the car."

She said something.

"Please talk with me for a minute."

She said something.

"All right then. I'll call you in the morning."

She said something.

He said, "Goodbye . . . sweet."

THE NEXT MORNING WAS A SATURDAY, and I thought Mother and Daddy would never get up. I hadn't learned to tell time. I was wild to know what was in the little white box My Granddaddy had given me, and I was desperate because I knew Mama Linnet would soon leave. She would go as early as she could to the train station, to shop the Farmers' Market there.

I was not allowed to wake my parents. I got dressed and waited until I could tolerate it no more, then went downstairs alone.

Mama Linnet was not gone, thank goodness, she was still in the kitchen, taking biscuits from the oven. Saturdays and Sundays were the help's days off, and meals were only for boarders. She didn't actually serve meals on the weekends, only prepared the food and left it in the kitchen for self-serving. Breakfast from 7:00 to 9:00 A.M., lunch noon to 2:00, supper 4:00 to 6:00. One of Daddy's new jobs on weekends was to wash dishes and tidy up after each meal, and lay out and heat the food for the coming meal. Half the time Mama Linnet let him out of it.

"Where is my present?" I said to her. I was bobbing up and down.

"It's nice to say Good Morning first, honey. I'll get it for you."

My Granddaddy had given me a gold heart and chain necklace, made for a little girl.

"Oh my," Mama Linnet said.

"Put it on me. Please."

She did, and said, "Isn't that beautiful. You are the prettiest girl in the world and it suits you exactly right. Come look in the mirror." We went to her apartment, to her dressing table. She took her brush and comb to my short hair while I leaned close to the mirror and looked at my locket.

"My Granddaddy is a good granddaddy!" I said.

"This is expensive jewelry," she said. "It's the kind to take care of. If you do, it will always be beautiful. You can wear it at special times while you're a little girl, and then when you're grown up and you have a little girl, you can give it to her. So wear it this morning and then ask your mother to put it away for you until tomorrow. You can wear it to Sunday School and church."

I started to cloud up. "I want to wear it all the time."

"If your mother says so, you can wear it whenever you're in the house if you want to. You've got it on now. See?"

BEFORE MY HAIR accident I had played outside a lot, sometimes with the help's kids and their cousins if they were out of school and stayed a while after lunch. But now I couldn't run and play with them like a hoyden, and I watched the bunch of them mosey away down the sidewalk, weaving and wandering in and out of each other's paths, some of them skipping and singing, and I wanted to go with them. The idea of school in the fall was like a promised island full of happy children, off somewhere in a golden mist. Before the accident, I had been promised it many times. After the accident, I failed to notice that no one was mentioning my going to school come fall.

As I got stronger, in the absence of any other child except occasionally Roger/Tian, who did not consider himself a child, I played by myself. They said I was not yet recovered enough to skate—that is, to strap my four-wheeled skates onto my Buster Brown shoes and struggle up and down the tilted squares of sidewalk displaced by tree roots, to the ends of our street and back. And forth again, and back again. No skating now, though. And now no matter what, I was not supposed to cross the street, or turn the corners of the block, or go into the alley behind the back yard, or the garages there.

So, my having nothing to do, it happened that I found myself not only inside the forbidden garage, but holding a box of matches and an open pack of Lucky Strike cigarettes. They had been left there, up on a crossbeam. A man would have to reach above his head to get them. I had spied them because when I opened the door the beam of daylight lit up the white cigarette pack with its red circle. I climbed on the hood of a truck to get them.

Monkey see, monkey do. Almost. Back on solid ground I managed to get a match lit with my still-clumsy fingers, and to light one of the cigarettes with little sucks of my mouth, and then properly shake the flame out and throw the match away. Next I was gagging and coughing and tearing-up and drooling, with smoke in my nose, and paper and loose tobacco in my mouth trying to crawl down my throat. I had just dropped the burning cigarette when I saw the shape of a bear. Then I realized it must be a man, a Japanese man I was sure. His looming figure was black against the glare of the half-open door.

I don't know how long he had been standing there looking at me. He came in without saying a word, and dragged shut the door behind him, so that it latched with a clank. In the near dark I could see only that he wore round-toed boots—which I took to be a soldier's boots—as he stomped out the cigarette which had rolled close to a truck. Then he reached down and grabbed me around my chest pulling me up against his big chest, squeezing so hard with his hairy arm that I couldn't breathe. He covered my nose and mouth with his hand. I was struggling, and still gagging from the tobacco, and kicking with my legs. He squeezed harder, and whispered, "Be still, you hear." Except for the gagging I went limp from fear and lack of breath. With his free hand he did something to his belt and pants, and worked my panties down, and then leaned us against the truck fender, mashing me in between, and did things to me with his fingers. It hurt.

When he finished but while he was still holding me, he whispered, "You know who I am?" He loosened the hand covering my mouth, but left it there.

I didn't move or even shake my head.

He jerked his arm tighter again around me, and whispered, "I asked you. Do. You. Know. Who. I. Am?"

I shook my head No, and tried to say it.

"You better not know me. And you better not ever tell anybody about this, little girl, because if you do I'll kill your mother, and I'll kill your daddy. I'll catch 'em when nobody's looking and I'll kill 'em, and then I'll kill you, you hear?" he whispered. He tightened his arm, "You hear?"

I nodded my head Yes.

He said, "Besides that, ain't nobody would believe you, this happened. You ain't even bleedin'. I'm that good."

He carried me to the back of the garage and put me on my feet and pushed the back of my head so that my face was in a corner, scraped against the rough wood. "Don't you move. You stay right there," he whispered. Then he walked to the door, opened it only enough for a quick little bit of sunlight to shine in for a second, and was gone.

I stayed the way he left me for a long time. I don't know how long. Then the door came all the way wide open, letting in a lot of light, and in a minute Miss Abien's voice was behind me, saying, "Missy. Come outa there. Your mama's calling you."

I walked slowly, carefully, still stunned, out of the dark and across the back yard to the house, making sure I couldn't see him anywhere.

Mother's voice was like a drink of water when I was thirsty, calling from our upstairs window. "Mary Mavis, if you're out there playing in that backyard, you come in here right now please. We can't find you. It's almost suppertime. You come in, now."

I didn't know enough to realize, then, that a Japanese man wouldn't have been speaking English.

DURING MY CHILDHOOD I never told anyone about this. For days I didn't speak if I didn't have to, because I was afraid somebody might ask something that would cause me to let out the secret of what happened in the garage. And I was watchful and easily startled. Only Mother and Mama Linnet noticed, and because of the spooked ways I had been acting for the past few weeks, they didn't think much about it.

———

MOTHER PLAYED bridge three times a week: once at The Bridge House, once at the Women's City Club, and once with her family. She had grown up playing bridge. When she played with her relatives she and Daddy both went, and they took me. This was at Mimi's and Pawpaw's house on Sunday afternoons.

The grownups would be my aunts Delta and Omega and their identical twin husbands Jack and John, then Mimi and Pawpaw, and Mother and Daddy. Enough for two tables. Daddy said the reason Mother married him was to make a fourth. He hadn't known bridge until he met Mother but he was a natural card player and Pawpaw said he was just too damn lucky. If Daddy wasn't winning he put his handkerchief on his head to change his luck and sometimes turned the table so everyone faced another direction. Then soon he and his partner would start winning. Mother liked it that Daddy won so much, but some of the others got jealous. When that happened Daddy would tease and carry on with whoever the sourpuss was, and put them back in a good mood.

I dreaded Sunday afternoons. I was half afraid of Mimi, who was tall and big, and who called Mother 'Child' and me 'Little Child'. I had nothing to do after I used every page of the new coloring book Mother supplied me with weekly. There were no children to play with because my twin aunts and twin uncles hadn't had any. Daddy privately said they had been married plenty long enough and he was beginning to wonder why, and Mother told him that was none of our business.

AT FOURTH and Victory only Mother, Daddy, and Miss Claire knew how to play bridge: three. No one had much time for bridge except Mother. She wanted to teach Miss Lucy, to make four. Miss Lucy might have wanted to learn. She took the books Mother pushed on her, and later she told Mother she found a book in the library for beginners and was studying that in bed at night. When Mother tried to give her lessons neither of them realized the problem was that Mother was talking over Miss Lucy's head.

Almost the same look Miss Lucy had when she tried at bridge, she had when she came back from The Home and her vegetable husband. Many other times too, living seemed to strain her. And sometimes for a minute or two she would seem to be in a different world. Those times, she looked one hundred percent angry, and relaxed about it. Miss Savory said Miss Lucy was born with a cob up her butt.

7

MISS LUCY CAUGHT MAMA LINNET IN THE DOWNSTAIRS HALL one day and asked her for an arrangement like Miss Claire's, to do some of the boarding house work in exchange for part of her rent, because she had just learned her schoolteaching job was gone. But Mama Linnet had to say no. She took a long time explaining why to Miss Lucy, and said she wished she could, because she understood what it means and what a shock it is to have your job evaporate all of a sudden.

"But you do it for Claire," Miss Lucy said, as if Mama Linnet hadn't just explained it.

"She asked first, before you came here," Mama Linnet said. "Also she has a child."

"I have a disabled husband," Miss Lucy said. "But now I want you to know: I have a little money, I don't want you to be looking for somebody to take my room because you might think I can't pay my rent, I can."

"Did you not tell me your husband gets a pension? But the main thing is, I simply am not able to offer you work, not at this time, because there isn't enough money for it. There are bills I wouldn't be able to pay."

Miss Lucy said, "You said, 'at this time' ... "

"I did say that. There is something that might come to pass. It's too early to talk about it, I've just started finding out about it. If it works out, then I would need more help, and I would talk to you about it."

"You would want me, then?" said Miss Lucy.

"Yes, of course I would. You're completely dependable and very smart. And you're a good person, which is the most important thing."

Miss Lucy's shoulders let down from her ears a little and she almost smiled. She said, "I'll be keeping my fingers crossed about whatever it is. Meantime, if you get in a bind and I can help out let me know. For free, I mean."

MAMA LINNET'S thing that might come to pass was operating the Tea Room at the Women's City Club. The contract was up for grabs. It took her less than a week to get it.

She told Daddy, "I have my ducks in a row."

The three of us were sitting at the white enameled work-table in the kitchen early the next Saturday morning. It was the middle of September but summer was still hanging on, and this day was hot already. The ceiling fan only pushed the heat back down on us. Mama Linnet was sitting on a stool, peeling potatoes from a bushel basket which sat on another stool beside her.

"Will it make us lots of money?" Daddy said.

She got an additional potato which she put in front of him along with another paring knife.

"It should make a profit," she said.

Daddy ignored his potato. "Who let it go? And why?" he said.

"A man and his wife and daughter. They had it about a year and a half. He said they were losing money."

"Uh oh," Daddy said.

"There's more to that story. He didn't care to show me his books. I got to wondering if he had any books. Everything is helter-skelter in the kitchen and pantries over there. They don't seem to know how to run a food business. For a fact it was the Women's City Club that decided against renewing the contract, not him."

I had always wished to be let to peel potatoes. My hands were too little. Also now my fingers still didn't move exactly the way they had before the accident. I reached slowly, so as not to be noticed, for the potato that Daddy was not going to peel, and the knife.

"Look here, darlin'," Mama Linnet said, "a new book of paper dolls." They had been in the drawer waiting for me. I forgot potato peeling.

"Mama, how is it you know how to keep books?" Daddy said.

"I asked someone to show me."

"Who?" he said.

"Sister Parker. She and Brother Parker had the store where I used to work. Do you remember them?"

"I do," he said. "I remember they are the countriest people I ever met ... who would guess she could keep books! And Brother Parker, he couldn't even read and write, I found that out by accident one day. I embarrassed him but I didn't mean to. Did you keep the books at the store?"

"No. After I got this place she showed me."

"When did this happen? I don't remember you taking bookkeeping lessons," he said.

"It wasn't lessons. I went out to see them one afternoon and she showed me."

"One lesson?" he said, shaking his head in wonder. "A woman with a sixth-grade education learned to keep books in one lesson from an old woman from the sticks?"

Mama Linnet rested her potato and knife on the table and looked directly at Daddy. She said, "Yes, son, that's what happened. Sister Parker showed me how to keep books in one sitting. She's a smart person, and a good teacher. About a lot of things, not just keeping books. As for me, no I don't have the education I wish I had, or I'm sure you wish I had, but The Dear Lord gives me sense enough to do the things I need to do."

"He sure does," Daddy said, shaking his head again.

They didn't talk any more for a while. Then Daddy made drum sounds on the table with his fingers. He said, "Cesarine will be wondering what happened to me," and stood up.

Mama Linnet said, "I was hoping you could help me with the Farmers' Market this morning. We need a lot of things."

"Aw Mama, I can't," he said.

"Are you and Cesarine going somewhere?"

"I am, she's not," he said.

"Is it something you could put off 'til this afternoon? I need some help with the heavy things."

"Mama, you make me feel just terrible. I wish you'd said something earlier. It's not something I can put off," he said.

"Can I go?" I said to him.

"Not this time, punkin," he said.

"Please, Daddy! I want to go fishing with My Grand-daddy too. He wants me to. I know he does. Please?"

"Are you going fishing with your father?" she said to him.

"Yes Ma'am," was all he said to her. To me he said, "No, Mary Mavis."

I started crying.

"Do you want to go with me?" she said to me.

"I want to go fishing with My Granddaddy," I said between my sobs.

"Well, I'll be leaving right away," she said. "You can't go with your Daddy. Think about whether you want to go to the Farmers' Market with me."

She got up and lifted the big pot of potatoes she had peeled so far, and put the pot in one side of the sink, moved the faucet over it, and ran cold water until it covered the potatoes. Then she moved the faucet to the other side and rinsed her hands, using only as much water as she had to, and dried them on a bleached dishtowel that had once been a flour sack. She took off her apron and hung it on a nail. I knew she would be gone fast.

I was still crying but I said, "I do want to go."

"You and your Daddy go upstairs and be sure it's all right with your mother," she said.

MAMA LINNET'S car was a black Buick Special with four doors and a big trunk space. It was two years old when she bought it, and was now three, and she all but loved it. She had made them put new tires and belts and hoses on before she would buy it. Her buying the car turned out especially foresighted because of the shortages that would be caused by the war. It would become worth two and then three times more than she paid for it.

When she hauled anything in the Buick, bushels of vegetables and crates of chickens from the Farmers' Market and the like, she covered the leather seats with mattress ticking. The only person she let drive it besides herself was Daddy if they went somewhere together. Rarely, she let him take it by himself if his reason was truly important. She did offer to let Daddy teach Mother to drive, but Mother said she didn't need to because she had a husband.

COMING BACK FROM THE FARMERS' Market, with the windows open in the hot car, I could barely fit in the little space left for me in the front seat, between Mama Linnet and two scratchy burlap sacks filled with ears of corn that smelled delicate and sweet. It wasn't delicate, it was late corn, but the grower had come down on his price because the time was past noon and he didn't want to go back home with it.

She would not allow me to sit in the back seat beside the crate of live brown chickens, and said not to be looking at them. It was unusual for her to straight out tell me not to do a thing. About the chickens, it was because she wanted to prevent my getting to know them and then having a heartache and a fit when she and Miss Savory had to kill them. Since I couldn't hang over the seat and pet the chickens, I could only look to the front and sides out the car windows as best I could, unable to see much. The human heart being what it is, what I happened to see was My Granddaddy. He was driving past us in his truck, going the other way, with Daddy beside him.

I scrambled up over the bags of corn and went three-fourths out the car window yelling "Granddaddy!" Mama Linnet leaned far over to reach for me, causing her to wrench the steering wheel at the same time she hit the brakes. The tires screamed and the car veered hard.

Mama Linnet grabbed for my skirttail and missed, but then before I fell all the way out of the car window she managed to catch a handful of my dress and yanked me backward. We had turned around and come to a stop headed in the wrong direction. I was still trying to get my bearings when Granddaddy put his pretty head in Mama Linnet's open window.

"Pet?" he said to her.

I had scared her to tears, and she didn't answer him for a minute.

He opened the car door beside her.

She said, "Shut the door, Hampton. I'm all right."

I said, "It's my fault, Granddaddy. I scared her."

"You scared me too," he said. "I saw you in my rear-view mirror. Don't be pulling that trick any more, you hear ?"

"Yessir but can I go fishing with you?"

He looked at Mama Linnet. "Can she go fishing with me?"

"She has a father," she said. "That's him over there." She pointed to Daddy, who was on my side of the car looking in. Her hand was shaking and her voice too.

Daddy said, "Yes. Hell. Yes."

Granddaddy stood up straight and gave him a look over the top of the car.

"I'm sorry I cussed, Mama," Daddy said. "And you too, punkin."

Granddaddy stooped down again and looked around

inside the car. "Linnet, darlin', what are you doing with all this stuff loaded in here?" he said.

"It's for the meals I fix and sell," she said.

"Who got it in here?" he said.

"I did, Hampton," she said.

"And you'll be getting it out?" He answered his own question. "By yourself." He stood up again and looked at Daddy. "Son, I hope you can tell me you didn't know about this."

Nothing about Daddy moved. Not his body, not his face. Not his eyes that, this time, looked straight into Granddaddy's eyes. They stared at each other for a long time.

It was Mama Linnet who broke the spell. "That's enough, please," she said to the air around us.

"Pet," Granddaddy said, "Would you let the boy drive you home in my truck and I'll drive your car home?"

She did agree to that, and let his arm steady her as she got out and stepped from her car and to his truck.

I rode with him. When we all got back to Fourth and Victory and she got out of the truck, she made a little gesture to motion him away and walked by herself from the parking lot, up the back stairs and into the house, where she poured herself a cup of cold coffee and sat on her kitchen stool with it while the two men hauled in the shopping goods and put them where she told them to. After that was done My Granddaddy took Daddy and me fishing.

<hr />

I COULD TELL Mama Linnet had a love for Granddaddy that she didn't have for anybody else. Her voice was different when she talked to him. She was almost always calm with everyone, but with him her tone was also more tender, whether she was pleased or put out with him. The ways she held her body were different when he was near her, either more relaxed or else more tight. She was not one to touch anybody except me or Daddy, but many times I noticed she almost touched Granddaddy and then realized it just in time to stop.

———

I PLANNED it out ahead of time, and one day my chance came for only the two of us to be in the kitchen.

"I know a secret, about you," I said to her.

"You do, do you? You want to tell me?" she said.

"You love Granddaddy."

She thought that over.

She said, "Yes, I do my best to love everybody. That's what we're supposed to do."

"No, I mean you love him better than anybody except me. You love him and me both better than anybody else."

"We're supposed to love God better than anybody, and that's what I try to do," she said.

"But the people that are here," I said. I made it a demand: "You know."

She stopped dodging, mostly. "Yes I know. And I love you both—and your father too—better than tongue can tell. I love each of you in a different way."

"The way you love Granddaddy is that you're *in love* with him."

"Five-year-old people haven't had a chance to be in love yet, so maybe you might not know all about that?"

"I know you're *in love* with him. And I know he's *in love* with you. That's not a secret. Everybody knows it. Everybody knows Dr. Haynes Senior is *in love* with you too and he has a lot of money, but I know you're not *in love* with him. So if you're *not in love* with him and you *are in love* with Granddaddy, why won't you marry Granddaddy back?" I said. "That's what I want to know."

"You had this talk in mind ahead of time."

"Please marry him back. I want him to live here."

"Honey, in the first place I *am* married to your Granddaddy, and I always will be. So long as we both shall live, and on beyond that. Every marriage is for life in the eyes of God, and since you want to know I will tell you that the marriage —the love—that binds Hampton and me is more even than that, and it will last beyond this earthly life."

She almost started to cry, but then got herself back, and said with a frog in her throat, "So that's not the question. Whether we could ever live together again is the question. And I know you don't understand why we don't live together, and I'm not free to tell you."

"I know he went away and left you to get a job and he drank alcohol. But he's back now and he probably doesn't drink alcohol anymore."

"Where did you hear all that? Your father?"

I nodded, and kept it to myself that also Miss Savory had had quite a bit to say on it, out loud and to somebody else.

"Well. I don't want to talk about this anymore right now," she said.

"Would you study and pray on it? Please?"

"Oh honey, I study and pray on what I ought to do about everything about every one of you it seems like day and night," she said.

WE WERE METHODISTS. Mama Linnet said it many times, "We Are Methodists." She meant, we-in-our-genes. As it was in the beginning, is now and ever shall be, world without end. It mattered not that Daddy married a Baptist and went to church with his wife when they went at all.

Mama Linnet's religious system was that after you are older than a little girl nobody gets to tell you what to believe or do. Your main job in life is to find out for yourself what to believe and do. The way to find out is to study and pray on whatever comes up until God tells you in secret. And no matter what, everything will be all right because God loves you. If you are still a little girl the last part is all you really have to know.

She didn't personally bother about the fine points in the Apostle's Creed—which she did know by heart, though—or about the Trinity. And especially not the Holy Ghost. She had a Bible, everyone did, even Roger/Tian who said his father and he were not Christians, but that I was to keep that a secret. But I never saw Mama Linnet read her Bible, and she didn't often read much else except the newspaper if she had time. She told me Bible stories which I later learned were mixed up. In one of her stories there was a snip from *Tales of the Arabian Nights*. By habit she hummed her favorite hymn, "What a Friend We Have in Jesus," whenever she did physical work, which was all the time. She couldn't carry a tune, so you would only have known what it was when she periodically broke out with the words.

She was against meanness, thievery, lying, Catholicism, and alcohol. However, she considered that people who actually were mean, thieves, liars, Catholics, and drinkers were only misguided.

Not that she abided outrageous behavior.

Her belief about prayer was that for yourself you should first pray for wisdom. She could quote the Bible correctly on that, Solomon's prayer, "Give to Thy servant an understanding heart." After that it was all right to ask for anything you or anybody else really needed. And it was fine to talk to Jesus about anything at all, because He was your best friend.

She went to Sunday School and church every week she could, because that was the Lord's due and also she enjoyed it, and it was almost her only opportunity for dressing up and seeing friends and just people socially. Usually she took me.

THE FIRST METHODIST CHURCH had a separate building for Sunday School before church. When my class of small children ended I always waited for Mama Linnet to come from her class and get me. That Sunday, my teacher had distributed little white New Testaments to us kids. I saw that mine had my name in gold. I was beside myself.

Mama Linnet had probably paid for the book and the name-printing, but she acted surprised and proud of me. She indicated that I had earned my New Testament by being smart and learning in Sunday School, and that made me proud of myself and I didn't think about it, that everyone got one. Then we walked together under a long green awning that ended close to the church's front doors. Big organ music was already spilling out.

Soon as we got inside the church I spied the back of Granddaddy's head, quicker than if he had been lit by a spotlight. I jerked Mama Linnet's dress. "My Granddaddy's here!" I whispered, and pointed.

She barely hesitated and then kept walking, stopping at the first pew with room for us, which was a good way in back of him, and tried to steer me in first.

I balked. "No. Let's sit with him," I whispered.

"We'll sit here."

I started to whine. "I want to sit with him!"

"Sit down."

"Can I just show him how nice I look in my New Testament and my locket? I'll come right back."

"Oh go on and sit with him!" she said, and sat where she was.

———

TONY BISHOP HAD NO MORE GOT DRAFTED than a monkey. That's what Granddaddy told Daddy, who told Mama Linnet. Granddaddy had found out the truth: Mr. Tony had thought he would need to leave town because of someone he was afraid of. But then it turned out he didn't need to go. My Granddaddy said Mama Linnet could expect Mr. Tony to make up some story and try to back out of leaving Fourth and Victory. And sure enough, pretty soon Mr. Tony told everybody he'd been notified his draft notice was a mistake.

———

MAMA LINNET LET Mr. Tony stay. When she told Daddy that, in the kitchen, he put down his coffee cup so fast it sloshed. He said, "You let him stay? With two men on our waiting list, you let *him* stay?"

She said, "I'm not taken with either of those men. They don't always pay their bills, I found that out. Tony Bishop has always paid on time. And he's cleaner than most men, and he keeps the rules. A bird in the hand."

"He's phony as a three-dollar bill. What's the real reason you're letting him stay?" Daddy said.

"What has changed, that I should make him leave? "

"The man is trouble on the hoof," he said.

He's not been any trouble to me."

"What about the fact he stole the money?" he said.

"Why is it you think he did?"

"I know he did," he said.

"You don't. But anyway I've decided."

Daddy was so exasperated he got sarcastic about the wrong thing. He said, "Oh I'm sure you studied and prayed on it."

She waited a long time to answer, staring at him until he fidgeted. Then she said, "Yes. I did."

MISS SAVORY and Daddy were always at odds. You might think it would be her fault because she was one to speak her mind, and enjoyed being funny at it, and would just as soon fight as not, where Daddy normally got along with every-body. But on the other hand, Miss Savory minded her own business more than he did. Just because she existed, though, she got under his skin like poison ivy, and it was more than he could do to leave her alone. No matter that she was always busy, cooking or washing or cleaning or ironing. No matter that she kept her back turned to him if he came nearby, and hardly looked his way unless she forgot herself. He would pick at her until they ended up in a fuss. Neither of them ever won, it never ended, because Mama Linnet would step in and make them hush, and then tell Daddy he needed to go somewhere else. Which is what he often really wanted anyway. This went on like a broken record.

One day he came back from work about ten in the morning because he had spilled something down the front of his shirt. Mother was gone to play bridge at the Women's City Club that day, and when he went upstairs to change he found that she had not yet ironed his next shirt. He brought it down and tried to give it to Miss Savory, who was on the screened-in back porch, under its ceiling fan, ironing the stacks of tablecloths and napkins that would be needed at noon.

She ignored the shirt in his outstretched hand and kept ironing. She said, "Miss Lewis told me to get on these table linens and finish them, and not let nobody nor nothing stop me no matter what."

"She didn't mean me," he said, putting the shirt directly under her face.

"She said nobody and she meant nobody," she said.

"Listen, I'm the man of this house, and you work here, and if I say your work is to iron my shirt, that's what it is." He banged the shirt down onto the middle of the ironing board and stepped back with his arms crossed and his feet apart.

She kept her eyes down while with one hand she pitched his shirt into a laundry basket alongside, and kept ironing with her other hand.

"Mama!" he yelled. When Mama Linnet didn't show up right away he yelled again louder.

Mama Linnet came to the doorway behind him and sized up the situation before he knew she was there. "Patrick, come out here please," she said, and disappeared back into the hall. He followed her out there.

Miss Savory and I heard everything they said.

Mama Linnet let him rave for a little. Soon, though, she said he had the option of going upstairs and ironing his own shirt, whereas she had no option for getting the table linens ready on time unless Miss Savory ironed on without stopping.

"I have had it!" he said. "This is the last straw. Either she goes or I go."

"Well, you know I can't do without Savory," she said.

There was a pause. Then Daddy's stomping footsteps went off down the hall. I turned to look at Miss Savory expecting to see the face of someone who had won a prize, but she was bent over the ironing board looking as serious as a person could and still be laughing without making a sound.

After the shirt ironing showdown Daddy left Miss Savory alone. He now behaved toward her the same as she toward him: they ignored each other as much as they could.

This leaving alone came with good timing because Mama Linnet had to be away a lot, setting up the Tea Room business at the Women's City Club.

Miss Savory added Saturdays to her work week and Miss Claire also took on more hours of work, to make up for Mama Linnet's absences.

8

MAMA LINNET MADE GOOD ON HER PROMISE TO ASK MISS Lucy to help. She called her into the sitting room one night after supper and asked her to sit down. The chairs and couch there were big and plush but Miss Lucy might as well have been sitting in the electric chair. Mama Linnet told her about the Tea Room and asked her to work there, and said, "I would understand if you can't see your way to do it. You would have to quit your job at The Home, you couldn't do both. I would need you Mondays through Fridays full time. The pay would be thirty cents an hour. That isn't much but it would cover your room and board and some extra. You'll want to study and pray on it, I expect."

Miss Lucy squeaked and sprang up and leaped toward Mama Linnet, stopping just in front of her. She scared us both. Mama Linnet slanted backward in her chair and put her hands over her chest, looking up.

"You will never regret this," Miss Lucy said.

MOTHER DIDN'T KNOW Mama Linnet had taken on the Tea Room, and Miss Lucy was accidentally the first person to tell her. Mother was sewing in our apartment and Miss Lucy returned the loaned bridge books. She explained about her new job and used it as an excuse to stop trying to learn to play. She was extra nervous, and talked a lot at first.

"I'm so grateful to Mrs. Lewis," Miss Lucy said. "I feel like she saved my life, almost. I guess I could have lived through the rest of the summer having to see what goes on at that Home all day every day and my husband having to be there helpless, but now I don't have to, and I can't tell you what a relief it is."

Mother said, "*The Women's City Club* Tea Room? Are you *sure?*"

"Well . . . I think so," Miss Lucy said. Mother had jolted her out of being certain about that. Then, "Yes. I remember exactly what she said. I thought you knew, I didn't know it was a secret. I don't want to be a tale teller. Please don't tell her I told you, please don't. . . . But no, it can't be a secret because Savory and Claire, and even little Mary Mavis know about it. Oh. I'm putting one foot in it right after the other. I am so sorry. I don't know what to say." She talked on that way trying to ease Mother's feelings, but Mother was looking mad and madder in silence, and then began to cry, and waved Miss Lucy away. Miss Lucy quit talking and hurried down the hall to her room and shut the door. After she left, Mother asked me through her tears if I knew about the Tea Room, and I said I did.

"Why didn't you tell me?" she said.

I too started to cry and said the truth, "I didn't know you wanted me to. I'm sorry. I'm sorry."

She put aside my new dress she had been sewing and

came to me on the couch and snuggled me to her, putting butterfly kisses and tears on my healing head, saying she was sorry she hurt my feelings and nothing was my fault or could ever be my fault, and that I was her good, good, girl. A relief like honey flowed through me and I hugged close as I could against her thin body.

———

MOTHER DID NOT TALK to Daddy about the Tea Room until that night when they thought I was asleep. In their room with the door shut, their voices grew from whispers to talking.

"*I play bridge there*, is why," she said. "I would be embarrassed."

"Play somewhere else then," he said.

"You always will not understand! There is no place else. My friends are there."

"You play at the Bridge House too. You could play there twice a week instead of once," he said.

"The Bridge House is for lessons, the Women's City Club is for socializing, and you know it."

"What I know is, you and your 'friends' want to keep pretending you have money, and when they find out it's your mother-in-law serving their lunch, you'll all have to face up to it that you don't, that you're married to a man who came up the hard way and hasn't made his mark yet. I'm only twenty-three years old." he said.

"I do too have money," she said. "I have my inheritance."

"Not yet, you don't," he said.

"I will."

"Maybe you will, maybe you won't. I won't go into that

again. Right now what you've got is me, and your mother-in-law. What is it you want me to do, anyway?"

"Tell her not to do it."

"Tell her to give up making money when we need it? Not to mention, I could tell her 'till I'm blue in the face and she would still do it."

Mother made a little moaning cry and said, "What am I going to do?"

———

MAMA LINNET HAD a pay phone installed in Fourth and Victory's downstairs hall, near the doorway to the dining room. It was popular right away, and the boarders and the help began to know more about one another from over-hearing and eavesdropping. Mother waited for times when the hall would be empty, she hoped, and then used the pay phone to call out. She let her friends assume she had a personal phone. But she didn't give that number to her friends because no telling who at Fourth and Victory would answer, or what they would say. Although using the pay phone was awkward for her sometimes, she preferred it to asking Mama Linnet for the use of her personal phone since there was no way she could pretend that wasn't asking for a favor.

Daddy had used the phone in Mama Linnet's apartment whenever he wanted, and the pay phone made no difference in that.

Mama Linnet had a party line, meaning she shared the use of the line, and its cost, with someone else, somewhere else. We knew only that it was a woman and she didn't use the line much. Neither did Mama Linnet use it much until

Dr. Haynes and My Granddaddy both started calling her. Even when she remembered I was present and avoided saying a name, I always knew, from her side of the conversation, that the caller was one of them, and which one. I kept an ear open for Granddaddy's calls, and begged to talk to him. She let me, and then left him talking to me while she went off and didn't come back. He called anyway at least once a day. Dr. Haynes did too but he never talked long, probably because half the people in town had picked him to be their doctor.

"How did you like my new truck out there?" My Granddaddy said to Mama Linnet.

"It's a nice truck. It looks brand new," she said.

It was late morning in the kitchen, with lunch preparation underway. He had come in and leaned against a wall out of the way, making easy talk to Mama Linnet, and including me. Miss Savory and Miss Claire were working in there, and after saying hello he and they ignored each other.

"Haven't had it long. You like it, though?" he said.

"It's nice, yes," she said.

"Good, because it's not mine, it's yours. I've still got my other one. No. No, don't say anything yet, let me tell you about it. Just listen, now. You need a truck, and that's a good one, and I want you to have it. And I've hired a man to come every Saturday and help you go to the market and haul your supplies and bring them in. I can't stand to think of you struggling that way." He took a folded paper from the wallet in his back pants pocket and unfolded it. "Here's the title. I've signed it, and you sign . . . here . . . and I'll take it down to the revenue office and get the license in your name. And insurance, I've tended to that. Here's a pen," he said.

She shook her head No at him.

"Think on it," he said. "You don't have to decide right now. I'll just leave it parked here and you see how you feel about it in a day or two."

"No, Hampton," she said.

"I'm hoping you won't completely waste a truck, because it's yours whether you'll drive it or not. And by the way, it's not for Pat: he can buy his own truck."

"I might have it hauled off," she said.

"If you do, darlin, have them send me the bill." He wrote something on the paper and examined it. "Uh-huh that's your signature all right. I'm going to license it now. "Bye, sweet girls," he said to her and me, and he put the truck key on the worktable and left.

The truck stayed unused for a long time. Daddy tried again and again to get her to let him drive it, but she would not. He got exasperated, saying it *needed* driving, and so forth, but she kept to her same policy: if he had some really good reason then he could drive her Buick. She kept the keys to both vehicles locked in her new safe. She would not give him the combination to the safe. That was another thing he didn't like, and had several reasons against. She said to him, "The combination is in my safety deposit box at the bank. They know me and they know you. If I die or lose my mind they will let you or your father get into the box."

―――――――

OMAR PHELPS' trucks had been gone from the garages since just after Mr. Tony's going-away party. Without a word, Mr.

Phelps and his latest hired man had driven them off in tandem as usual . . . but this time never came back. He still had a week left on a garage rental month and his two-nights-a-week porch sleeping privilege. Mama Linnet hadn't heard from him, and had long since counted him gone for good. She now moved her Buick and the red truck Granddaddy gave her into the garages, and liked this so much she stopped advertising the space for rent.

When she took me with her on trips in the Buick, she was a little puzzled at first that I wouldn't go in the garage to get in the car. I balked and waited in the alley until she had backed the car out. She asked me why, and I whispered, "It's dark in there," and she took that as reason enough.

MOTHER'S FEARS about her reputation at the Women's City Club disturbed her more every day. When I was around her, I was not just edgy and indrawn, I was also sad because she was. The first week, she skipped her routine day to be at the Club. The next week, on that day she dressed to go but then sat down with her pocketbook in her lap and stared at the wall until past time to leave. Then she changed back into a housedress and lay on the bed with her eyes closed.

The thought came to me how to cheer her up. I left her lying there and worked my way downstairs and into Mama Linnet's apartment. I opened her desk and borrowed the big flashlight she kept there, and made my way unnoticed out of the house and to the cellar. Down in it, I was braver without Mother than I had been with her. I was determined to get one of the big vases for her.

I made it almost to them, but now some new obstacle lay

in the way, stretched lengthwise in the narrow walk space between the stacks of shelves. It was necessary to step up on the new mound to get to the vases. Holding to a shelf for balance I put one foot on the big long lump, and stopped. A grisly feeling traveled through my shoe to my brain. Slowly I removed my foot. I was afraid to shine the flashlight on the thing but I did it anyway. When I saw what it was I inched away backward until I could turn and get up the stairs and out of there.

In the parking lot I sat on the running board of a car. I was shivering in the warm September sunshine.

Roger/Tian came loping home across the lot and almost passed me. He stopped. "What'samatter?" he said. I didn't answer, and he said, "Are you sick? You look funny."

"I'm scared," I said.

"What are you scared of?" he said. "Tell me. I'll protect you."

I knew he couldn't protect me from having found a dead man in the cellar. But to tell him would be a relief. "They're here," I said.

"Who?" he said.

"The Japanese."

He glanced quickly around and squatted down beside me. "Where are they?" he whispered.

"I don't know where they are. They killed somebody," I said.

"Who told you?" he said.

"Nobody. I saw who they killed."

"Who is it?"

"I don't know. A dead man."

"Where?" He said.

"In the cellar."

"Did the police come?" he said.

"They don't know it. I'm scared to tell anybody."

"Is he still there? The dead man?" he said, and I nodded.

"Show me," he said, and took my hand.

I followed Roger/Tian and did as he did, stooping and ducking through the half-dozen parked cars and along the house's wall until we came to the cellar. There I balked. But he told me, "You have to," and so I followed him down into the dark place and he held my hand and I led him to the body. He had the flashlight and after he saw the corpse, the beam of light began to shake. He swallowed out loud and then breathed in and out several times. Then he said in a loud whisper, "Mister! Hey! Mister!"

"He can't hear you, he's dead," I said.

"I have to be sure. He could be just unconscious."

The corpse was lying face down. Its middle was covered by a throw rug, so that only the back of the head and shoulders showed at the top and then the trouser legs and shoes on the feet at the bottom. Something was wrong about the head. Roger/Tian used the flashlight with his shaking hands to tap the sole of the nearest shoe, calling softly, "Mister!" Next he gave me the light and ordered me to hold it steady. I saw that he was about to try and turn the man over. But when he touched the stone flesh of the corpse's shoulder he quickly stood up. "He is dead," he said.

He stayed motionless and silent for a long time.

Finally I said, "What are we doing?"

As if I had waked him he said, "Come on." He took the flashlight from me and led the way toward the steps, and we went up, into the sunny back yard, blinking at the light and the normal-looking world we stood in.

"Don't tell anybody," he said. "I'm going to find Dr. Haynes. He'll know what to do."

"Don't go! They might be going to kill everybody! Me!"

"Dr. Haynes is the one to tell first. Your job is to not talk to anybody. You hide someplace until I get back."

ON THE TOPMOST floor of the house, halfway down the hall, a set of stairs enclosed in a dark tunnel led up to the attic. I climbed the steps, which seemed to have grown since the last time, but when I reached up to open the door it was padlocked. I sat on the top step, wider than the others, to think of another hiding place. Next I felt all my strength draining away, and I turned sideways and propped myself so that I was half lying down. After a moment I slid on down into either unconsciousness or sleep.

Maybe I heard them calling my name, but if so, that became part of my dreams.

When I woke, it was to the sound of many footsteps below in the hall, some of them heavy, some light, and they slowed as they came near the attic stairs. "If we're starting at the top, the attic is first," Daddy said; but then he said, "No. We can skip that. Mama put a lock on that door." The grouped footfalls sped up again, going away, and stopped at our apartment door, and I heard its hinges, then a long silence until the people came back out into the hall, Daddy saying, "Okay. Not in there. Now the bathroom."

The search party was Daddy, Mother, and a man I didn't recognize by his voice. He spoke softly, and didn't say much. I listened to their search until they had looked in all the rooms on that floor and gone down to the floor below. The sounds dwindled to silence.

I didn't know they were looking for me, I thought they were looking for the Japanese, and when they didn't find any on our floor I felt safer. My hands and arms were weak and my legs had gone undependable again, but I eased down the stairs, went into the bathroom, and got a drink of water out of the faucet. In the hall I took out the key to our apartment that Daddy kept hidden in a hole in the wooden paneling near our door. Inside, at the window the gloom of night was coming. I took three fig newtons from the tin where Mother kept them, and got my pillow. Returning to the attic stairway even more slowly than I had come, I worked my way up one step at a time, backward, to my dark warm little platform. After I ate the cookies sleep came again.

TOWARD MORNING THEY FOUND ME. A man said my name and picked me up. My mind stayed more asleep than awake, but I saw his uniform and he sounded familiar and friendly, and I understood he was a policeman and not a Japanese killer. I let sleep take me completely again as he carried me from the attic stairs. When he brought me into the kitchen downstairs, Mama Linnet, Mother, and Daddy all cried out with gladness, waking me some. Daddy took me from the policeman into his own arms and stood rocking himself and me, and I was aware of that too before slipping back into sleep.

The next afternoon when they woke me I was in my own couch bed in our apartment. A man was sitting in a chair beside me, holding my wrist and shaking my hand, calling my name. I wasn't scared but I didn't know him. I looked around and saw Daddy.

"It's Dr. Haynes Junior, honey," Daddy said. "Can you wake up for Daddy?"

I tried to sit up but couldn't make it.

"She's had a relapse, hasn't she? That's it, isn't it?" Daddy said. He started to cry and put his face in his hands.

"It appears she might have," the young doctor said.

"May I have a drink of water?" I said to Daddy.

"Mama! Cesarine!" he said, strangling through his tears, "Come in here, she's awake. She's talking. She wants water."

I DID NOT ASK who the dead man was, nor even wonder. He was a dead man, yes, but he could not be really a person because I knew only live people. Bugs died. Birds died. I once had seen a decomposing cat. But I didn't know, and didn't want to know, any dead people. It was Mother, despite her own distraction, who eventually noticed there was a piece missing.

"It was Tony Bishop," she told me gently. "Honey? It was Tony Bishop." When I still didn't act as if I had heard, she said, "You remember him don't you?"

"I remember him and he's not dead."

She understood somehow. Over the next couple of days, with just the two of us again together alone so much in our apartment, she sometimes came out of her own misery enough to say little things that eased me some, but I didn't move Tony Bishop out of my world and into death. And my worst fears were still inside, twisting like snakes. Eventually a hope managed to get born within that mess, and I asked a big question, pulling it out of its terrible ghostliness. "The police caught them didn't they?" I said to Mother.

She didn't know I meant The Japanese, and I didn't realize she didn't know.

She said, "Not yet, but ... "

I squealed and drew into myself.

" ... But they will. They'll catch them, honey! You don't have to be afraid."

"Dadeee," I said, although he wasn't there.

That night I heard her say to Daddy, talking too fast in a voice that was too high, "I don't care what Dr. Haynes Junior says, he has no common sense. I know my own child, and it's not just that she's had a relapse and is in shock because Tony Bishop's dead, and she'll get better. She *won't* get better unless somebody does something. She doesn't even understand he's dead yet. What's the matter is, she's scared something awful is going to happen to all of us. She's scared nearly to death. It's not just a saying. She's so scared she could die of it. It's even worse whenever you're out of her sight. We're lucky she's alive. In the morning I'm going to start finding some way to help her. She can't live on like this."

BEFORE SUNUP THE NEXT MORNING, Mother, for the first time ever, went directly herself to ask Mama Linnet for something. She knocked on Mama Linnet's door and asked if she knew of anything to help me with my nerves.

And Mama Linnet was like minded with Mother about my condition. That morning she drove off in her Buick and didn't come back until late afternoon. She brought back something she made a tea of, and carried a quart jar of it up to us, with a tablespoon.

She told Mother, "It's strong. Just two tablespoonfuls every two hours, three times, to see how she does with it. That's what Sister Parker said. Then if she seems nearly the same or no better, up it to three spoonfuls every two hours. Or if it makes her groggy, cut it back to one. Or stop altogether if you think you should."

Mother repeated it back in her tight voice. Mama Linnet said that was right, but Mother wanted to recite it again. And then again.

Mama Linnet said, "Would you want to write it down?"

Mother tried that, but her hands were shaking. Mama Linnet gently took the pencil and wrote the instructions herself, and Mother thanked her.

MOTHER'S METHOD of telling certain things and not others was adopted and put to use by everyone when it came to what they told and did not tell Dr. Haynes Junior. Without a word to each other about it, they all, including Mama Linnet, kept quiet to him about Sister Parker's potion.

9

I HAD BY THAT AGE ABSORBED BASIC READING BECAUSE PEOPLE read to me. My grownups knew I could read and they thought it was smart of me, but they tended to forget it. And probably it never dawned on them that I regularly figured out the words to most everything on at least the front page of the newspaper, even though a lot of it made no sense.

It was in the paper that Mr. Tony's body had been found under the house and murder was suspected. I got the part about the body and the investigation, but not the part about who was dead. Seeing his name in black and white did not make it real.

It was real to the meal customers, though. Three or four of the regulars stayed away but most others came with their curiosity showing. "What it says in the paper is all we know," Daddy told the help to say to people—and to keep saying. But the truth was, the police had found out more than was in the paper. It had been for sure a murder, a stabbing, done in the garage. Whoever did it was strong enough to drag the body quickly and quietly to the cellar and hide it there.

———

"THEY DON'T KNOW it was the Japanese," Roger/Tian whispered to me about the police when he finally got a chance. He had come to see me, and Mother used the opportunity to lie down in the bedroom and shut the door.

"Tell them," I said.

"I did, but they don't believe me. Now my mother and Dr. Haynes Senior both have forbidden me to say it again. Even Dr. Haynes Senior doesn't believe me."

———

THAT NIGHT, in the middle of the night, Mama Linnet heard men talking low, out in the parking lot. She got her flashlight and twenty-two rifle and slipped out there in her robe. It was Granddaddy and two policemen having a quiet conversation.

Next morning Mother—and I—learned from Daddy that Granddaddy was spending his nights out there in his truck, keeping an eye on the house.

Mama Linnet said, "Since it's my house, it would seem they could at least let me know about it. I might have shot somebody."

Daddy said to Mother, "He thinks somebody might either try to sneak into the house, or sneak out. I bet he knows something and won't say what it is."

"Or," Mother said faintly, "Maybe he wants not to be under suspicion himself."

To that, Daddy said nothing.

I took some comfort in it, thinking My Granddaddy was out there watching over us in the night.

AFTER TWO WEEKS the police declared themselves done with Mr. Tony's body, but his mother could not afford to have him shipped home. She sent an envelope addressed To Whom It May Concern in care of the police department, with eighteen dollars in it and a short note asking for him to have a Christian burial "as nice as possible."

Our county had a paupers' cemetery, located just outside our city's limits. He would be buried in a concrete box, same as everyone there. Mama Linnet chose his burial clothes from his closet and arranged for our pastor to do a graveside service.

Mama Linnet had to insist that Daddy go. Mother pulled herself together enough to go willingly because of Miss Sara Ann.

All the women were to squeeze into the Buick, driven by Daddy. Granddaddy was go alone in his truck.

Miss Sara Ann was the only one of the women who didn't have a black outfit to wear when somebody died. She had been upset about that, and Mama Linnet somehow at the last minute the day before, located friends with a black dress and purse and shoes the right size that she could borrow.

Then on the morning of the service Miss Sara Ann went across the street to Mrs. Tabor's and asked for flowers. There were still late summer blooms, enough to make a large bouquet. Next there was quite a flurry throughout Fourth and Victory about finding a suitable ribbon for the flowers, which turned into finding any ribbon at all. Eventually, with Miss Sara Ann approaching closer and closer to hysteria, someone came up with a blue one.

"Why don't you let Hampton take the flowers in the truck?" Mama Linnet suggested.

Miss Sara Ann lifted her chin high to one side and closed her eyes and managed to shake her head No.

So the flowers rode in Miss Sara Ann's arms in the middle of the back seat of car, spilling over into the faces and laps of Miss Claire and Miss Lucy, making them have to fend off the blooms and leaves, and getting pollen and little bugs on their carefully kept black clothes, and making Mother and Miss Lucy sneeze, all the way to the cemetery.

At the end of the service Miss Sara Ann handed the bouquet to Granddaddy. He asked her to hold his big tan hat and then got on his knees in the wet dirt, in his beautiful dark blue suit, to place the flowers carefully down onto the concrete casket. He also got mud on his hat because she dropped it when she swooned. This was how Miss Lucy later told it to The Lawyer Cato, who was unable to get off work that day.

THAT DAY OF THE FUNERAL, Miss Savory stayed at Fourth and Victory with me while Mother and Daddy and Mama Linnet and the boarders went to the cemetery. After they left, she carried a rocking chair all the way up from the downstairs parlor to our apartment. When we were alone she put the chair beside my couch bed and rocked and hummed softly. Her voice was low pitched. After a while she said, "How about I rock you?" and she gave me a hand to climb in her lap. Her body was bony but she knew how to hold a little girl. She had a paper fan on a stick, and she kept us cooled.

She didn't talk, and seemed to be in deep thought,

crooning her song with no tune and no words. So we passed a while neither asleep nor awake.

Then she said, "Lord, I almost forgot to give you your medicine," and she sat me on my bed, and got the jar of medicine and a spoon. "You don't seem to mind it," she said when I swallowed it, and she smelled the liquid in the jar.

"It tastes funny but it's kind of good," I said. "You want some?"

She considered it.

"I won't tell anybody," I said.

She gave one of her quick laughs like a little puff. "'S'all right if you tell it. If you happen to." I got one of our special looks and I knew she'd rather I didn't tell. "I'll just have me some," she said. "My nerves could use settlin' too, that's for . . . sure." She took a sip out of the jar, and then another, then cleaned the rim with her apron hem. Her tongue and lips made smacks to catch the last of the flavor. "I know that from somewhere," she said, "Somebody give me that long time ago. *Long* time ago. Or seasoned something with it. Can't remember what it is." It surprised her that she couldn't place it.

"You hungry, Baby?" She said.

"What do we have?" I said. I hadn't been hungry but now I was interested.

"Well, we have some Jell-O with peaches, and we have some baked chicken legs, and we have some, ah, biscuits! I could toast you biscuits with butter and honey, and . . . " she went on naming other things she knew I liked.

"It's all downstairs," I said, and started to cry and hold on tight to her.

"I ain't gonna leave you," she said.

"I'm so hungry," I cried.

"I'm gonna take you with me," she said. "Put you in my kitchen for a little while. Do you good." She was not a lot bigger than a child, but she picked me up as if I were nothing, and carried me downstairs and fed me, and carried me up again and fanned and hummed me and my happy stomach to sleep.

THIS DAY WAS some kind of turning point. Gradually I began to get better. Awareness that Mr. Tony was dead must have finally begun in my mind, because I did not ask or wonder why I never saw him again.

NOTHING WAS enough to get between Mama Linnet and her intent to take over the Women's City Club Tea Room, and do it without losing any of the month's revenue at Fourth and Victory. Not a murder and its hubbub at her house. Not the nervous breakdown of her dear and only grandchild. Not the impending nervous breakdown of her daughter-in-law. Not the attentions and contentions of her separated husband plus another suitor. All of these together were no match for her will. And thanks to herself and to Miss Savory, Miss Claire, and Miss Lucy, who rolled up their sleeves and stood by her, she did it.

MY GRANDMOTHER'S success with the Tea Room made my mother's anxieties come true. And it did not help Mother's social standing that the murder mystery was a lingering focus of attention for the small city. Her bridge cohorts shunned her openly, and she was not strong enough to stand that. She mostly sat at her sewing machine, not sewing. Or sometimes she sat beside me wherever in our apartment I sat or lay. Sometimes she went to bed. Wherever she was, she often had tears on her face. When she tried to do anything she lost track of her purpose. Her body grew still and her eyes stared into distance. She stayed that way for long times if I didn't or couldn't break the spell.

DADDY WAS gentle and pampering to Mother at first. But when nothing he said or did was any help, he got testy. After a few days and nights he told her sharply that she wasn't trying to help herself and until she did nobody else could help her either. At that she stopped speaking to him at all, or much to anyone else. Not that she seemed angry; just, she now looked always away from us.

Sister Parker's medicine had already been a great help to me, and it might have helped Mother except she would not take it. By the time Daddy thought of giving it to her she was refusing all food and drink except rarely some sips of water.

MAMA LINNET WAS NOT available for Daddy to fall back on. He asked her to postpone what she was doing at the Women's City Club so as to take care of Mother and me.

"I can't do it, son. And I can't spare anyone to do it. You'll have to take off work," she said.

"Your work's not as important as my work," he said.

She was very tired.

"It is more important," she said. "Your work is not what feeds us all, and keeps a roof over our heads, and lets us live in cleanness and decency, and lets us not have to beg or borrow to stay alive, and lets us share with others who need it, and lets us give our tithe to Our Lord and Savior, and lets us put back something for emergencies. And first, last, and most of all, my work is what lets us pay for a doctor and a hospital if any of us need it. I will never again have someone I love die in my arms because I have no money. Whatever it is you do with the money from your job, it's not any of those things, and those are the things that matter. So yes, my work is more important."

Apparently he could not find anything to say. They sat there silently on either side of our little drop-leaf table for a while. Then she said, "Had you thought of asking Cesarine's mother if she can help?"

STARTING the next afternoon Mother stayed at Mimi's and Pawpaw's. To recover herself, everyone said.

IT WAS unanimous and unspoken that I should stay, not go with mother. So when Daddy packed her clothes and drove her to her parents', Mama Linnet moved me downstairs to her own apartment. The help could tend me there and easily look in on me when I rested, or if I got too lonesome they fixed me a pallet under the kitchen worktable. When their kids came to the house they were let in to the apartment to talk and play quietly with me. But the children weren't there much because school had started—which I didn't realize.

IT WAS when I asked about the kids' absences that I found out school had started and I wasn't in it. I had a full-blown fit.

"Why?" I shrieked to Mama Linnet, who happened to be there at the time. "Why can't I go? Please please let me go to school."

But she only got alarmed about me, and tried to hush me, and gave me an extra dose of my Special Tea to calm me down, and put off my questions, saying I could go when my health was better.

I then later, dampened down some, tried to get Daddy's permission. "When? When will I be better enough? Can it be tomorrow?"

Neither of them would give me a straight answer. Later I heard the two of them talking in the hall.

Mama Linnet said, "When she's strong enough I'll ask Sara Ann if she'll teach her. Or Lucy. I'll pay them. She'll probably be able to keep up with First Grade."

From Mama Linnet's apartment I screamed to them, "I don't want to have school at home, I want to have it at school."

Daddy yelled back, "Okay, Miss-Cut-Off-Your-Nose-To-Spite-Your-Face: you won't have it at all, then. Go to sleep. I don't want to hear any more out of you."

Mama Linnet said, "Both of you hush. Pat, control yourself, you're a grown man."

I yelled again, "If I have to have school at home I want it to be Miss Sara Ann."

THE POLICE TALKED with every grownup, one by one, who lived or worked at Fourth and Victory. Mostly this was done in the sitting room, and it took several days. It made everybody nervous except Mama Linnet. Not that they talked with her very long. They went light on all the women. But for Daddy and The Lawyer Cato they came back a second time each. Daddy told them he had not paid enough attention to Mr. Tony to have any thoughts about him at all, good or bad. At the end of that part of the investigation, according to Daddy who got his police information from My Granddaddy, they still had no suspect.

They did have a clue about the motive for the murder, but they didn't get that from Fourth and Victory.

They had learned he was not from St. Louis as he had claimed, and his money and movie star clothes had not come from his parents, as we already suspected. He was from Kansas City. His father was dead, and his mother was dirt poor and hadn't heard from him in a long time. He was known to the police up there as having been probably in a ring of thieves and fences.

"I told you so! I told you so!" Daddy said, standing in the doorway to the kitchen, giving the news to Mama Linnet one night when she was trying to get the last of the tidy up done. "I was right, he was a born crook, and I saw it from day one. I've never understood why you couldn't see it."

"Well he's gone now, so we can let it rest."

"But you were bound and determined to give him the benefit of the doubt every single time. Like the time he ... "

"Son." she said. "Let it rest."

DADDY WAS NOT AROUND MUCH at that time. Weekdays, after he got off work he came and ate supper fast and then went straight to Mimi's and Pawpaw's to be with Mother. The four of them played cards if Mother felt up to it, or sometimes he took her to a movie, and sometimes he borrowed the Buick and took us for rides to get Mother out of the house and give the two of us a chance to see each other. He tried bringing her to our apartment once but she only sat down on their bed and cried. Weekends he spent a lot of time with Mother, but also went fishing with My Granddaddy. He came home mostly to eat and sleep. He looked in on me every day but he didn't stay long. If I asked for Mother he said she was still sick but doing better but she couldn't come home yet.

I missed her, and I missed him. But if I cried about it to him, that only made him leave sooner.

Another person who wasn't around was Dr. Haynes Senior.

"Why can't he be the one to come?" I asked Mama Linnet. "He's my real doctor."

"They're both your real doctors. They're partners. Dr. Haynes Senior is supervising your case. Yours and your mother's both. He's sending Dr. Haynes Junior in his place, but he's watching over what's going on. Dr. Haynes Junior tells him everything, and he makes sure he agrees with what Dr. Haynes Junior thinks is best to do."

"But why?"

"Dr. Haynes Senior has a lot of patients to see and operate on," is all she would say.

Who didn't come around me at all, for a long time, was Roger/Tian. I gradually realized it and began to miss him. I asked for him and the adults said maybe he would come pretty soon, but he didn't.

I HAVE since looked up exactly what was going on overseas and in the US during this time when I was five going on six. Most of Europe was at war because of the Nazis in Germany and the Fascists in Italy. The Japanese had invaded Manchuria, Mongolia, China, and had made a pact with Germany and Italy and, unbeknownst, were studying Pearl Harbor.

But at the time, the impact of this on our lives had still been slight. Except for the threat of the military draft, my grownups felt it most that certain things were getting scarce to buy—when there was money to buy anything. Granddaddy was the only man who said we would get in the war. He didn't explain it, he just said it. He had been in the Navy when we fought the Germans in World War I.

Daddy was one of sixteen and a half million men who had registered for the draft the year before when it had become the law. Since then Uncle Sam had taken only three men we could say we knew. The chance of being drafted made men nervous if they didn't want to go and didn't have an in with their local draft board. But others did want to go because it was manly and romantic and better than being jobless and maybe half hungry. Plus, being selected would not mean going in harm's way, everybody but my grandfather said. It would mean only being part of Preparedness, our USA showing strength. We weren't in the war. We were doing our part by sending supplies for England and China and Russia to fight with, and showing we could fight if we wanted to. The newspapers and radio and movie news shorts told us pieces of what was going on in the other side of the world. This gave the men grist for repeating things to each other or arguing.

THAT WAS the extent of concern about the war for most people I knew, until the day Daddy looked at his mail and the blood drained out of his face because he had been drafted.

There it was in his hand.

OCT 7, 1941
   (date of mailing)

ORDER TO REPORT FOR INDUCTION

THE PRESIDENT *of the United States*

TO PATRICK DANIEL LEWIS

• • •

ORDER NO. *1215*

GREETING:

HAVING SUBMITTED yourself to a local board composed of your neighbors for the purpose of determining your availability for training and service in the land or naval forces of the United States, you are hereby notified that you have now been selected for training and service therein.

YOU WILL, therefore, report to the local board named above at
      Rock Island Railroad Station, Little Rock, Arkansas
      (Place of Reporting)

AT 7:15 A. M., on the 20th day of October , 1941

THIS LOCAL BOARD will furnish transportation to an Induction station. You will there be examined, and, if accepted for training and service, you will then be inducted into the land or naval forces...

...AND SO ON. It was signed by a member of the local draft board, who was a man Daddy knew of.

"Hell, this is not right," he said to the air.

He and I were in the hall, just inside the front door,

where a basket on a table was the place Miss Savory put everybody's incoming mail.

I said, "What, Daddy? . . . What, Daddy? . . . What, Daddy?"

"Be quiet, I have to think."

He didn't think long. He hurried down the hall, passing the pay phone, to Mama Linnet's apartment, snatched up her telephone, and said into it, "'Scuse me for interrupting, Missus, I have to make an emergency call. Could you hang up please. . . . No, there's nothing you can help with. Just kindly hang up."

Then he dialed Curtis Haskell. "Boss? It's me. I came home for lunch and I've got a draft notice. . . . What do you mean? . . . No you didn't tell me that. You told me there were a couple new members of the local board, but you never told me *that*. What do I need to do? . . . No, I mean what do I do to straighten this out? Do I have to write some kind of letter to the whole board, or can I just talk to somebody face to face, or what? . . . Appeal to a *Regional* board? Curtis, are you pulling a trick on me? Because this is not funny." There was a longer pause, then, before Daddy spoke again. "Stop talking to me about holding my job for when I come back. The law says you have to do that anyway. Quit trying to sound so great about it. You make me sick."

He jammed the two pieces of the phone together again and slammed it back down on Mama Linnet's bedside table. Next he picked it back up again and tried to call someone else who didn't answer. Then he left, walking fast to the front door and out, with not a word to me.

"DID MR. PAT TALK TO YOU?" Miss Savory asked Mama Linnet when she got back from the Women's City Club two hours later.

"No. Was he looking for me?"

"He went tearin' off at noon, 'thout any lunch, I bet looking for you. He got drafted."

"Oh Dear Jesus," Mama Linnet said.

"I knew when I seen the outside of the envelope. And sure 'nough that's what it was. He's upset. Don't tell him I told you." Miss Savory went on to tell her also about Daddy's conversation with Curtis Haskell, and said, "It sounds t'me like Mr. Haskell's been pullin' the wool over his eyes and he's got a good chance of really havin' to go."

THE NEXT AFTERNOON my grandparents and Daddy had a talk on the front porch, just the three of them. And me. Granddaddy hoped Mama Linnet would sit beside him in the swing but she took a chair. He sat in the swing with me in his lap because when they had tried to get rid of me I threw my arms around his neck and put my face against him and tuned up to cry. Daddy walked back and forth until Granddaddy said he wished he would sit down and then he took the other chair.

Granddaddy told him he should stop thrashing around and straighten up and go on into the service. When Daddy said, What about my wife and mother and child?, Granddaddy said it didn't look to him like any one of us was actually dependent on him. And he said we would be just as fine without him as the wives and mothers and children of the other men.

He said Daddy should go on to the induction center and show right away that he had a good attitude and was educated and smart, and try to get in the Navy. He said learn everything you can because we will be right in the middle of the war before long. And try to become a commissioned officer, he would really like to see Daddy as a naval officer, and it would be important to Daddy himself to be an officer instead of a swabby or a grunt. He said he himself never had a chance to be an officer when he was in the last war since he didn't have the education and was only sixteen when he enlisted. But he did make Chief Petty Officer and was proud of that but he expected more of Daddy. Then he said to Mama Linnet, "What's your opinion, pet?"

She said, "I think this is something you would know best about."

10

———

MOTHER AND DADDY SAID THEIR GOODBYES TO EACH OTHER AT Mimi's and Pawpaw's.

Mama Linnet and I drove him to the station and saw him get onto the train along with a dozen other men. I didn't cry about Daddy because I was scared of being so close to the huge locomotive hissing out steam, and because I didn't know this was the end of an era in my life.

———

THE NEXT AFTERNOON Mama Linnet took me with her on the short walk to Main Street, to a dry goods store where she bought small amounts of cotton material in solid colors of red, white, and blue. She knew in her head exactly how much she wanted of each. Back home, she got out a pattern she had drawn and cut the night before on an old newspaper, and now used a dining room table to cut the material into its pieces. There were hardly any scraps. Her old treadle sewing machine lived in a corner of my bedroom, and she pulled it out under the ceiling light, and whirred away. In half an hour there was a beautiful oblong banner nearly as tall as I was. It had a blood-red border, a pure white background, and in the middle a true blue star the size of my two hands. It had gold braid at the top, to hang from.

I wanted to have it, to run around with it and wave it in the air, but she said no. "This blue star: that's your father. We are a blue-star family because we have a man in the service. We'll hang this in the front window so that everybody who passes by can see it."

I was impressed about my father and our new status.

Then she sat down and sewed another one.

She said, "Tomorrow I'll take you to see your mother and you can give this to her."

DADDY PHONED us usually once a week, on Saturday evenings. I'd know who it was when Mama Linnet would say to the operator, "Yes I'll accept the collect call." One night she told him she had taken out a mortgage and bought Fourth and Victory. He must have said something about biting off more than she could chew because she said she thought she had judged that all right. She also said, "No, honey, I haven't rented out your apartment. We'll keep that for you and your family's home." She laughed. "Unless a better home comes along." After they talked it was my time. A few short few minutes when he used his gift of gab to draw me out.

He also wrote letters to me after she told him it was not enough for her to read me her letters. Mine were only some lines not geared to a child, about what he had been doing in the army. He could talk a good game but not write one. Probably they were copies of parts of his letters to Mother and Mama Linnet. Still I was proud whenever there was an envelope from him addressed to me.

ON A DAY in early November Granddaddy came to Fourth and Victory again. After we hugged and I didn't want to let go, his tone of voice was no nonsense when he said to go on and play, he and Mama Linnet wanted a private conversation. My feelings were hurt and I was confused because he had never been gruff with me before, but I obeyed.

No one else was in the dining room, and they sat there. When I left he closed the hall door behind me but of course the other door was the half-door, the swinging door to the kitchen, where I headed as fast as I could go. I was thinking if I waited and listened for the right time, I could get back in there with them.

From the kitchen I was amazed to hear him tell her a lie: she asked if he had been drinking and he said no. I knew he had because I had smelled it. I recognized it because of Mother and Daddy secretly sharing their nips at special times, no matter that Mother was a Baptist. When I heard him tell this lie I felt locked up inside, and I had no name for that.

I didn't realize she knew the smell of alcohol better than I did. Asking him was her way of bringing it up.

BEFORE THAT DAY when Granddaddy came to Fourth and Victory drunk, in my own mind I had been on his side about the alcohol. I classified Mama Linnet's objection as one of her unexplainable religious beliefs.

But that day he was drinking and lying to her about it, and making her cry. And he looked like Granddaddy but did not seem like him at all. Everything about him was slow and heavy, and all of his fun was gone.

Sitting beside her at a table he said, "You need to stop this. I've done everything I know to do. You are my wife and I need you to be my wife and love me, and let me love you and take care of you. I can take care of you again now. Be my queen again. You'll never need to turn your hand to work from this minute on. We can go back to the way it was before we lost everything, I have it all back now, except you."

"Oh, Hampton, you don't. What you have is a steady job making nice money, and you're going to lose that if you keep drinking."

"No, for one thing I've got some savings. I've learned to save, you won't have to fuss at me about that anymore. And I've got a beautiful little piece of land just outside of town that I picked because I knew you'd like it. It's waiting on us, we can build a good house and raise some cattle, and take that little girl with us and give her the best any child could have . . . "

She broke in and said, "Stop." She was crying. She put her fingers of both hands across his lips.

He swiped her hands down and said, "You don't understand. I'm trying to tell you something you don't know, something I've . . . Pet, I might not make it without you. You are my love and I need you and I'm not sure I'm gonna make it." And he started crying.

"I do know. My darling. My darling."

"Then how can you hold yourself away from me this way. The one thing I need."

She stood up. "*Stop drinking*," she said. "I will not talk to you about this again until you *stop drinking* completely for one year. You're going to eventually kill yourself if you don't."

"Come back to me so that I *can* do it. Without you I can't. And don't talk to me anymore about praying my way out of this. Who cares if God loves me if *you* won't love me."

"You drank before we married. You drank when we were married. It's what kept us from getting through the worst times, we could have made it through except you just drank more and more. You are drinking now. And if we got back together now you would drink ever after and eventually ruin us both. I will not live with that. I will not live with you drunk, drugged, like you are now instead of my real Hampton, my beautiful Hampton. Wanting me back is the only thing that might make you stop drinking."

"You'll marry your boyfriend the doctor, is what you'll do."

He might as well have hit her.

"That doesn't deserve an answer," she said. "Have I asked you for a divorce?"

"We'll see," he said.

"Stop insulting us both. You need to go. If you love me don't come here drinking again. I can't bear it and I don't want Mary Mavis exposed to it."

He got up and left without another word. His unequal footsteps sounded like an injured giant's going down the hall to the front door.

THE NEXT TIME I saw Daddy was just before Thanksgiving. He was a soldier in a crisp tan uniform, spiffy and more handsome than ever. Somehow he was a few years older than just the weeks since he'd gone. He was cheerful again and something else: bright-eyed and bushy-tailed. His body was harder, fuller. He walked faster. The Navy hadn't needed anybody else right then, and he was in the Third Infantry and would go to an Army training camp when he left us this time. On this furlough he laughed and talked and ate and told stories and played with me, but something was different. A part of his mind was somewhere else. I was never to have the whole of him again.

Mother, I think, would have had all of him except that she was not together at that time.

———

MAMA LINNET RENTED Mr. Tony's room to a teenage couple with a new baby girl. They were straight out of the country. Sister and Brother Parker had asked Mama Linnet to take them in because they had no place to go. Their names were Janna and Tom McNee, and the baby's name was Tonna.

Tom couldn't read and write but I didn't know that for a while. Jana covered up for him.

Mama Linnet made a trial agreement to let them live and eat at Fourth and Victory in exchange for working three hours a day each. Tom's work was to be a general handyman and start repairing and painting the long-neglected house. He was also to assign an hour's useful work to every hobo who came to the house asking for a meal, and be the supervisor. Janna's work was to sweep and mop everything. This was a trial arrangement, to last a month.

Mama Linnet even added in a little cash money, which thrilled them. They had arrived with thirty cents.

They were both hard workers—Tom champed at the bit to work because it was what made him happy—and when their first month was up Mama Linnet renewed their room and board agreement indefinitely.

MAMA LINNET'S workload load had grown lighter because of Janna and Tom McNee and Miss Lucy pitching in. She often, now, let Miss Savory and Miss Claire run her off from the kitchen shutdown chores at night. She and I would go early to her apartment where she propped her feet up and sipped coffee while we listened to shows on her radio, or sometimes she wrote letters or read the newspaper, or made telephone calls to sick people from First Methodist Church. Or received a few phone calls.

She also had some breathing room during the days because she didn't need to be personally at the Women's City Club every single minute as she had at first. Miss Lucy was a natural organizer and great at following directions. She watched how Mama Linnet liked things to be, and made them so, such as: "Put the lettuce leaf curved up like a cup on the plate and then spoon in the chicken salad so the salad will look smaller." The idea being, society ladies like to pretend they eat like birds while still getting a lot. This, by the way, was the opposite of how it was done for Fourth and Victory, where putting the bulge upwards made a medium amount of filling look bigger.

Or, "Any kind of sandwich looks elegant once you cut

away the crust and quarter it to make little triangles and add a toothpick with an olive on it. But save the crusts."

Or, "At least once a week one of them will tell you something she would like better, some way you could improve the menu, and so forth. Just smile and say thank you and say you'll work on that. Do not, do not, take it personally. They think it's their duty. Let them say it, it's part of it. It's good for business." And Miss Lucy was able to do that, somehow gritting her teeth without showing it.

Miss Lucy truly liked producing and serving the Tea Room food: pretty plates of finger sandwiches, celery stuffed with pimento cheese, sliced fresh fruit, fancy crackers with spreads, teacup bowls of bisque. She was also good at numbers and keeping the inventory and the books. She seemed tireless. The place was making a good profit. Mama Linnet was quickly turning over the meal planning and management to her. The head work, not just the body work.

Miss Lucy's weakness, though, was that none of the other help liked working with her. Her talent for rubbing everybody the wrong way was probably the real reason the school system didn't want her back. What the school administrator had told her was, they were moving toward having only teachers with college degrees. Moving toward. Miss Sara Ann didn't have a degree and they were taking *her* back.

Miss Lucy drove even Miss Claire past her patience. And if it should come to hiring someone new to be Miss Lucy's assistant, plenty of people would take the job but who in their right mind could last? They would start looking for any other job right away. She was too bossy to be a boss. Mama Linnet began to teach her about this, though Miss Lucy didn't realize it.

THE LAWYER CATO and the new and eager Tom McNee were both exempt from the draft. The lawyer, because of his bad leg. I happened to know he tried to enlist anyway, and got turned down. He didn't want that known. Tom was disqualified because he couldn't read, and we didn't mention that either.

Tom and The Lawyer Cato steadied the male boardership at Fourth and Victory after Mr. Tony's death. I thought of them as my good friends, and that's the way they treated me. I followed Tom around quite a bit during the daytimes and asked questions and chatted with him while he hammered or painted some part of the neglected house or did winter cleanup of the yard. Weekday afternoons, instead of waiting for Daddy as I used to, I waited for The Lawyer Cato to come home from work, and greeted him with a hug. He liked that, even though he had to be careful bending down to accept. He grew out of his shyness with me and though I was still the one to do most of our talking out on the porch or at meals in the dining room, he said enough that I finally realized he was really smart.

THE POLICE TOLD Mama Linnet they had no new information about the murder. I was not surprised since Roger/Tian and I were the only ones who knew the Japanese had done it.

Miss Sara Ann had been tutoring me since early October, about a month, and I was about to learn to write. This was the only thing I was mildly interested in.

We were taking it easy because I was frail. Also she was not all that interested in my lessons. Each day by the time she came to me she'd already had a full day at the school plus her visit with her mother and her little dog or girl. And she had the take-home tasks that teachers do. She did those while she was teaching me.

If Mr. Tony had been still alive she wouldn't have had time for me at all. And if she hadn't declared to herself and everybody else that she was in mourning for him, she would have been going out with her girlfriends to meet men.

We spent about an hour together three weekdays in the evenings. Those times were, for me, at least a diversion from my fears and worries. She with her big blue eyes and I with something close to a desire to learn to write. We alternated subjects by the day. Mondays were for Reading, although she had no new storybooks and I could already read the many that I had. Tuesdays, Arithmetic, which was not thrilling but since it made use of a lot of rote memory, it came easy. And then best of all, Wednesday and Writing. Which, it turned out, was printing. She explained printing came before writing, or cursive as she said its name was. I had not known there were two kinds of writing, and I liked that idea. She assigned light homework, which I always did, sometimes twice or more if it involved the alphabet and printing.

But my longing to go to school with other children continued. Increased. My schoolbooks and supplies became also props in secret imaginary scenes with classmates when I was alone in Mama Linnet's apartment. This pretending was some diversion from my dark thoughts, but not enough.

A FEELING GREW between my two grandmothers: cooperation. Before, there had been a stiffness, generated by Mimi. She took a superior stance toward everybody who was not her blood kin. In the case of Mama Linnet that began to fade. Each time we went to see Mother on Sunday afternoons, before we left Mama Linnet found a different way to say gently to Mother that our apartment was waiting for her whenever she was ready. Mother would usually say something neutral, but Mimi always said it was truly appreciated.

ROGER/TIAN slipped in one day, excited, to tell me in secret that he and his mother had had another letter from his father. Mr. Lee somehow sent letters so that they could not be traced to him. Roger/Tian said that was hard to do and his father couldn't do it often. This letter told them that something important was about to happen that would probably make the United States join the war to help China and its allies. His own location had changed, he said, although of course he still could not let them know where he was.

Roger/Tian said, "*Now* something will be done about them! The Japanese are going to find out they can't just march around murdering everybody anymore."

"What else did he say?" I asked.

"He still doesn't know when he can come for us. He thinks it might be a long time. He arranged for us to get some money. I bet it's a lot."

MISS SARA ANN found some time to resume going out with friends. She was recovering from her mourning for Mr. Tony.

"That Sara Ann's seein' Hampton Lewis. Sure as I'm settin' here talkin' to you," Miss Savory said to Miss Claire in the kitchen.

"Surely they wouldn't do that."

"I know they are. I'll get proof of it once she starts showing up with him at them clubs she goes to. I got friends who work them clubs. She's man crazy."

"As buttoned-down as people are here, how does she keep her teaching job if she goes to clubs?"

"How do you think? Her bosses is men."

MISS ABIEN'S work hours grew from only laundry mornings to full mornings five days a week. She became what Miss Claire called, with a little smile, Our Sue Chef. That's what I thought she was saying. The rest of us didn't know that term. Potato peeler, string bean stringer, trash burner, dish washer —all as assigned by Miss Savory only. If anyone else spoke to Miss Abien it made her freeze with her eyes wide open the way a cow does when it sees something new. She worked seriously and paid attention only to the task. My Accident with the laundry wringer had had a lasting effect on Miss Abien. As much as possible, she kept away from me. Even when Miss Savory told her to, she would only pretend to come and see about me. If I spoke to her she would say, always, "All right Missy."

"Miss Abien do you know where Miss Claire is?"

"All right Missy."

Miss Savory scolded her. "You got to quit that. She don't understand. You hurt her feelings acting that way! I ain't having it. She is all of our job to take care of like she was our own. That means you too."

It didn't do any good, and I soon got used to the way Miss Abien was. I didn't care much about anything, anyway, outside my fears.

MISS CLAIRE WAS QUIET, and I had not yet focused on her as a person, out of the jumble of more showy folks and events at Fourth and Victory. I was not old enough to wonder what might be going on in the mind and heart of a woman who had been a performing artist in another world, and whose husband was a Chinese genius and absent, and whose son was precocious and rambunctious and was of mixed race and thus was half-hated whenever he left the house. And a woman who couldn't guess when or if their next dollar would come.

ON DECEMBER 7 the Japanese bombed Pearl Harbor. The day after that, the United States declared war on them, and then also on Germany and Italy.

"What did I tell you," Roger/Tian said. "My father has ways of knowing things other people don't."

MY ADULTS WERE SO astounded with the news of Pearl Harbor they forgot themselves and talked openly in my hearing about how terrible it was. How many men had been killed, and in what gruesome ways. Trapped in their ships and drowned. Exploded. Burned alive. Their conversation was full of this, and what it might mean in our lives and the lives of the men in service. Roger/Tian was encouraged. I was horrified.

My grasp of what had happened was a ghostly proof of the terrors I had recently almost climbed out of. Now I was slipping underneath them again. I felt I might be killed in some way like the terrifying ways of Pearl Harbor, and so might my loves and friends. Any of us, all of us. And Daddy was gone. And Granddaddy was gone. And Mother was gone. I kept myself in Mama Linnet's apartment now all day, with the door open so I could listen, but usually with my eyes shut, my body curled in a ball with a cover over me in her easy chair or in her bed. Sister Parker's potion returned, but it was a gradual medicine. Whoever could, looked in on me, many short visits taken from their busy workdays. At night Mama Linnet put me in her bed to sleep, holding me in her arms. The first night of this episode, she had started to recite for me, just after I had stopped her from turning out the light, my Now I Lay Me Down to Sleep prayer. But when she got to *If I Should Die Before I Wake* I stiffened and screamed, "No praying! No praying!" After that, last thing at nights, she half-sang the Itsy Bitsy Spider song softly against my head. This substitute was far from comforting to me but I think it was to her. I squeezed tight to her and let it be.

CHRISTMAS 1941 CAME and went like a shadow. I had stopped believing in Santa Claus the year before without realizing it. Now the magic didn't come and I missed it all the more because my fears and fatigues were still with me.

Mama Linnet had no Christmas spirit either. Weeks before, she had sent holiday boxes to her son in the service. Now all she could do about him was hope without really expecting it that he could get a phone call through. That didn't happen.

On Christmas Eve afternoon Mama Linnet drove me to Mimi's and Pawpaw's and left me there to spend a few hours with Mother and them. A month earlier, Mama Linnet had bought my presents for Mother and Daddy. For Mother, she had chosen Chanel No. 5 eau de toilette, and told me it was what Mother wore. When I gave the little box to Mother, she liked it mildly. Her present to me was a red velvet dress she had made, but when I took it out of the box and she held it up against me, it was too small. She started crying and said she was worthless, and went to her room and shut the door. Mimi and Pawpaw quickly pointed me to a big white box under their tree. It turned out to have a baby doll in it. I had sense enough to sing-song, "This is nice. Thank you, Mimi. Thank you Pawpaw," and to keep it to myself that I already had three nearly identical baby dolls and didn't care a bit for them.

Back home at Fourth and Victory, on Christmas morning I got the cowboy boots and a holster and toy pistol I had once begged for. Somehow Mama Linnet had managed to get them. Also, with my gun there was a surprise red roll of caps. After I shot the first cap I couldn't bring myself to squeeze the trigger again. I took some pleasure in clomping around in my western gear but the new soon wore off and Christmastime went all the way flat for me.

———

BUT BEFORE THE holidays were over excitement replaced the doldrums.

Mama Linnet liked to read the whole newspaper, time permitting, meaning the want ads too. She kept an eye on it that Pearl Harbor was causing small businesses to go up for sale because the owners, or other crucial men, were heading into service. And bingo, there it was. Fourth and Victory's nearest competitor for the meals business, the Rock Hut Cafe, was on the market.

11

MAMA LINNET ALREADY KNEW ALL ABOUT THE ROCK HUT Cafe: how many ate there, who they were, what they ate, why they ate there, what they paid. It was located four blocks away from Fourth and Victory, across the street from the Post Office. It was a short-order one-room food establishment in its own wee sandstone building. It had an orange-red neon sign, two picture windows with red and white checkered curtains, and a black cooking grill almost the length of the room. In front of the grill was an equally long red-topped counter where people could sit on red-topped swivel stools. Also in the room were four square tables with red and white checkerboard oilcloth covers, four red-seated chairs to each table, and a fat red-and-chrome jukebox. *And:* Beside the jukebox was a pinball machine which came to life like a fantasy, with many colors and enchanting sounds. It cost a nickel to play. Or a slug.

The owner wanted to sell the establishment fast, and Mama Linnet snatched it with a cash down payment and a promise agreement drawn up by The Lawyer Cato. Most people in transition didn't have any cash, the very thing they needed most, but Mama Linnet nowadays kept enough to get the attention of a seller if she wanted to.

———

THE DAY after Christmas she already had the keys, and she took us on a walk up to see the new place, a parade of us in our winter coats although it was barely cold: Mama Linnet holding my hand, Miss Claire and Roger/Tian, Miss Savory and Miss Abien, Tom with Janna carrying little bundled-up Tonna, and The Lawyer Cato. The only ones absent were Miss Sara Ann who was staying at her mother's for the holidays, and Miss Lucy who was with her vegetable husband. We got most of the way there before I ran out of steam, and then Tom carried me piggyback.

Mama Linnet had put up a sign on the front: *UNDER NEW MANAGEMENT - OPEN AGAIN JAN. 5.*

"Mrs. Lewis, how can you get it open that fast? That's next week," Miss Claire said.

"A week and three days. I *have* to do it or the customers will start going somewhere else and get out of the habit. Everything's here and ready. I bought it lock stock and barrel. The waitress wants to stay on, her name is Ydean Boxley. She also knows how to work the cash register. She'll do all right I hope, I don't know much about her. I can be here a lot of the time for the first couple of weeks to work out the problems. There's not much to do except buy what's needed in the way of fresh food, and find a dependable fry cook."

"Ah kin cook," Tom said.

We all looked at him.

"Ah kin. Ah know mah way around this," he indicated the grill and all that was behind it. "Ah done it before. Ah *like* tuh cook. Ah'd appreciate having 'at job, Miz Lewis, Ah'd like tuh say Ah was somethin' in p'ticlar an' not just a odd jobs man." He looked to Mama Linnet and cocked his head. "Want me tuh show ye?"

"No, you don't have to do that. If you say you can do it, I believe you. But Tom, I'm going to need you to keep on working at Fourth and Victory," she said.

"Ah kin do both. Miz Lewis, you don't know this about me, but since two years ago when my daddy and mother was kilt in a accident and we lost everything, there weren't a day in my life I didn't work two jobs' worth. We all did. If you'll give me this short-order job I'll make you glad you did, and Ah'll do mah other work on mah off time. You wouldn't have to pay me till you see I'm worth it."

"I'll pay you starting tomorrow and if it doesn't work out we'll make adjustments," she said.

WHILE THIS TURN of events was playing out I had dragged a chair between the jukebox and the pinball machine, to climb up and look inside them. I was fascinated and mystified by what I saw, and was saying, "What do these do? . . . What do these do?" with no one listening.

Finally Mama Linnet gave me her attention. "Does anybody know how to play this?" she said about the pinball machine. She opened her purse, then her coin purse, and gave me a nickel.

"I'll show you," The Lawyer Cato said in his growl. He

dragged the chair with me standing on it to the front of the machine. He said, "Pull this out. Put the nickel in this little round place here. Now push the whole thing in. Get ready." As the machine chimed and turned colors and the silver ball popped up into view at the top and started to roll and bump its way downhill through the obstacles, and the bells rang and the buzzers buzzed, he took my hands and held my two index fingers to show me about punching the side buttons that worked the flippers and made the ball ricochet up for a do-over.

Then and there I began to get well again. I asked for another nickel and played more. And then more. They had to pry me away. "I'll bring you back tomorrow after church," Mama Linnet said. "Then you can play all you want."

Miss Savory said, "Miz Lewis, you gonna be out a lot of nickels, looks like."

"A nice thing is," Mama Linnet said, "all the nickels in that machine will end up with me."

The pin ball machine may have been my salvation. That night I went to sleep thinking about it, and the next morning it was the first thing on my mind. My fears were not gone but they were weakened, displaced, their habits were broken. I was better. Mama Linnet thanked God out loud in her relief that there was something I wanted so much it took me out of myself, and she saw to it that I was taken to the Rock Hut Cafe for twenty-five cents worth of plays almost every weekday. It was Miss Abien's job to walk me to the Cafe, wait there sitting or standing in a corner for me to play out my nickels, then walk me back. In all the trips she never would talk to me. It was more than a month before the fascination began to dim for me. By mid-February I was agreeable to go only a couple of days a week, and thereafter I was satisfied to play the machine only whenever I happened to be there because Mama Linnet or someone else was going.

———

THE PASTOR of the First Methodist Church didn't like the jukebox and pinball machine. He phoned Mama Linnet and asked to come and visit with her, which had never happened before. Soon one afternoon they were talking in the sitting room.

He was about the same age as Mama Linnet and was married to a woman she liked. He was a friendly man. You don't get selected to be the pastor of the city's downtown Methodist Church unless you know how to get along with people, and he did. Also to support him in this meeting he had his position as a pastor—*the* pastor—and what he thought was his duty.

Mama Linnet was shored up by her own convictions, though. Also she was smarter. And probably he was attracted to her, and probably she knew it.

They both were calm through the whole stalemate. He was smooth, and she was sweet.

He said he knew she wouldn't allow the pinball for actual gambling, his concern was the image of it, the possibilities of bad influence from the near-gambling and the jukebox's modern popular music, one thing leading to another the way they do, and she being a woman alone and the sponsor of it. One of the Church's most valuable women, he said. She told him of course no one is ever alone, and we are all valuable, and that he was right: she would never countenance gambling, much less trashy music. Near the end she said if it would help she could promise that none of the proceeds from the machines would ever get into the church's collection.

Afterward she explained this matter to me in case I might overhear something about it. At the end of what she said about it, she told me it was also a good example of how you must never let anyone, even your pastor, or maybe especially your pastor, tell you what is right and wrong for you. After you reach the age of reason.

"That's how Catholics do, but We Are Methodists. I know in my heart and mind there is no evil in my jukebox and pinball machine or my customers who play them."

"Or me," I said.

"Or you," she said. "Especially you."

"How old is the age of reason?" I said.

EVERY SUNDAY AFTERNOON Mama Linnet drove me to Mimi's and Pawpaw's to see Mother, as she had done since Daddy left for the service. We stayed for an hour or two. My maternal grandparents did their best to find topics to visit with her about while I sat on Mother's lap and showed her my pretend-school papers. Sometimes we soaked each other up, but other times she was not really there. When the time for the visits was over nobody in the room minded bringing it to a close.

ANOTHER SIX WEEKS, and winter and spring were playing tug of war. The Rock Hut Cafe was doing more business than it ever had. Mama Linnet knew she would have her down payment back in three months. Tom and Ydean had been a team from the start, and they took over and ran the place without much need of Mama Linnet. Both of them were funny and likable. They treated the customers like family. Janna was suspicious of Ydean where Tom was concerned.

MAMA LINNET PRAYED SILENTLY SITTING in her desk chair with her feet propped on her bed, "Dear Lord, You showed me how to get past it when You took my precious Dennis back to You. And You showed me how to get past Hampton's sickness, so far. And a big theft, and a murder, that each one like to have ruined me. And I can never thank You enough. And if it is Thy will, Lord, show me how to get past this Rationing. I ask in Jesus name, Amen." Then she tilted her face again and said, "And please help me remember that the reason for Rationing is to keep our son fed and clothed and safe."

This was at the end of the day that she had gone to apply and get her Ration Book One.

Same as we had a Local Draft Board, now we had a Local Rationing Board. We had been told in advance by newspapers, radio, billboards, movie announcers, and posters that on a given Saturday an adult from each family should go to the primary school closest to where they lived, to get a Ration Book with Ration Coupons in it. Representatives of the Local Board would be there to take applications and give out the Books.

In our case, the school was Carter Elementary. Snow came only two or three times in our winters, and the time was almost in spring, but it had started snowing before daylight, and was still snowing hard on the morning Mama Linnet walked to the school. She arrived at seven thirty, knowing the doors wouldn't open for another hour. Already there was a line, and more kept coming, and they all stood until eight thirty in the snow, some with galoshes and over-coats and umbrellas, and some with just their wet only pair of shoes and two layers of sweaters and a scarf on their head. Or less.

Once in, they were directed to take a number and sit in the school's auditorium. Mama Linnet was lucky to get a seat. People came until they had to line up around the walls, with the line going out the door, down the hall, and out onto the playground.

A teacher-volunteer handed Mama Linnet a clipboard, a pencil, and some mimeographed papers. There were not enough clipboards, and the volunteer asked her to signal when she was finished with hers. Mama Linnet made sure it was all right to use her own fountain pen, and then read the instructions and filled out the application. And waited.

Up on the stage were three big wooden desks, spaced apart and spotlit from overhead. Each desk had two chairs. At nine o'clock three men in business suits walked down the center aisle, climbed the stage stairs, and walked with loud steps across the hollow wooden floor to their places behind the desks.

When it was Mama Linnet's turn, about ten thirty, the man behind her desk was Dolph Burnley.

Mr. Burnley was a big man who was losing his hair early. What little he had left, he oiled and combed into long see-through strands on his white scalp. He needed glasses but didn't wear any. Most of the town knew him at least vaguely, or knew of him, because he was a native son who had a dozen kids and had lost his wife to cancer two years before, and had cried for a year. He managed by himself to keep all the kids at home and together.

Before Rationing, his former job had been in the Post Office. One of his duties there was to make people fill out long forms. For instance, if you said you didn't get enough stamps for your money but you decided it wasn't worth a half day of forms, he wouldn't let you go. He was determined to fill out the government's bottom line and he stood ready to make a federal case of it.

When it was finally Mama Linnet's turn to get her Ration book from Mr. Burnley, she explained that the form didn't fit what she needed to apply for. She not only needed coupons for herself and her granddaughter, she needed enough to feed at least twenty meal customers three times a day, plus weekend meals for five boarding house occupants and one baby, plus a total of twelve meals a week for the help and their children, which was understood as part of their pay; plus a short-order cafe. She didn't even mention free meals for three or four hoboes a week.

He listened but didn't say a word. Then he put his face close to some colored papers on his desk and squinted at them to make sure they were right. He put those in a booklet cover, and handed that to her. He said, "This is your Ration Book One. It has coupons in it for one adult and one child. Yourself and your granddaughter. Which is what you declared as the family you're the head of."

He also told her she could only have one car sticker and

gasoline stamps for only one. He reminded her she had declared she owned ten car tires, and the limit was five.

She said, "You don't understand. If I can't buy the food for my businesses, I'll go out of business. Let me go back over it all and explain better."

"Miz Lewis, we can't give out Ration stamps like it was a free-for-all. Our nation is in a war. And our local organization is expected to show our patriotism. You'll have to have proof about your businesses, and file Applications for Exceptions."

"Oh good, I have the proof," she said, and opened the snap of her pocketbook to get the papers. "I have a business license for both of my businesses."

"No. This is Individual and Family Day only. Business Exceptions is next Saturday," he said.

She looked at him. Finally she said, "Will you be here that day?"

"Yes, but I may not be the one you see. We can't pick who we see. Nepotism and cronyism is against the law."

"I don't know what those are," she said.

"Playing favorites. No can do. And I don't want to get your hopes up about Exceptions. Just because you apply for Exceptions doesn't mean you get approved. Most people won't. Not first time around, anyway."

"Will you tell me now everything I'll need to bring, to apply for Exceptions?" she said.

"No. Because what we are doing today is helping everybody we can to apply for their Individual or Families, and I need to get on with it. As you can see. But you can come to our offices this week, Monday through Friday, and ask for me, and I can walk you through it then. We're located in the Post Office."

And so she came home with a book of Ration coupons that would allow her to buy, for herself and me only, food and other essentials amounting to about half of what we had been used to.

Also in the book was a set of printed warnings: It was against the law to sell or give away coupons, or even use anyone else's. The penalty for coupon fraud was ten thousand dollars or ten years in prison, or both.

Rationing would start in two weeks.

AND SO THE War was not only taking away our men, it was now reducing how much anybody could get of whatever mattered. Rationing came fast and rough, as if our government suddenly frowned on us. The disapproving tone of it was in the signs and posters that appeared in public places, lecturing and chastising us in unsympathetic ways:

"Do with less—so they'll have enough!" with a picture of a smiling soldier in his helmet, holding out his aluminum food cup.

Or *"When you ride ALONE you ride with Hitler! . . . Join a Car-Sharing Club TODAY!"* with a ghostly Hitler sitting in your front passenger seat.

Every person—and some businesses, but not all—got Ration coupons allowing the buying of much less than they were used to. Food, shoes, cloth, paper, cars, gas, anything made of rubber or metal. You name it, you couldn't get much of it.

Sugar was the first and maybe the most disturbing loss for most people—and for most food businesses. You could get about a tenth of what you wanted. For any cake or pie that should have been good and sweet, the options were to have something tiny, or else something not really sweet and not very good. Small bakeries were among the first businesses to go under.

For canned goods, each person got forty-eight Ration points a month. That amounted to about, say, one can of peas, one of corn, one of tomatoes. Yes, per month.

Coffee: severely restricted.

And the list went on. Flour. Potatoes. Chocolate. Beef...

Our government was stockpiling the bigger portion of these goods. They were needed to feed the servicemen and keep them in clothes and gear, and weapons and transportation. Only the lesser portion was left for civilians to buy.

Also the government set the price for almost everything. It was now not just unpatriotic to charge more than the set price, it was illegal.

And it was illegal and immoral to *pay* more. There was a special poster for this: a picture of a saintly-looking young housewife in a white ruffled apron, holding up her right hand in oath-taking, saying, *"I pay no more than top legal prices. I accept no rationed goods without giving up ration stamps."*

Mama Linnet looked at this poster and said, "I don't believe in swearing anything ahead of time. You never know what you or somebody you care about might come up against."

Nevertheless, she turned her back on the black market as much as anybody could.

She called the boarders together again for a meeting in the dining room, on the next Saturday morning. Miss Claire, who also brought Roger/Tian, Miss Sara Ann, Miss Lucy, and Tom and Janna with baby Tonna, and The Lawyer Cato.

She told them that soon she wouldn't be able to feed them anymore unless they were willing to meet two conditions. One was to contribute their food coupons into a household pool. For this, they would need to let her tell them what to buy, and then they themselves would each have to go to the store and buy it. Once a week.

Tom said, "Janna, did you get them coopon thangs yit?"

Janna said, "Miz Lewis we have our Ration Book and you can count our coupons in."

The Lawyer Cato, who was sitting as far away from Miss Sara Ann and as close to Miss Lucy as he could, said, "Ahhm. I was under the impression I wouldn't need any, because of your food establishment here . . . "

"Have you applied for your Ration Book at all?" Mama Linnet said to him.

He hemhawed No.

Mama Linnet said, forgetting herself, "Mr. Cato, for goodness sake. What can you be thinking? You're going to need at least gas for your car . . . but anyway, if I'm to see to your meals then I'll need you to contribute your food coupons."

Janna said, "Men just do not care to understand what is going on."

The Lawyer Cato said he would get his coupons and consider them as belonging to the house.

Miss Lucy said, "Count me in."

Miss Claire said she had her and Roger's coupons to give. Roger/Tian looked bored but in secret he was relieved to know his mother had taken care of the matter of this Rationing that had gone right over his head. He liked to picture himself as the man of the family, with his father away.

Miss Sara Ann said her situation was so complicated she didn't know what to do. She had declared herself head of a household: herself, Loretta—whom she didn't identify—and her mother. "What do y'all think?" she asked the whole group.

Mama Linnet said, "Sara Ann, all you need to do is, in your mind and in your Ration Book, separate your own coupons from the others, and decide whether you want to contribute only yours. I would not be asking for Loretta's—your little girl's? Yes—or your mother's. Just please tell me by tomorrow."

She went on, "And that brings me to the second condition. If I'm to keep on with your meals, we'll have to have Victory Gardens, and you'll each have to do part of that work. You'll have to pitch in with some of your time for the gardens two or three times a week. For a long time. The foreseeable future. It's a bigger decision than it sounds like."

"Now *that* ah kin do." Tom said with a big smile.

"*Gardens*?" Miss Lucy said. "How many? Where would they be?"

"One here that will take up the back yard, and the other, an acre out on Hayes Road that someone is loaning me. It has a year-around creek close by to get water from." Mama Linnet said.

She went on to say to them all, "The garden work needs to start right away. I've got cool-weather seeds that will need to be sprouting indoors, and I want those plants in the ground by mid-April. Also we will be raising our own chickens."

"I'm asking you to sleep on it and tell me tomorrow whether you're in or out for the victory gardens. If it's out, I'll understand and we'll work out a different price for your room and board."

"Mrs. Lewis?" Miss Lucy said, "How did you get enough coupons for the outside-customers' meals here? And at the Tea Room? And the Rock Hut?"

Mama Linnet said, "I can't get those until next week." Under the table she had her fingers crossed.

12

I BEGAN GOING TO SUNDAY SCHOOL AGAIN THAT SPRING, although not church yet.

My tutoring lessons had fizzled out. Mama Linnet was the one who put a stop to them and that was because Miss Sara Ann had reduced them to two days a week and then soon down to one or none, undependable. Mama Linnet didn't like seeing me expect Miss Sara Ann and then be disappointed when she didn't come. Miss Sara Ann said her mother was sick and needed her many of the afternoons and nights.

"That's BS," Miss Savory told Miss Claire. "Ain't nobody sick. He picks her up at the school when she gets off—somebody does, I know for a fact—and I bet she's with him 'til probably he drops her off someplace close enough to walk here and play like she took the bus."

Miss Sara Ann began to use the pay phone in the hall to talk in a whisper to someone for ten or fifteen minutes at night, two or three nights a week. She turned her face to the wall with her back to Mama Linnet's closed door, one hand cupped over her mouth. She had never before used the phone much. Mama Linnet and I could not help knowing she was there, since our door's transom was always open. What she said, whispering and murmuring, we didn't know except for the moments she forgot herself. One night while Miss Sara Ann was on the phone, Mama Linnet dialed a number on her own phone and after getting a busy signal she slowly put her finger on the pad and hung up. Next night, same thing.

———

I HAD NOT SEEN or heard from Granddaddy in more than six months. "Has he been drafted?" I asked Mama Linnet. She said he was too old. I said in puzzlement that he was not old, and she agreed, and explained the draft had an age limit.

"Where is he, then?" I asked.

"He's out of town a lot. His work takes him different places."

"What is his work?"

"He operates a big steam shovel. The biggest there is. A power shovel, they call them now, they're not run by steam anymore. It digs out dirt by the truckloads, and big rocks, to get all that out of the way if they want to put in highway or a building. Not many can do what he does. He's a master at it." She was smiling, thinking of him at it.

But there was something new Mama Linnet didn't know: he *was* in the Service. The Navy had formed the Seabees, and Granddaddy enlisted. Age didn't matter with them, and skill did. He knew somebody who was Somebody, and he had already gone to Rhode Island. There he would help build a base where more Seabees would come to train and then they would all go where the war was. They would build airstrips, bridges, roads, for the fighting men.

She found out about it only when he sent her a three-page letter that made her cry. Part of it said,

"*...I am no use to you or myself. Maybe I can be of use to our country for at least a while. And maybe help keep you and our little girl safe from these evil bxxxxxxs. If it happens they take me out then they will only have done for me what it turns out I could not do for myself...*"

She forgot what she had been doing before the mail came, and sat down at her desk in her apartment and wrote him a long letter right back.

The next afternoon our blue-star banner had a second star.

———

DADDY WENT to Officer Candidate School. When he finished there, he came home for almost a month. Mother was some-what better. Not well but better. She came temporarily back to Fourth and Victory and the three of us had a fairytale time of days and nights in our apartment, a family again. Each of us had changed enough to be almost new to each other.

They say if you lose yourself you should go back to where you last had yourself, and I think this is what Mother was trying to do. She bought some material and patterns for a little girl who was no longer barely five but now almost six-and-a-half and would need up-to-date school clothes in a few months, and took my new measurements, and sewed efficiently. Daddy slept late, and ate all the home cooking he could get, read the newspaper with his feet propped up, sometimes helped out with boarding house chores or getting supplies, and went to see old friends.

We all three accompanied Mama Linnet on her over-seeing rounds to the Rock Hut and the Tea Room—Mother went to the Tea Room without saying a word about it. Mama Linnet let Daddy take her Buick whenever he wanted. She told him to remember there was gas rationing. Regardless, Daddy insisted on giving Mother driving lessons because he said she might need to know how in case of emergency, and she did learn how and got a license, although she didn't like driving.

———

THE WEATHER WAS fresh and sunny, not yet hot, and Mother, Daddy, and I walked to the zoo and movies, and once in the evening Daddy drove us to the airport to watch the half-dozen planes that landed and took off between sundown and dark, until the mosquitoes began to bite. If we three went downtown Mother dressed up, and dressed me up, and we felt like a spiffy threesome strolling on the street with Daddy in uniform as a Second Lieutenant.

There were other soldiers and sailors home on furlough, and when enlisted men passed us they saluted Daddy. Mother and I were impressed that he was so important. He had to pull his hand away from mine each time, to respond.

Daddy enjoyed the comradeship at the Rock Hut Cafe, and took Mother and me to eat and hang out there. He laughed and bragged on my scores on the pinball machine, and then showed me some tricks that let me score higher. He liked music. He got coins out of the cash register and played the jukebox. His favorite was "Praise the Lord and Pass the

Ammunition." He took Mother dancing two nights, as if they were courting again.

HE KNEW that a few weeks after he got back to his base he would be on his way to Europe. He told us this but soft-pedaled it. He said he liked the kind of work he had trained for, which was Artillery.

Mother surprised us all by saying to him, "I want to go back to your base with you. I want to be with you until you have to go overseas."

"Honey, I . . . well, I guess . . . maybe we could find some-place for you to stay. That would be just a chance, though. Every Tom, Dick, and Harry's wife and kids are there already, looking for any kind of place. Sweetheart, do you think you're up to this?"

"I can stay in a hotel at first. After all, we have a lot of money saved."

"We do?" he said.

"Of course. What do you think I've been doing with the allotment money for Mary Mavis and me?"

"I thought you'd been spending it," he said.

"On what? You know I'm not a spendthrift."

It was almost like the old days, between them.

"On what you need to live," he said.

"What would I need, living at home? My parents certainly would not expect me to pay room and board."

"And you haven't been paying my mother anything for keeping Mary Mavis?" he said.

"I never thought you wanted me to: *you* never did."

DADDY TOOK himself seriously as an officer and a gentleman. The next day he told Mama Linnet he didn't want his daughter being a charity case, he would send my allotment checks to her in the future. Her response was that he should stop talking that way, none of our family ever was or would be a charity case so long as there was breath in her body. She told him he ought to see she loved me more than words could say and would take care of me unto eternity if need be; but she would like to have my allotments to put in a savings account for me.

The question was never brought up, whether I should go with Mother and Daddy to his Army base. Mama Linnet and I saw them both off on the train.

MAMA LINNET MAGNETIZED MOST MEN. They reacted in various ways, some being honestly over-friendly, and others turning contrary or odd. The honest ones were easiest to deal with. She was good at being sweet to them while letting them know they needed to move on. Sometimes she had to let them know several times before it took, but that was all right. It was the ones who were mad at her because of their attraction who were troublesome. Curtis Haskell was one of those. He came around periodically as a meal customer, with made-up excuses to talk to her in the kitchen where she had gone to try and get away, and tell her things she ought to do. She had secretly never liked him, and now she was also mad at him for the way he had treated her son, lying to pretend that he could keep Daddy from being drafted. So Curtis

Haskell's attraction to her was bothersome, but he was only one in a steady stream.

Part of her pull was physical. She was beautiful, face and body. Her plain style never could disguise it. She wore no makeup and usually kept her hair, which was light brown, pulled back in a bun. You could see three or four gray hairs. Like as not, she would be wearing a clean white bib apron over a print housedress. Her small perfect figure was concealed. To get to her blue-green eyes, you had to look through her wire-rimmed glasses. Her shoes were black lace-up oxfords with a two-inch heel. She had a good gold wristwatch she was careful of. She took it off and put it in a pocket anytime she had her hands near water. The watch was her only adornment on ordinary days.

She did like nice clothes and jewelry, though, and bought them with care, and wore them to church on Sundays. Her hands were little and she kept her nails manicured with clear polish.

Typically men were attracted to her in three phases. First they just liked her. Next they realized they were only seeing a little of something that seemed to have no bounds, and they wanted more. And when they found out for sure they couldn't have it, a few of them did colorful things.

WHEN SHE DECLINED Dr. Haynes Senior he was not dramatic; he just stopped coming around. Which is not necessarily to say he stopped intending to marry Mama Linnet. Whether he had taken No for an answer was anybody's guess, and people were guessing both ways at Fourth and Victory and throughout the city. He was our town's darling.

One of our two banks bore his mother's maiden name. On his father's side we had the Haynes Musical and Theatrical Auditorium and the Haynes Municipal Library. His medical education was the best the east had to offer. When he came home with a blueblood wife, they were invited everywhere that mattered. A year later they had a stillborn baby. About a year after the baby, she left him. People said it was because she was wild and fast, and he wasn't. We never knew the truth. She disappeared and left a cloud of rumors and never came back.

Dr. Haynes Junior was his nephew, not his son.

They said that after his wife divorced him he went through a spell of dating a few daughters of old-money families, but he didn't follow through with any of them. From the beginning of his career until now he had dodged a lot of debutantes and nurses aiming for him, but never come close to marrying again.

He had been our family's doctor since Daddy was about ten. That was as soon as Mama Linnet had scraped together enough money to have a doctor to take her child to if she let go everything else.

Miss Savory wondered to Miss Claire just how long Dr. Haynes Senior might have been in love with Mama Linnet. "It might'a been years. Now I think on it, I bet that's why he ain't married again. Don't write him off, he ain't done yet. Still water runs deep."

A SENSE of the would-be romance between Dr. Haynes and Mama Linnet had got around town, or at least enough of town that two different church friends of hers had hinted about it to her in a positive way. People's opinion as to whether it would be good or bad, was forming along yea and nay lines: yea with the working class, nay with the old money—much of which money was no longer there. Also there were still whispers about the murder. Mama Linnet had caught the public eye.

Our newspaper had a monthly article featuring notable local citizens. One day a reporter phoned Mama Linnet and asked if she would agree to be interviewed. "I don't know what you could possibly say about me," Mama Linnet said, but as she listened to the reporter her face changed from puzzled to pleased. She took an afternoon off later that week and had her picture taken in her good suit and hat by the town's portrait photographer. She was pretty to begin with, and the photographer was gifted. In a couple of months there in the rotogravure section of the Sunday paper was a three-column print of a charming picture of her with the caption, "Businesswoman Succeeds at Multiple Enterprises."

Not long after the newspaper article, Miss Lucy confided in Mama Linnet one day when they were in the Buick that she wished she could get a divorce from her vegetable husband. She wanted to take care of him all his life, but she wanted to be free to marry again and have the life she once thought she would. She didn't want to be alone forever. It was maybe not too late to have children, even, she said.

Mama Linnet was at a loss to respond because of her own separated but married condition. She said only, "I can understand how you would feel."

That was enough to take the lid off Miss Lucy's feelings, locked away a long time. She talked on, letting it all out.

At the end Mama Linnet said, "It's a hard decision. But first you would need to know whether you *can* get a divorce. I don't know what the law is about that, do you?"

And that led Miss Lucy to consult The Lawyer Cato.

On the front porch. On a delicate spring evening with a mockingbird singing high up somewhere near, to his mate.

"Is there someone you want to marry right now?" The Lawyer Cato said to her.

"Does that matter?" she said instantly.

"It does to me," he blurted out. He turned beet red.

"Explain to me why it matters," she said briskly, "I was speaking theoretically, but if timing is important I need to know."

He said, "Excuse me, I misspoke."

So began the courtship of two people who didn't know how. One of them didn't even know for a while that they were courting.

Miss Savory said to Mama Linnet about them, "Miz Lewis, I cain't stand it no more. What he sees in her I do not know, and she is a good ten years older than he is, but won't you please tell her he's sweet on her?"

"She's no more than five years older, and no I will not tell her," Mama Linnet said, "And I hope nobody else does. It's between the two of them."

"Then, cain't you tell *him* to tell her?"

But Mama Linnet said nothing to them and nothing about it. Her own situation kept her from knowing what would be moral to say. She did pray for their happiness.

We all saw them every day and their relationship on the thin edge. It was painful to watch.

THE LAWYER CATO was from of one of our state's landed families who had lost most of their land. They lived in one of the southernmost counties of our state, where he'd grown up as the youngest son of a clan who were losing their fortune. His parents grew old and died before they should have, prices dropped, markets closed, and, especially, *ventures failed,* as they say. He quietly watched all that. Probably when he was young his mind got trained to the careful side of everything.

His older brothers were responsible for the failed ventures. They also invested in him, as they saw it and said it, helping him get his education. He passed the bar just fine, but he was not offered a position in an established law firm, partly because of his shyness. All the firms were doing less than well. Probably his non-functioning knee didn't help, either. His family could not leverage him in anywhere. That was how they found out their extended influence had petered out completely.

He did go to work as a lawyer, but it was for the state, in the basement of the state capitol. So in his family's eyes he was a failed venture too. As a lawyer, he was certainly not the kind who could help restore them to their place. He repaid his brothers for his education as soon as he could, with interest. And he sent money each month toward the support of his two maiden sisters. But what his family said about him was, "At least he can support himself." He had two indulgences: his cigars, which he smoked only outside because of Mama Linnet's rules—and his car. He called it a British roadster. It was dark green. We called it The Racing Car. He parked it on our lot and covered it with a tarpaulin.

Whenever there was talk of the draft he said nothing. He told no one that he had tried to enlist the day after Pearl Harbor, but they had turned him down because of his impossible knee and his bad eyesight.

———

THE LAWYER CATO didn't leave us in sympathetic pain too long before doing something about Miss Lucy's blindness to his affection He must have realized he needed to paint with a much broader brush. He found out her birthday was coming soon—after all he was a lawyer—and when she came home that day there was a note in the mail basket, written in Miss Savory's big, beautifully careful script on a full page taken from my big-lined yellow school tablet. I was thrilled to participate.

Mrs. Weldon.
Somebody sent you Flowres they are
In the Kitchen.
PS Happy BD from us
Savory & Mary Mavis

THAT NIGHT MISS LUCY made a point of arriving at the dining room door as soon as The Lawyer Cato sat down, and she sat beside him. She said something to him that nobody else could hear. He blushed and smiled straight ahead, but leaned his head slightly to her and whispered back. Thereafter they were a twosome. On the porch, in the sitting room, in the dining room. They went out on dates to the movies. We were surprised that she had another personality when she was with him. Gentle in speech and body, smooth and reassuring to him. She lightly touched his arm a lot. He unfolded like a flower.

"Not in a million years would I ever a'thought it a' either one of 'em," Savory said.

MISS SARA ANN no longer mentioned her little dog-or-girl, and now she talked only about her little girl who was close to my age, Loretta. Miss Sara Ann said we should meet. She said we would go to the same school, come fall. Loretta would be in second grade. Miss Sara Ann had transferred her to Carter Elementary and she was going to school now, until summer recess in a few weeks. After first asking me whether I would like an outing with Loretta, and getting me excited, Miss Sara Ann took me by the hand and asked Mama Linnet if she could take us out for a Saturday. I was bouncing up and down at the thought, begging. Mama Linnet took a pause before she answered, then said only yes, it would be all right.

Miss Savory said afterward to Miss Claire, "That Sara Ann Martin's up to something."

WHEN THE SATURDAY outing day came Loretta and I did well enough as companions. We had in common that neither of us had enough to do and so were attracted by anything pleasant that was new. She talked a lot more than I did, and our looks were different. She was plump and dainty, and I was a skinny tomboy. Mama Linnet had given me a dollar bill, more than enough for two little girls' expenses, pinned to my dress in a little cloth purse. There was no children's movie that day. Miss Sara Ann took us to the three other places our city had for kids: the child section of the library, the zoo—including a ride on the miniature train that meandered through it, and lastly the merry-go-round in the Park by the zoo. The Park, which was open only on weekends, had two other amusements that we begged to go on but she wouldn't let us: the spook house and the bumper cars. After we knew we had done all that would be allowed, I told an idea I had been holding back. "Let's go to the Rock Hut Cafe and I can show Loretta how to play the pinball machine!"

Miss Sara Ann would not do that. Loretta wanted to, and I kept on describing it and how much fun it was. But no. Miss Sara Ann wouldn't say why.

Loretta and I both started to cry. But Miss Sara Ann was after all a schoolteacher, and crying children did not faze her. We were tired by then, and Miss Sara Ann ended the trip by taking us back to Fourth and Victory.

Back at home we still had time left before Miss Sara Ann was to take Loretta home. "Don't you have some dolls somewhere, I remember?" Miss Sara Ann said to me.

"Upstairs under my bed," I said.

"Could I see them?" Loretta said, and we went up and I unlocked our apartment and tugged out from under my parents' bed the long heavy cardboard box where my dolls were, and took off the lid.

"So many!" Loretta squealed. But she had some manners. "May I pick them up?" I said yes. She was enthralled. "This is an Eskimo," she said, turning it front to back. "This is Little

Red Riding Hood . . . this is a Mammy doll . . . this is . . . what is this?"

"A Hopi Indian man. His wife is in there too," I said.

"Oh my goodness. I wish I had these. How do you play with them?"

"I don't play with them."

"You don't? What do you do?"

"Sometimes I take them all out and look at them."

"I bet you play with *her*," she said, reaching into the box and pulling out a blonde princess in a pink silk polka-dot dress and silver slippers.

"No."

Loretta turned and looked at me, and said, "Why don't you play with them?"

"How?"

"You know. Make up things. Stories that they do."

That had never occurred to me. "They are to have and look at," I explained, "And count."

"How many do you have?"

"The next time I get one it will be a hundred."

"Where do you get them?"

"People give them to me. My mother and my grand-mother, and my other grandmother, gave me most of them. And they tell their friends if they go somewhere to bring me a doll from there."

She turned back to the box and pulled out Pinocchio, two feet tall, and stood him up on his jointed wooden legs, and put up his arms, delighted, and I was surprised to see that she was not scared of him. I saw the movie before I got him, and I half-thought he could come alive.

"If I had these I would play with them all the time," she said. "Could I play with some of them now?"

I said yes, and then watched and listened as she picked up a small Swiss skier with tongue blade skis and a nurse, much larger, in her white uniform and cap, and made them have a conversation and decide to get married. Then they suddenly had an infant daughter, a baby doll who was five times bigger than either of them, whose name was Loretta. "Here, you can be Baby Loretta," she said. But I said I didn't want to, and she went on to be the baby too.

Later when Miss Sara Ann called us downstairs because it was time for her to take Loretta home, Loretta said to her, "Mother Dear, we need to come back tomorrow. Mary Mavis has ninety-nine dolls and she doesn't know how to play with them." Then she said in a loud whisper, "I don't think she knows how to play with other little girls, either."

I said, "I do too! I play with other little girls all the time." I was thinking of my imaginary school friends but somehow I knew better than to say that.

13

For some of us there was a lot of waiting in the mid-year of 1942.

I wanted school to start. That would be on Tuesday, September 1, 1942, and I had a calendar to show it, with my red crayon lines drawn around that day's square. The Lawyer Cato had suggested that—he gave me the calendar, it was put out by a bread company—and also he said I could every night at bedtime mark through that day with a green X and then count the squares that were left. I did this each night, as if I had won a game.

Afternoons, I sat on the hall bench near the door, ready to show the result to The Lawyer Cato when he came home. He was the only one still enthused about my calendar after several days. He always sounded excited and proud when he counted by the weeks and said in his voice that was like a rumbling wagon, "Lookah there, only seventy-two days to go!" and " . . . only sixty-five more!"

Also I wanted Mother to come back home. I did not

exactly miss her, she had been at Mimi's apart from me too long for that, but it was as if something vague was wrong and I wished she were back at Mimi's.

Miss Lucy waited for The Lawyer Cato to say more than Would You Like To Go To the Show?

Miss Savory said Miss Sara Ann was waiting for the right time to ask Mama Linnet if she could bring Loretta to live at Fourth and Victory.

Mama Linnet waited to hear from Granddaddy and from Daddy. If there was a letter from Granddaddy she stopped whatever she was doing and took it into her apartment to read, and wrote part or all of a letter back to him right then.

Mother did come home soon, on short notice, after being gone only about two weeks. Daddy called two nights before, and whatever he said to Mama Linnet worried her. Mama Linnet didn't want to take me to the train station to meet her, but it worked out she had to. Also we picked up Mimi to go with us.

When the train pulled in and stopped and steamed and the people got off, no Mother. Both my grandmothers had a feeling she was in there. Mama Linnet kept me by the hand while Mimi went on board and found her and led her off the train.

When I saw her I didn't know what to think. She had been always picky about her looks, but now her clothes were dirty and didn't match, and her hair hadn't been washed or combed in a long time. She wouldn't talk. I'm not sure she completely recognized us. She didn't hug me. Mimi collected the suitcase, and when we got to the car she said, "Linnet, don't you think it would be best if we went straight to my house?"

I didn't see Mother again for two weeks, and at first I thought she was better because Mimi had spiffed up her clothes and hair. But she acted about the same poor way.

IT WAS by now over a year since My Accident. My hair was grown back enough to be cut evenly, and you would never have known the difference unless you knew it was shorter. It was light brown. I was too young to tend it myself and never gave it a thought. But the help said about it, when it was their time to shampoo it or try to comb it, "It's so thick! It's so curly!"

Mama Linnet said to them, "Yes and you haven't seen anything yet. Just think when it gets longer. My girl will have long beautiful hair," she said.

She said over and over that I was pretty, and so I assumed I was, and had no thoughts about it. That's a good way to start out in life.

EARLY ONE MORNING in the heat of mid-July Mrs. Tabor's maid came running across the street and into the house calling, "Miz Lewis! Where's Miz Lewis? I think Miz Tabor's dead!"

"Oh God," The Lawyer Cato said. He was eating breakfast in the dining room, and he threw his napkin in his plate and stood up so fast his water and his chair turned over. His limping footsteps shook the floor as he ran outside. Mama Linnet and the maid were not far behind.

After a long time, Mama Linnet came walking back to us, not fast and not slow. The help and the customers both were gathered on the porch waiting, and Mama Linnet addressed us as the captain of a ship might do.

She said, "Eleanor has passed away. We've called the police. That's what you have to do first. I need to go back over there. Lucy, why don't you come and see if you can help Willard. He's taking it hard."

Although we had known without much noting it that The Lawyer Cato had visited Mrs. Tabor's home now and then, none of us realized that in the year since they met they had grown close, the missing mother and the missing son to each other. On the day she died, when the hearse had come and gone and he finally came back across the street hand-in-hand with Miss Lucy, he was crying and undone.

Miss Lucy took him upstairs to his room, the first time ever she had set foot in there, and guided him onto his bed. She fetched him iced tea and a sandwich, and sat with him, putting fresh washcloths over his eyes until after dark when the supper customers and the help had gone. He came downstairs then, and we family and boarders had what amounted to a wake in the kitchen. He held back his tears through most of that, but when they did come he didn't even notice.

———

MRS. TABOR HAD WILLED her house and five thousand dollars to The Lawyer Cato. The police told him about it two days after she died. He didn't believe it at first. He had helped her re-do her will not six months before, and the last he knew, almost everything she had was to go to the First Baptist Church. But what he had done, unknowing, was to simplify her affairs so much it was easy for her to make another change. She just got another lawyer to substitute Willard Lawrence Cato for First Baptist Church, and also named him executor, and that was the will they found in her lock box.

So there he was. A young attorney with a paid-for house, a fortune of money in the bank, a steady income. And a girl-friend holding her breath.

ABOUT THE SAME time Eleanor Tabor died, Lucy Davis got a divorce from her vegetable husband. She didn't tell The Lawyer Cato, and she said to Mama Linnet that she didn't want him to know unless he committed himself to her. He was giving her no clue whether he wanted their romance to lead to anything further. He had not offered to help her get a divorce. He had not even told her for sure whether she had grounds for it, and that part worried her the most: that he certainly would have known, but would not tell her. She had gone over in her mind everything he'd done, everything he'd said, but she was still mystified as to what he was thinking or feeling. She said she wanted the divorce in case her existing marriage was a stumbling block for him, yes, but however it turned out with him—and her voice choked for just the one word "him"—she wanted to be free to have a life.

ONE SATURDAY about a month after Mrs. Tabor died, Mama
Linnet and I were on the way out the door to the farmer's
market when The Lawyer Cato caught us and asked Mama
Linnet to "discuss a little matter" with him in the empty
dining room. She asked if it could wait, and he said in a flus-
tered way that it wouldn't take long. So they sat down
together while I ambled around the room running my
fingers along the hanging edges of the tablecloths.

"Ah need to give you notice Ah'm going to move, Miz
Lewis," he said.

"You're going to live in your house, I expect."

"Yes'm. I'm giving you a month's notice past this month.
Here's the amount for that." He wrangled his billfold out of
his back pocket. He had already written a check, and found
it and put it on the table. He said, "But I won't actually be
here, starting tomorrow night." He added, "Not much to
move, I've discovered."

"Six weeks is generous notice. Our agreement only calls
for a month."

"It's non-negotiable. I want you to have plenty of elbowroom for picking my replacement. Get a better one," he said.

"That's not possible," she said in such a way that I knew
for the first time she was fond of him. I wondered if he knew.

"I have a favor to ask," he said. "Could I arrange with you
to get take-out meals? Three times a day. Mondays through
Fridays. Whatever you're serving. I would make it worth
your while. And if somebody could bring them to me across
the street I'd pay a delivery fee."

He suggested an amount for the whole thing, and Mama
Linnet said that would be fine. He said, "How about I pay
ahead a month at a time? Would that work?" She said yes,
and he wrote another check.

THE NEXT DAY while I was in church The Lawyer Cato moved the last of his belongings and his green racing car across the street. Because he was so nearby, I didn't realize he was gone from me. But no more greetings at the door, no more calendar countdowns. Two or three evenings later I asked Mama Linnet for permission to cross the street so I could visit with him. She told me I must wait to be invited.

NOR DID Willard Cato invite Miss Lucy to his house, or anywhere else. A week went by and he had not so much as come over to speak to her.

Two weeks.

We never saw her cry, her face was like a mask and so was her voice. Even I knew to be careful what I said to her. Of course we did our best not to mention him.

And during this time when we thought at any minute she might break, she kept on like a trooper. Never missed her work at the Tea Room, continued her daily visits to her help-less now-ex-husband, and at Fourth and Victory she filled in as needed in the evening work. She even managed to do a bit of good boarder's part in the small-talk visiting on the porch or in the sitting room. I think that was the hardest thing for her.

IT WAS Loretta who let the cat out of the bag.

Miss Sara Ann had brought her to play with me. Play

with my dolls, really, and I didn't want her to. The two of them had found me in the kitchen, sitting at the worktable, early in the afternoon. I had been talking with Miss Savory and Mama Linnet.

I said to Loretta, when she asked, "No. My dolls are tired. They want to stay asleep." That was a big stretch of the truth and it surprised me when I said it. To me dolls neither slept nor woke and had no desires. But Loretta and Miss Sara Ann thought I meant it. They tried to get around my stubbornness, but I won that one.

Miss Sara Ann said, "Then y'all can play paper dolls. Here's some brand-new ones." She took the skinny book of them out of the teacher's tote bag she carried, and gave them to Loretta, and left.

Loretta climbed up on a stool beside me.

So I sat sulking while she pushed and twisted two paper dolls free from their perforated prison in the book. A man and a woman. And guess what their names were.

"Hello, Mr. Cato," said the woman doll, bobbing up and down.

"Hello, Miz Martin," said the man doll, bobbing. "You can call me Will."

"Well, you can call me Sara Ann," said the woman doll.

"Lo-ord, Lord, *Lord!*" said Miss Savory.

Before she went home that night Miss Savory said to Mama Linnet, "I had it wrong! I had it wrong! I knew it was *some*body she was seeing, and I coulda swore it was Hampton Lewis. I all but told you that, but Thank-You-Jesus I didn't, because I was way off track. That'll teach me."

Mama Linnet didn't answer.

JANNA MCNEE TOLD Miss Lucy that The Lawyer Cato was dating Miss Sara Ann. Tom McNee had heard it from the men customers gossiping at the Rock Hut about Miss Sara Ann. He sat on the news for a while, but then Janna got it out of him. She had never liked Miss Sara Ann because of her being flirty with Tom.

Janna collared Miss Lucy in the downstairs hall and told her, "I just can't stand for you not to know: That Sara Ann Martin has her hooks in Willard Cato, and has had for a long time. They were seeing each other all along while he was dating you."

Later Janna said to Tom about Miss Lucy, "She was really good at playing like she didn't care what Willard Cato had done or might do forevermore. But I could tell: it broke her heart."

"*You* broke her heart," Tom said, and she didn't answer.

Everybody who lived or worked at Fourth and Victory started giving Miss Sara Ann the cold shoulder—except for Mama Linnet and maybe Miss Claire.

Soon even Miss Abien got bent out of shape about it. One morning she had The Lawyer Cato's breakfast sacks in hand and she waylaid Mama Linnet and slammed the sacks down on a table and said, "I ain't taking *him* no more food. You can just fire me."

Like lightning Miss Savory came out of nowhere and said to Miss Abien, "Shut your mouth."

To Mama Linnet Savory said, "Miz Lewis, she don't know what she's sayin' ner who she's saying' it to. There ain't gonna be no vexation, I'll run his meals over there."

"That will be fine, work it out however's best," Mama Linnet said.

Back to Abien Miss Savory said, "I'll be more than glad to have that whole dime tip three times a day that *somebody* is too uppity to take, after somebody *else* gave 'em the chance. It ain't just ever'place where the help gets to keep the tips."

Mama Linnet had picked up the sacks of food for The Lawyer Cato and was hefting them in her hands and looking at them as if she could see through the paper. She said, "It would behoove us to remember. Mr. Cato is paying top dollar for these meals. We can certainly use that money. They should be *good* meals and *plenty in there.* " She handed the sacks to Miss Savory.

"Yes'm," Miss Savory said.

———————

HERE ARE three letters from about that time.

They are from my family's keepsakes I gathered together after I was grown. They were in Mama Linnet's cedar chest.

The first, I found in a large hatbox together with items that had belonged to Granddaddy and generally pertained to his military service in both world wars: yellowed photos of him and his shipmates and later his work crew mates, and his service medals, and such. In that box was only this one letter. Other letters to him were in a different box.

The one from the hatbox is dated August 5, 1942, and it is from Miss Sara Ann. From its content, there likely were others she wrote before it. But only the one survived.

The most of what she said to Grandaddy was,

"*...and I know you will understand, because I know the truth is your heart belongs to someone else too. You never said it, but there is so much you never said. Thank you for being who you are* *and for helping me and Loretta when I needed it so badly. You are the kindest of men. And the most dashing. And the most fun. Thank you for those great times we had. But I know I could never hold you if She beckoned you. I do not want you to find out from someone else who I am seeing now. It is Willard Cato. As you know, he is a good man too. Not that he is like you in any other way. But I have to grow up sometime, don't I? You don't have to write me back, I almost hope you don't, but please do let me know this letter reached you. ...*"

The second, from another box, is a letter from Granddaddy to Mama Linnet, written from Guadalcanal.

23 August 1942

Dear Beautiful Wife,

Your last letter is in my pocket and the others put away. Please keep writing. They are the life of my heart. I am not drinking. There is not a lot to drink here ha ha. This is Sunday and we have a little time off. I went to church service. The chaplain is a Lutheran but he did OK. We are about two thirds done with our first objective which is the ▮▮▮▮▮▮ unless something else happens. We came in right behind the Marines and took it over from the Japs that were building it. Now they ▮▮▮▮▮▮ at night and it is two steps forward and one back but we are gaining. I will be glad when the real equipment gets here. The biggest thing they can give me to drive is a tractor.

Don't let the news make you worry. Seabees are not combat men. I am in more danger from the jungle rot ha ha. I got a letter from our son with most of it marked out and you probably know more than I do but I can not find out or figure out where his outfit might be sent except since he is Army it will be one fourth of the world away from me. And you and our girl are one half way. Sometimes I am thunder struck our life could get like this.

Anyway I am proud our son made Lt. Keep telling me what our girl is doing growing up so fast. She is a dandy. Give her a kiss from me every night. But keep the big girl kisses for yourself. I wish I could deliver them in person.

Your loving husband,

Hampton

Another is from Daddy, written by chance the same day. I know now that at that time Daddy was on a troop ship in the Atlantic, headed for England. He was in the Seventh Infantry Regiment of the Third Infantry Division. His regiment would stay on hold in England a while, then make a landing on November 8, 1942 on the northwest coast of Africa. He was unharmed in that battle. These troops later went on to take part in the invasion of Sicily, and then Palermo, and beyond.

23 August 1942

Dear Mother,

We are in the middle of ▆▆▆▆▆▆▆▆ *meaning a few more days to* ▆▆▆▆▆▆▆. *Probably the censors won't let any of that get through to you but you will know I tried. I will be glad when we get there because there is not much to do except think about whether the krauts might send us a* ▆▆▆▆▆▆▆. *There are some good fellow officers* ▆▆▆▆▆▆▆▆. *Some are West Point men. I wish there were some books or study materials about military tactics so I could continue to improve myself but no.*

How are you doing and Mary Mavis? Cesarine doesn't say much about her so it is up to you to keep telling me everything. Mimi writes once a month about Cesarine and I think she writes for Cesarine and it sounds like status quo. If ever it is not let me know. Also anything you hear from Dad let me know just in case. From the news I would guess the Seabees will be mostly in the South Pacific but who knows.

Tell everyone at 4th & Victory hello. Tell Willard I said he is one lucky man getting that house and money.

Your loving son, Pat

I<small>T WAS</small> the day school started! I was at last getting to go. That morning I couldn't get my clothes on fast enough, and forgot my shoes and socks until Savory noticed, and ate only snatches of my breakfast. I tagged around at Mama Linnet's skirttails each task she went to, saying, "Is it time yet? Is it time yet?"

Finally it was, and she took me by the shoulder, probably to hold me on the earth, and we started out walking the nine blocks to Carter Elementary.

I carried my new shiny metal Roy Rogers red lunch box she had let me choose. It was expensive. It had a half-size silver thermos inside.

"Pay attention," she said, "because after today you'll be coming by yourself. And going home by yourself. You don't want to get lost. You have to remember where the turns are."

"I know where it is," I said as if she were not quite bright.

"All right then, you lead me," she said.

And I did. I don't know how. I guess it was the pull of sheer desire.

Carter was the oldest elementary school in the city. It had been built to last, of thick white granite outside and thick dark wood inside. It sat on raised grounds a city block square, and all the way around was a white granite wall taller than I was. To get in from the sidewalk you went either to the front or the back, where the wall was cut and there were steps, and then along a concrete walkway to the front door. There was not as much room inside as you might have thought if you were going in there for the first time, and everything in it was plain and simple. But to me on that morning it was the place of dreams. (School was also Japanese-free, in my mind. Without thinking specifically about it, in my dreams I had made it a haven from my fears.)

Mama Linnet had to check me in and sign something before she could leave, and I could hardly wait for her to be gone so that it could all get started, whatever it was. And I was not disappointed.

Nor was the first grade teacher disappointed in me. Her name was Mrs. White.

I already knew how to mind, and sit still. I was clean. I was not shy, and would speak when spoken to. I was used to taking instruction on trust that it would end up making sense. I knew my numbers, my alphabet. I could read and to some extent write. I could draw a house, a man, a woman, a dog, a flower, and a sun. What Mrs. White had on her hands was a ready-made success looking up at her like a hungry sponge.

At recess bell all six rooms of grades of us poured through the doors and merged into one stream that parted outside into two streams, with the girls going to the east to their playground and the boys going west to theirs.

I said to the closest little girl, "Let's swing!" and started for it.

Those swings were hung on steel chains with long links going up fifteen feet to the welded steel-bar scaffold. A child who could get a swing and put energy into pumping could arc high enough to clear the ground by twelve feet or so. You had to be careful if you went that high because at the beginning of each downswing you were hair-raisingly weightless, and so were the seat and the chains. It was all too easy to get separated from the seat and find yourself hanging by your fingers as gravity pulled you down and made you too heavy, and/or to have a finger mashed or worse by the chain links clanking back together. And this did happen. But who cared. Not the kids, certainly, and not the adults, obviously.

But for a long time I still could not run fast enough to get a swing. There were only six on the girls' side.

This day I settled for the monkey bars. I climbed up although it was hard for me, and eventually hung upside-down by the backs of my knees, with my dress skirt falling down over my head. I was just realizing my legs were not strong enough for it, and wondering how I was going to get down, and then panicking, when I heard Loretta's voice close to my ear, saying, "That's not nice. Girls are not allowed to do that." A couple of seconds later I heard her farther away, screaming above the screech of the playground. "Look at Mary Mavis showing her underwear! Look."

I started yelling Help. I was lucky because the teacher on monitor duty happened to be near enough to notice I was doing something wrong. She helped me down and said, "Don't do that. It's not nice."

I stood unbalanced in mind and body while Loretta kept yelling about me to her pack of second-graders and the world. Part of what she said was that I didn't even know how to play with dolls, and another part was, "Her mother is crazy."

The bell rang and all the girls surged together funneling through the back door. I went the other way, heading down the nearby steps to the street. I had the single-minded urge to go home. It didn't occur to me I was leaving through the exit opposite from the way I came in. Also I was crying and could only half see, and for sure I wasn't thinking. I was probably several blocks out of sight of the school before I realized the surroundings were strange, and then knew I was lost.

14

I HAD NEVER BEEN LOST BEFORE. THE FIRE OF THE humiliations on the playground and now the fear of not knowing where home was were suffocating. And then the spooky dread of the Japanese whispered in my mind again. My knees shook and I collapsed on the curb, sobbing.

A black car crept slowly by, big and close. I closed my eyes. I could feel its heat on my legs and face. Then it stopped and the engine went silent except for a couple of clicks. Its door opened. Somebody came to me.

"Honey? What's the matter, darlin'?" a woman said.

She was not a Japanese. I didn't know her but she belonged. I said, through my gasps and hiccoughs, that I was lost and wanted to go home.

"Do you know where you live?"

"Fourth and Victory."

"I'll take you home, honey, it's not far, it's all right, don't cry. Here, get in the car."

"I can't! I'm not supposed to get in a car with strangers."

"It would be okay this one time," she said, and she tried to take my hand.

"No!" I screamed, and kept on screaming. I fell flat on my back on the strip of grass between the street and the sidewalk, screeching.

Another car pulled up and stopped. This time a man got out and came over. He said, "Who hit her? Was it you? How bad is she hurt?"

She eventually got him to understand and believe what the situation really was. Then he tried getting me in his car by giving me a direct order, and next he intended to pick me up and put me in there, but the lady stopped him. Between them they decided she should stay with me while he drove to my address and got someone I knew.

It was Miss Savory. When they came back she jumped out of his car while it was still rolling, and dropped on her knees beside me and began gathering my limp body until she had me all, saying, "My baby," over and over.

The man said, "She's not hurt. I told you."

She didn't answer him but she knew I was hurt in my heart.

WHEN WE GOT HOME Mama Linnet was already there. Every day she made rounds in the Buick, going from Fourth and Victory to the Women's City Club, to the Rock Hut, and to the bank or to buy necessary things. Miss Savory had telephoned and found her when the man came and said I was screaming on the street and refused to be helped.

After Miss Savory handed me over to Mama Linnet inside the house, Mama Linnet thanked the man and asked his name. He took out a white card from a brown case in his suit jacket. She smiled at him, and I knew from the change in the tone of his voice he would try to hang around. But she thanked him again and Miss Savory opened the door for him, and he left awkwardly.

Mama Linnet put me down to stand on my own, but I was wobbly. She took one of my hands, and Abien—who had come into the hall to watch like a half-tame cat—of her own free will took the other hand, and I made it into Mama Linnet's apartment. Miss Claire was also standing by to be sure I was all right.

By then the first of the noon meal customers were coming in. Mama Linnet released everybody to their work, except she asked Miss Savory to bring me some soup and a glass of milk. As I ate, slowly, Mama Linnet steadied my hand, and let me finish only half the bowl, and got me to tell her what happened.

Near the end, I started crying again and said, "I don't want to go to school anymore."

She said—and her words were like a salve to me—"You don't have to."

Miss Savory came in then to retrieve my lunch dishes. I was saying to Mama Linnet, "Is Mother crazy?"

"She Definitely Is Not Crazy. Loretta doesn't know anything about your mother. She's never even seen her. That is something somebody would say just to be mean. Your mother had scarlet fever when she was a child, and it went into rheumatic fever, and left her with a weak heart and a nervous condition. She takes things harder than most people do. And when things happen that aren't good, it takes her longer to get over them. That's all."

I took that in. Then I said, "Do I take after my mother?"

After a long pause she said, "In some ways you do, in some you don't. Same as everybody with their parents. For instance, your hair is curly and hers is straight, and your eyes are green and hers are . . . I don't remember what color they are, but they're not green."

"Do I take after her nervous condition?"

She paused again, then said, "No."

She went on to say, "Loretta made a very bad mistake to say what she did, and to do it in such a hateful way. She may not have realized how much it would hurt you, I don't know, she's only still a child. But my darling girl your nerves are just fine, and your feelings will mend. At least they will a lot. You're going to feel better. I promise."

Miss Savory had stopped frozen. When she didn't move to get the dishes, just stood there for a long time, Mama Linnet said, "Savory?" and broke the spell. Miss Savory placed my dishes on the tray and took it out.

MAMA LINNET HAD BEEN calm through all this disturbance. Even I could never have guessed at first that she was furious. She said later it was all she could do to keep from going right then to Miss Sara Ann's school and snatching her out of her classroom. But she waited until Miss Sara Ann got home to tell her what happened and give her in writing a month's notice to move.

Miss Sara Ann said, "Miz Lewis, *please.* I'll see Loretta never says anything like that again. She's just a child. I can't imagine how she even thought that up. *Please* don't throw me out."

"She's bound to have heard it from you. That's why I'm

giving you notice. I'll not have someone living under my roof telling mean lies about my family. It's not just what your *child* did, it's what *you* did."

"But I *didn't!*" Miss Sara Ann said. "Cesarine is my closest friend. Or at least she was, before she got sick and had to leave . . . She has been nothing but sweet to me from the day I came here. I know she's not crazy and I would never say that about her. Please believe me."

Then she added, "Miz Lewis, can you not give me the benefit of the doubt?"

Something about that slipped through Mama Linnet's anger and gave her pause. She said, "I'm going to study and pray on this. I'll give you my answer in a day or two."

———

THE NEXT AFTERNOON Miss Sara Ann asked to speak to Mama Linnet and said, "I need to tell you something. I can only hope you'll believe me, and you won't like it. I talked to Loretta about how bad she had been, and asked her how she got the idea that Cesarine was crazy. She said she heard Savory say it."

———

THAT NIGHT after the work was done and they were alone, Mama Linnet asked Miss Savory if she was the one who said it.

Miss Savory said, "I did say it. Am I fired?"

Mama Linnet said, "As of this minute. I'll get you your wages."

THE NEXT DAY Mama Linnet was doing Miss Savory's work. And Miss Abien's. If Savory was fired, Abien was not about to be there.

Miss Claire tried to go to bat for Miss Savory, telling Mama Linnet how it happened, that Savory was just letting off steam in confidence to Claire. It was a while back, after Cesarine had treated Savory in a high-handed way. And neither Savory nor Claire had known Loretta was anywhere near, to hear.

"Thank you for telling me—finally." Mama Linnet said.

"Mrs. Lewis, you already know a lot of things we hear in this house are best forgotten. Frankly, I never gave it a thought—although you might not like hearing that either. The point is, Savory would lay down her life for you or Mary Mavis. Surely you know she would never intentionally hurt you."

Mama Linnet said, "I know. But she did hurt us. Through sheer uncalled-for big mouth carelessness. I've had my fill of it."

BUT WHEN MAMA LINNET fired Miss Savory she hadn't taken into account my grief at losing her.

It was the last straw for me. I lay around or sat around and cried for two days and nights. I wouldn't eat, and barely drank. She kept an electric fan blowing gently on me because I was continually hot and flushed. She gave me Sister Parker's medicine, increasing up to the maximum dose. Then she reduced it because it was only making me stupid and maybe sick. I retched and choked every now and then, though practically nothing was in my stomach. I wouldn't talk, except to say, "I want Savory."

MAMA LINNET WAS AGAIN SCARED for me. First thing Monday morning she called in Dr. Haynes Senior.

He came as soon as he could, which was at noon. He warmed his stethoscope in his hand and gave me a brief check-over, and tried to get me to talk. Then he and Mama Linnet had a long private talk in the dining room while he ate lunch.

Whatever he said, she chose to take it as an order.

As soon as he left, she got her purse and keys. On the way out she told Miss Claire, "I have no option but to find Savory and try and get her back."

She returned at dusk, hot and frustrated. She had eventually found Miss Savory's house, she was pretty sure, but it looked empty. Asking the neighbors had been useless and exasperating. But she was careful to show she was not defeated. She said, "We'll get your Savory back, Lord willing. I'll go again tomorrow."

But she couldn't find Miss Savory, who, with Antoine and Abien, were just gone, that was it.

I GRADUALLY, as they say, adjusted. Over the next month or so I once again made progress bit by bit, gaining toward but not yet reaching the normal stamina of a six-and-a-half year old. Mama Linnet went to see Mrs. White at Carter, and was pleased to hear what she already knew: I would still be ahead of most of the children in my First Grade, even if I had to stay out a few weeks longer.

But in October I returned to school on time. For the next month, even though Mama Linnet was hard pressed for time because she was short of help, she drove me to Carter every morning and was there waiting for me afternoons. She had prepared me with rote things to say if Loretta acted up again, but Loretta didn't. I was allowed to go outside with the other kids, but I was forbidden for a month to run, climb, jump rope, or play anything more strenuous than Ring Around the Rosie or Farmer in the Dell.

Loretta, for the first several days, said nothing to me—or about me, that I know of. Then she tried to get me to talk to her, as if nothing had happened. But Mama Linnet had prepared me for that too, and I turned my back and walked away without saying anything. Then occasionally I saw her whispering to her friends, and I knew it was about me because they looked in my direction.

Mama Linnet told me that someday I would need to forgive Loretta but it needn't be right now. If I would just not do or say anything mean to her, that would be a good Christian for the time being.

She had called off Miss Sara Ann's eviction as soon as the actual guilty party was known, but there was stiffness between them.

THE RESIDENCY of the house was now down to Miss Claire and Roger/Tian, Miss Sara Ann, Miss Lucy, Janna and Tom and their little Tonna, and Mama Linnet and me. No bachelors, and Mama Linnet was not in a hurry to rent those rooms until she could hire more help of the dependable kind.

She had been intending to hire more help anyway, and now that the absence of Savory and Abien seemed permanent, help was a must. It would take two people to replace Savory alone. In looking at prospects for full-time employees, Mama Linnet passed over the three part-time women who already came on laundry days. She said they knew where Savory was but pretended they didn't, and because they were lying, every time she talked to one of them it was like swallowing a bone. She kept them on, though, and acted the same toward them in their pay and food privileges and her politeness.

To get job applicants all you had to do was put up a Help Wanted sign. She already had a sign, three-foot square, up in the attic, and Tom hung it below the establishment sign out front. Miss Claire and Miss Lucy were glad to see it go up because they had once again pitched in and joined Mama Linnet in working themselves half to death. Three days later Mama Linnet had taken her pick of about fifteen women. And she had splurged, or so we thought. She hired not two, not three, but four. We had, now, three new smart, strong, eager-to-please women in the Fourth and Victory staff, plus another one to help Miss Lucy at the Tea Room.

I have the letters Mama Linnet wrote to Daddy, outlining all these and future happenings in a plain way, not as gossip. I think she wrote so much not only to carefully tell him what happened with me, but also to help him feel he was still a part of us all.

Miss Sara Ann kept to herself. If it were true that she had been on the verge of asking Mama Linnet to bring Loretta to live with her, she said nothing about that now. She was present in the house in the evenings, more than ever. However, she stayed in her room. If she and The Lawyer Cato were dating, it couldn't have been often.

Around Halloween it leaked out from the Rock Hut customers that Miss Sara Ann and The Lawyer Cato were no longer seeing each other.

Janna, who had never picked up any tact in her sixteen-and-a-half years of life, now made double-sure Miss Sara Ann knew better than to even say hello or please pass the salt to Tom.

And then Miss Lucy confided in Mama Linnet that The Lawyer Cato was trying to start up again with her. She said, "Why couldn't he have just gone on his way and left me alone? I had gotten back to myself and straightened up. Now here I am again wondering night and day what to do."

15

IT WAS MORE THAN A YEAR SINCE MR. TONY'S MURDER. THAT topic didn't come up much any more at Fourth and Victory, except occasionally someone would say how much better it would feel to know the murderer was caught and not running around loose. My heart always clenched at that, and my lips too, and I guessed it was the same with Roger/Tian. But we two did not speak to each other anymore of the killer Japanese, or of anything else if Roger/Tian could help it. There was no little-boyness left in him now. And I somehow knew he thought my frail health was his fault for scaring me about the Japanese. He avoided me, and I gave up trying to get him to be friends again.

Roger/Tian was fourteen then, in the tenth grade. That was the first year in high school in our system. He was doing well there, for a half-Chinese person in a hidebound society.

He had already taken his hardest knocks in junior high —nobody called him "That big little half-Jap boy" any more, at least they did know now he was Chinese—and he went on into high school among classmates who were his friends, or, at worst, who were used to him. He was always big for his age, and now he was maturing early and looked sixteen. More handsome every day, and with an open personality. His athletic powers didn't hurt, either. He was already a starter in football, and there still to come were basketball and track. Our town had only one high school, so there was enough money for extramural teams in three sports. Boys' sports, that is. For girls, track only.

Baseball for our city was left to Dr. Haynes' Blues team. He was still Roger/Tian's mentor in all things including sports, and the team trained, in one way or another, year around. Also Roger/Tian still did odd jobs for him two days a week after school. He gave his earnings to his mother, but she returned about a third of it as an allowance. So he usually had money in his pocket, which will tell itself no matter who you are or how quiet about it.

As to Roger/Tian's father, no word had come from him in months. And no money.

I heard Janna say to Tom, "Oh Tom! There ain't no Mister Lee! Do I have to draw you a pitcher?"

He smiled and said, "You don't know. There was wunst, for sure."

THE CHIEF of Police came to Fourth and Victory to talk to Mama Linnet. He had phoned first, and it startled her, and she offered to go to the Station, but he said no, he'd come to her.

He could have sent one of his men. But six months before, when he was still fairly new to his job and the city, he had seen her writeup and picture in the paper, and had heard the rumors about her maybe turning down Dr. Haynes Senior. His name was Donavan Symmonds and he was married, but had been half-mindedly half-waiting for an excuse to meet Linnet Lewis. He came alone.

They were about of an age, and he was a large, good-looking man with a deep voice. He wore his uniform. She had put on a dressy dress, and she showed him to the sitting room and then left and came back with a cloth-covered tray holding a little pewter pot of precious coffee, a cup and saucer and spoon, two precious lumps of sugar, a little pitcher of thick cream, a little slice of pound cake, and a white cloth napkin. He made himself at home with all this.

Then he put down the napkin and asked her what she knew about Omar Phelps. He said, "I understand he lived here for a while last year."

She told him Mr. Phelps hadn't lived there, only slept two nights a week on the screened-in porch and kept his trucks in the garage. She said he'd paid on time in cash, left without notice but not owing anything, and that that was all she knew. She asked why.

"We're looking for him. Turns out he's a black-market dealer, Mrs. Lewis. Cigarettes, whiskey, diesel fuel, and beef, mostly. The federal government is after him, and they've asked us in on it. Also we found out that he's a pervert."

"What does that mean, please?" She said.

"He's been arrested for . . . liking children more than any man should. When was the last time you saw him?" he said.

"Give me a minute, please. I need to get all this together in my head."

"I'm sure it's a surprise, knowing you were giving shelter to a criminal," he said.

"I don't think you need to put it that way, Chief

Symmonds. I was not giving shelter to him any more than to anybody else who rents here. Less, in fact. And yes, I am surprised."

He said, "I wasn't meaning to hint anything about you yourself, I was just making a friendly comment. Call me Donavan and I'll call you Linnet. We know you've never had anything to do with anything illegal. We've known that since Tony Bishop was murdered. We were obliged to find out."

"Chief Symmonds, what went through my mind first is the shock of knowing I let somebody like him come near my little granddaughter, and second that I rented my garage to somebody who might have kept truckloads of diesel fuel or alcohol closed up in there and blown us all to kingdom come."

"Yes. Now . . . " he said.

"And third, here I am finding out I've been investigated by the police. There was no need to go snooping around, talking about me with other people. I'm very disappointed about that. You could have simply come here and asked me anything you want to know." Her voice was getting louder.

"Here I am, doing exactly that. Mrs. Lewis you know we have to do our duty." He caught himself before he said more. It was probably the first and only time he'd come close to apologizing for investigating somebody.

She said, "And the next thing I thought of is, if Omar Phelps is such a criminal did he have anything to do with Tony Bishop's murder?"

"We're trying to answer that same question," he said. "Did the two of them associate with each other, to your knowledge?"

"I never saw them even talk to each other. The only time they would have been in the same room, that I know of, is maybe sometimes at meals here. No wait . . . one time some-body had a going-away party here for Tony Bishop, and Omar Phelps came to that. But he happened to be in town that night and it would have been natural for anybody here to drop in on the party."

"A going-away party. So did Tony Bishop go away and then come back, or what? Because we know he was still living here when he was murdered," he said.

"He never left. He thought he was drafted and then found out they made a mistake."

"That's peculiar, I'll check it out," he said, and jabbed a note into a little booklet. "Well. Going all the way back, which one of them came here first?" he said.

"Tony Bishop. I had a room-for-rent sign out front, and he knocked on the door. He was clean and spoke well, and had cash in advance, so I leased a month of room and board to him, and after that he stayed on. That was in late summer, year before last. It was hot, and I had to buy another electric fan so there would be one in that room."

"And after that, when was it Omar Phelps came here, and how did that come about?"

"Omar Phelps just showed up one day, about three months after Tony Bishop came. It was not quite winter. He asked about the garages. I don't know how he knew about them. I hadn't thought of renting them before, and I liked the idea of that money. He didn't have a place to stay, and he asked might he sleep in the garage. He only needed some-place to sleep and eat twice a week, and then be on the road in one or the other of his trucks. So since the weather was about to get cold I made him a price for sleeping on my screened-in porch and eating when he was here, and let him use the public bathroom in the hall."

He said, "Let me ask you one more thing. Is there anybody who was here when Phelps and Bishop were here, who's not here now?"

"I'm thinking. Oh. Only Savory, and Abien. Savory was my main cook and my mainstay help. And Abien was I think her sister or cousin, and she was part of the help too. In her own way. They didn't live here but they were here all day every weekday. I fired Savory a couple of months ago. I wish I hadn't. And Abien went when Savory did."

"How did that come about, that you fired . . . Savory, is that the name?" he said.

She leaned forward, and said, "How strange this is. I thought about asking the police to help me with it, but I decided it wouldn't do any good. And now here you are, the Chief of Police himself, *asking* about it. The Lord works in mysterious ways."

And she told him, "I fired Savory for having a big mouth, and I want her back. We love her. I shouldn't have treated her that way. You don't fire friends. But I was mad, and I let that take over instead of taking it to the Lord. And she is a very proud person. And now we're all paying for what I did. My little granddaughter is very attached to her." She produced a Kleenex and blotted her eyes and nose.

"What is it the police could do to help you?" he said.

"Find her! I can't find her. If I could talk to her, I think we could get back together."

"I can have somebody look into it. He took up his booklet again. Okay, her first name is Savory, what's her last name?"

"Chardin. That's C-h-a-r-d-i-n. And the other one's name is, first name A-b-i-e-n and last name A-s-t-i-e-r."

"What race are they?" he said.

"I think they might be from some race I don't know of.

Savory's address was in the Negro part of town, but they don't look Negro. They both had a kind of accent to certain things they said. Not everything. It's hard to describe. Their skin could be any race, and so could their hair. Savory has green eyes. A lot of times she acts like she was born the Queen of Sheba. Whatever is their race, it showed up in Savory's cooking. Everybody loved it."

"Were they from New Orleans?" he said.

"I don't know. Why?" she said.

He told her there were important things he still wanted to say: "We're pretty sure Phelps and Bishop were partners. Bishop was the front man, the salesman. He scouted out businesses that would be likely prospects to buy and sell their particular goods on the sly, and he made the deals, we think. Phelps got the commodities and trucked them in. We do know that for sure. May be still trucking them in, we're watching to see. And maybe the two of them got at odds somehow. Maybe each one wanted to be top dog. Mrs. Lewis, I need to know about it in case Phelps shows up here again or you see him somewhere."

She said, "So yes, this is not a dream. Here I am after trying to do right by everybody, finding out I might be thought of all over town and throughout the federal government as giving shelter to not just one but *two* crooks. And to boot, one of them may be a murderer, and that other thing you said."

He went on, "Let me repeat that we have confidence in you, and plenty of reasons to back that up, and we will be sharing that with the federal investigators, so I think you can put your mind at rest as to how they will regard you. But the last thing I wanted to say, Mrs. Lewis, is that while these feds are in town you should be very—*very*—careful not to buy anything you shouldn't. And the same goes for everybody who lives here."

FEDERAL INVESTIGATION OR NOT, Mama Linnet decided she should begin doing business as a corporation. She had heard vaguely of advantages, and she consulted The Lawyer Cato. He advised her and did the legal work, and she hired a book-keeper he recommended, a moonlighter acquaintance from his job at the State Capitol, who set up her books and kept them for a small fee, which took a load off her and Miss Lucy too. She was now Lewis Enterprises.

In November she made a down payment on a big house, a distress sale, which was located one block down and around the corner from Fourth and Victory. With Tom as the carpenter and someone he knew as the plumber, she turned it into four small makeshift apartments. She made the rent reasonable, and by word-of-mouth the place filled up right away with decent people. It was her first business gamble that had nothing to do with meals. After the initial money outlay, she was set to make three times as much as the house payment each month, with little effort on her part. She said to God, "Dear Lord, I know it couldn't really be this easy to make money but thank you even if it turns out it's not."

She kept her operations as close to home as she could, mostly because of gasoline rationing. She walked wherever she had to go, in all kinds of weather. If there were items to carry, she pushed them in a baby buggy. The Tea Room was her farthest business, three-quarters of a mile. And because Miss Lucy managed it so well it was the one she had to visit least, usually only two or three times a week.

Busy as she was, she sat back once in a while to take a look at her businesses with an eye toward improvements. Usually that meant a decision about spending money: hiring someone or buying something. And then next she would study and pray on whatever it was. She decided yes on two secondhand refrigerators, one for Fourth and Victory and one for the Rock Hut. But after pestering the Rationing Board she could only get one. She chose Fourth and Victory as its home. Then she persuaded the Women's City Club executive board to buy a refrigerator for the Tea Room. They gave her the old one, for the cost of hauling it off, and she had Tom haul it in her truck to the Rock Hut.

The refrigerators relieved her and her employees from depending on iceboxes to keep the foodstuffs cold. She kept the iceboxes, though, and kept them operative, not only for the ice but in case a refrigerator went on the blink. And she tried her best—but failed—to get a modern automatic washing machine for the screened-in porch at Fourth and Victory.

THE LAWYER CATO continued to ask Miss Lucy on dates, unsuccessfully. But that didn't faze him. He regularly called for her on the house phone, mailed notes to her, sent her flowers. A few times he crossed the street trying but failing to talk with her face to face. We noticed he never came in person when Miss Sara Ann was at home. Miss Lucy was polite in turning him down, and each time he acted as if it were the first time, and took it graciously. And he gave her to know that he would keep on asking until she accepted or said stop.

Miss Lucy said to Mama Linnet, "He doesn't talk like himself. He's smooth as silk. What do you make of that?"

"Maybe he's been practicing. He's working hard at this. I'd say he'd be due some credit for that. It's a compliment to you." Mama Linnet said.

"Has he talked to you about this?" Miss Lucy said.

"I think Willard would do almost anything to correct his course with you. It takes more character to admit a mistake and correct it than if there had never been a mistake. Besides which, you now know for a fact that with open eyes he chooses you over . . . anyone else."

"Linnet, has *she* ever talked to you about it?"

"No."

After a little while Miss Lucy said, "If I knew he loved me it would make all the difference."

"How can you not know whether somebody loves you?" Mama Linnet said.

"You maybe can tell that, I can't. If he's practicing, I wish he'd try saying something in the ballpark of 'I love you.' Never ever has he said anything close."

Mama Linnet said, "I bet he will."

DADDY AND GRANDDADDY were both in harm's way, Granddaddy the most, as best we could tell. Daddy was in North Africa, and it was cloudy to most Americans what exactly our troops were doing there. But it was clear the dangers Granddaddy was exposed to on Guadalcanal were extreme. Mama Linnet did everything she could to keep these two men real to me and at the same time downplay the risk they were in. She didn't succeed in preventing my fears for them, since war news was everywhere.

Also I was secretly so afraid of the Japanese that to know Granddaddy was near their land was enough to make me terrified for him. As I should have been, and as Mama Linnet secretly was.

The Japanese had been driven off Guadalcanal and were determined to get it back, or least to keep the US from being able to use it as the crucial base it was. Every kind of fighting went on there and in the waters around it. Ships' cannons, airplane bombing and strafing, land artillery, bazookas, grenades, hand-to-hand. And worst of all, to a little girl's mind, flame throwers. This warfare was constant and we saw it in the movie newsreels.

Granddaddy wrote two or three times every week, saying he had not a scratch, and furthermore had managed to avoid the jungle disease that was taking down so many Seabees and fighting men. He never again, after his very first letter, referred to any half-hope that the war might kill him. He said he and his mates were working until they dropped, and it was like a dream because they rebuilt the same things over and over and the Japanese persistently tore them up again. Many of his letters came uncensored, or mostly so. They each read about the same. Here was a man who was going to write his wife, no matter what, and no matter that there was nothing new to say. Although he wrote often, we got the letters in batches with scary spaces of time between, once as long as three weeks. This went on during September, October, and half of November 1942, and then his letters stopped for a week . . . a month . . .

IN EARLY DECEMBER on a Sunday afternoon Mama Linnet's telephone woke her from her doze in her desk chair. I was taking up her bed, preferring it to my own in my little annex room. I sprawled with my shoes off on her white bedspread, reading my funnybook. One funny book was my every-Sunday indulgence paid for by Mama Linnet after I selected it with terrible care from its rivals in the rack inside the door of the drug store on our route home from Sunday School and church.

She roused and answered the ring.

"Hampton? Is that you? . . . Speak louder, sweet. Where are you? . . . Are you in the United States? . . . What hospital? . . . How bad is it? . . . No, you have to tell me . . . I need you to talk louder if you can, sweet . . . Is there anybody there who could help you talk to me? . . . Hello, yes, this is his wife, are you his doctor? . . . Oh, John, are you his room-mate? . . . You're in a hallway? He sounds like he needs a doctor right now, can you help him? . . ." and soon they ended that call.

She turned to me and said, "Your grandfather is back safe in the United States. He has a little wound in his legs and he's in Walter Reed Hospital. That's in Washington, D.C. I'm going there. I'll leave tonight if I can get the right train."

"I want to go!" I said.

"I can't take you this time."

"Yes!" I screamed.

"I don't know what-all I'll need to do up there. I don't know how long I'll be there. There would be nobody up there to watch you for me."

"Don't leave me! I won't have anybody! I'm scared!" I screamed. I came up off the bed and threw myself at her, clinging like a huge baby monkey.

She petted my hair, and eventually she spoke, said not to cry, she would take me.

ON OUR WAY to D.C. the trains were packed with young soldiers and sailors. Most of the men were on leave, often short leave, trying to get home if only for a day. Home might be clear across the nation. Or else they were trying to return to base before their AWOL deadline put them in the brig. The train seats were taken, the aisles were taken. The boys in the aisles sat on their duffel bags if space allowed, or just stood and leaned.

But each time we boarded a train and Mama Linnet steered me by one hand ahead of her up the little steps, tugging her big brown suitcase behind us, the sea of navy blue and khaki parted for her as if she were a queen. The only boys who didn't jump up and try to make us take their seats were the ones who hadn't seen us yet. Whoever the women of their hearts actually were, Mama Linnet was the substitute on the train ride. The men couldn't do enough for me either, but it was mostly because I was hers. One time she nodded off and I was awake, and they talked me out of our double seat so that she could stretch out a little. To entertain me they taught me to play gin rummy in a little pushed-back space they made in the aisle beside her.

WE ARRIVED in D.C. late in a morning, in the slush of a snow, and took a cab straight to the hospital. There, we were up against something she had warned me might happen: they wouldn't let children past the lobby. Somehow she talked a woman at a desk behind glass into babysitting me. She paid her on the sly.

More than two hours dragged by before she came back, and I had been quietly crying for an hour. I had refused to talk to the nice big woman who was helping us. Mama Linnet asked her if she knew a cheap decent hotel nearby, and she said she did except it was not really cheap if you were used to small town prices. She said a lot of people asked her that question.

By the end of our third day in this big unknown city Mama Linnet had got enough information from Granddaddy and his doctors to make a plan.

His legs were terribly wounded. He had had basic emergency surgery on both of them overseas, and the doctors now said he should not have any more operations for the time being. At worst he might not walk again. At best it would be three to six months before it could be known whether he would.

Also she suspected something might be wrong with his mind, although the doctors brushed that off. She thought it might be shell shock.

She prepared in her mind to change the direction of her life, putting all her other responsibilities and aims into the background so that she could devote herself to helping him heal. She stood ready to give up all that she had worked for plus her hard-earned personal independence, if need be, for him.

She was determined to get him home and to a hospital there as soon as she could talk the doctors into letting him go. She didn't trust these doctors. They were always in a hurry and sometimes didn't tell her everything.

It took Mama Linnet two weeks to get everything in hand, and then she and I left D.C. on the train to go home.

GRANDDADDY WAS SHIPPED home in an airplane. Mama Linnet was able to make this happen only because Granddaddy knew someone who knew Someone. As he always did. He had a lot of friends. He arrived the day after we did, and was taken in an ambulance from the airport to the Baptist Hospital.

He was discharged from the Seabees, and for once he listened to Mama Linnet and put his pride down and accepted a disability pension. He said he did that only to ease her mind, that he had plenty of money stashed away and would be on his feet again faster than the doctors said.

Mama Linnet had arranged for a specialist doctor for him, one who was, as Granddaddy put it, "Not that highfalutin guy who wants to marry you."

For two weeks she went to the hospital briefly in the mornings and again late every afternoon, when she stayed with him until early evening. But as he began to get a little stronger and she tried to talk of his coming to Fourth and Victory to finish his recovery, he wouldn't speak about that. She insisted they discuss it, and he said, "I'm not coming to you as a cripple. When I get back on my feet is when we'll get back together."

She said several times in different ways, "You can't stay in the hospital until you fully recover, it will be too long, they won't allow it. And if you won't let me take care of you and help you, then who will it be? Where will you go? Someone will have to be with you. Also someone will have to see to your money for you."

"I'll take care of myself when the time comes," he said, or, "I can make my own arrangements."

She had kissed him only once in all this time, and that was in D.C. when she first found his hospital room, where he was sleeping. After that she had not touched him again unless by accident while fetching him something or smoothing his pillow or covers.

Now, twice in two days, sitting at his bedside, she caught the smell of alcohol. But hospitals have alcohol, and at first she dismissed her alarm. He always had buddies, though, popping up wherever he was. Some here at home had happened to come to see him while she was there.

So the day came when she broke routine and went to the hospital in the middle of the day, and instead of going to his room she stayed in the waiting room on his floor and sat in a chair with a view of his door. Soon one of his boyhood friends—Mama Linnet knew the man, but he didn't notice her—went in briefly, and came out and left.

Next came Miss Sara Ann. She stayed in his room for the length of time a teacher could, on a lunch hour. When she came out she saw Mama Linnet. Their gazes locked. Miss Sara Ann's step missed a beat, then she walked on pretending they hadn't seen each other.

As soon as Miss Sara Ann was gone Mama Linnet went to Granddaddy and said for him to tell her the truth.

He didn't even sit up in the bed. He said, "I'll probably

get a divorce and marry her." He opened his mouth to go on, but she told him she didn't want to hear it.

She said, "Tell her to get out of my house before dark."

He tried to complain it was impossible, and she said she didn't want to hear that either, and turned to go. But he grabbed her arm.

"There's something you don't know," he said. "I didn't know how to tell you. I can never come back to you as your husband. I have the Bad Disease."

Her legs shook and she crumpled onto the visitor chair.

"I've had it for a while."

Her voice was thin as a child's. She said, "They've got penicillin now."

"The shots are not helping me. I've had it too long. It's in my nerves, they think."

"If this is true, why did your doctors not tell me?" she said.

"I told them not to."

"Hampton, I can't talk to you anymore right now. I don't know if I'll be back," she said.

She left the room and walked down the hall carefully because of still feeling faint. But halfway she stopped, and turned around and went back to him. She stood holding her pocketbook under one arm and with her free hand steadying herself by holding onto his bed rail. She looked down into his face.

"If you can never be a husband to me, what about her?" she said.

He only stared into her eyes.

"She has it too? Is that it?" she said.

He put his gaze on the far wall and remained silent.

BACK AT FOURTH AND VICTORY, dark came and Miss Sara Ann had not set foot there. Mama Linnet unlocked the door to Miss Sara Ann's room, and went downstairs and waited for Tom to come home. She told him, without explanation, to take Miss Sara Ann's clothes and every other possession to the alley and put them beside the trash barrels. She said, "If they're still there tomorrow night, burn them."

After he got past his shock he said, "Miz Lewis, I'd never side against you on anythang but I don't think I could burn somebody's thangs."

She said, "That's fine. Just get them out. I'll burn them myself."

But Tom, or somebody, managed to get word to Miss Sara Ann. That night about midnight a truck stopped in the alley with its headlights still on, and Mama Linnet watched the silhouettes of a woman and a man getting her things.

MAMA LINNET BURNED sage in the empty room that had been Miss Sara Ann's. I was stumped as I watched her walking slowly around, carrying a white plate to catch the little ashes, waving and blowing the smoke into the very corners, and the back of the closet, and the empty opened drawers. Never had she done this when a renter left, and I asked her why.

She said, "I'm . . . fumigating it, you could say."

"What's that?"

"Getting rid of anything bad that might still be in here," she said.

"Like roaches?"

"Not exactly," she said.

"Like germs? Why wasn't the Lysol enough? You washed everything. Twice."

"Sometimes you need the old ways. This is what my grandmother would have done. Your great-great-grandmother. She was Cherokee Indian."

MAMA LINNET RECEIVED A DIVORCE NOTICE.

She took the paper across the street to consult with The Lawyer Cato, who told her, "If you want to let him get this divorce you can take the do-nothing option. But if you want to contest it, I'll help you."

"I don't want to contest it," she said.

"Then please accept my concurring opinion. Setting him free once and for all is a good move."

"Hampton can pretend he's free if he wants to. What God has joined together no man can put asunder. But also I believe in rendering unto Caesar," she said. "My legal affairs will be a lot simpler once he's not in there to be considered. I want you to remove him soon as you can, starting with my will."

Mama Linnet and The Lawyer Cato were talking in his comfortable sunny parlor. He had kept the room furnished as Eleanor Tabor left it except for clearing knickknacks off the long white marble-topped coffee table. He used that as a makeshift desk at times like this. He liked this room better than the office, which was toward the back of the house. He now sat relaxed on the sofa, which was upholstered in silk brocade, and she sat on one of a pair of velvet chairs.

After she had consulted him about her own business she didn't move to leave. Instead she told him there was something else they needed to talk about. But she didn't go on.

After waiting, he said, "Mrs. Lewis, you know I'm not good at feelings. I would help you tell me whatever it is, if I could."

"I know," she said. "Hampton has the Bad Disease."

He said nothing.

"And it's likely Sara Ann has it."

He said nothing.

"Willard, you've dated her," she said. "And now you're dating Lucy."

He said nothing. Finally, as if waking someone from a stupor, she said, "Willard!"

He in fact did startle. Then he said, "You have my word there's nothing to worry about where I'm concerned. Between Sara Ann and me, to be perfectly frank. And so nothing where Lucy's concerned. I know you and Lucy are good friends. Are you going to tell her? I beg you not. My situation with her is . . . not as clear as I would like. That's due to my own mistake, which I can't explain even to myself. But Lucy and I have been doing a lot better. I was considering proposing marriage at some point. This news would throw her for another loop. Could you at least wait a while?"

"What if I asked you to swear on the Bible that you didn't . . . have relations . . . with Sara Ann?" she said.

"I would do that. Just a minute."

Without giving her a chance to reply he left the room and almost immediately came back with a huge black Bible. He thrust it into the space between them with one hand underneath it and the other on top, and said, "I swear to you before God that I what I told you is the truth."

She said, "Goodness. All right. My lips are sealed. And Willard, I have two suggestions. One is, tell Lucy outright that you love her: say, 'I love you.' No lawyer talk, just 'I love you.' Practice that out loud by yourself first, so you can be sure you can say it. Say it to her today or at very most tomorrow. The other thing is, stop waiting to propose. Give her a day or two after you tell her you love her, and then ask her to marry you. And do it in a romantic way."

"Could you help me with exactly what to say when I propose?" he said.

CHIEF SYMMONDS TRIED three times in one day to telephone Mama Linnet with news about Savory. It was about six months after their first talk, and she had long since assumed he'd dismissed the problem. He phoned again, after hours, but before going home to his wife.

"She finally surfaced in New Orleans. I was pretty sure she'd be there, but nothing showed up until recently. She took over a little restaurant, and her name's beginning to show up in records for taxes and permits and inspections and so forth. The food is out of this world."

"You've been there?" Linnet said.

"I was down there about something else."

"Did you talk to her? Does she know I want to get in touch?" she said.

"I told her you regret what happened, and that you were worried about the little girl missing her so much. She didn't have a lot to say. Maybe after she thinks on it she'll get in touch. But I'd be surprised if she'd leave there. That restaurant will be on the map soon as a place to eat. She's already making money."

"What's the name of it?" she said.

"*Cyrille's.* She gave it that name after she took over. Cyrille is her middle name, and was her mother's and grandmother's name. Probably you knew all that."

"I didn't. You must have done a lot of research," she said.

"She's an interesting person." He paused there but didn't go on with that. He said, "I got a few of her mimeographed menus, with the address and phone, and I'll have my secretary mail you a couple. She said give one to the little girl. Or I could bring it to you on my way home if you'd rather."

"Oh Chief Symmonds, thank you so much for all you've done for us. I wouldn't want to put you out more. The mail will be fine," she said.

16

Miss Claire had taken up the task of answering the doorbell after Savory left. On a clear morning early in May of 1943 it rang, and when she went there and peered through the lace curtain on the door window she saw an Asian man in a business suit holding a small suitcase. He was too short to be her husband. Her heart surged from hope and dread. She asked him in and when he identified himself she led him to the sitting room. Thirty minutes later she followed him back to the door. Tears drenched her face, and this time it was she who carried the suitcase. He left with only a few more words, and she shut the door slowly, and locked it only after she had watched him walk away down the sidewalk and around the corner, out of sight. Then she turned to the stairs and carried the light belongings of her dead husband up to the room she and her son had been calling their temporary home.

She waited until that night to tell Roger/Tian about the plane crash.

And she waited until the next month, when his school let

out for the summer, to tell him he would have to get a full-time job. And that he might have to keep it, they maybe couldn't afford for him to go back to school in the fall for his high school junior year.

———

ROGER/TIAN asked Dr. Haynes Senior for help finding a full-time job, and that night the doctor showed up as a paying customer for supper at Fourth and Victory. When Miss Claire brought food for the table where he sat, he made an appointment to speak with her after she finished her duties. He had come in his car. He had unlimited gasoline because he was a doctor, and he left after he ate, and came back two hours later, well after dark. He and Claire sat alone on the front porch and talked for an hour in the near-dark.

The next day Dr. Haynes Senior phoned Mama Linnet.

"Yes, Harry," she answered.

"I need to ask about something I heard. Whether it's true. Rumor has it that Hampton Lewis is saying he's divorced."

"He will be, yes, when the papers go through," she said.

"May I ask if you're all right with that?"

"Are you all right with your broken marriage? How could anybody be?" she said.

"What I mean is, could this make things different between you and me? All the things I've said to you before are still true." And once started, he couldn't stop. "I love you. I'll always love you. I want to lay myself and everything I've got at your feet. I don't want you to work another day in your life. And I think you love me, or could if you'd let yourself, and I know you like me, and that's enough to start out with. I want you to marry me. It doesn't have to be right now. You're probably still getting your balance back after Hampton, and his injuries, and his alcoholism, and his divorce, and all that. I can wait if you say you'll marry me."

"No," she said.

"Why?"

"If I married you I couldn't be myself anymore. I'm just beginning to be myself, and I want to keep on. I don't expect you to understand that, or agree it's true," she said.

"If you married me you could be anything you want, do anything you want, any time you want."

"I know you think that." She took a breath and said, "Harry, you're the finest man I've ever known. I'm very honored by your proposal, but I can't."

DR. HAYNES SENIOR phoned Mama Linnet again one night soon after she had told him no, and this time his words in her ear were as if from a different man. Their conversation was short, and when they hung up she sat looking at the black phone a few seconds before getting up. Then she went upstairs and knocked on Miss Claire's door, and together they took a trip to the kitchen for a quiet talk.

Dr. Haynes Senior came calling for Miss Claire soon, one evening in late May. He wore a tuxedo that had been tailored precisely for his tall thin body. He was exactly on time, and Roger/Tian let him in. Miss Claire was waiting at the top of the stairs in a floor-length black satin dress and matching shoes, with a simple tiara in her hair. She carried a small jeweled bag. She came down the wooden staircase with her dancer's grace, and as she neared the bottom steps the doctor lifted his hand and her fingers took it. Roger/Tian watched as the doctor placed her shawl wrap around her bare shoulders, as she took his arm, and as the elegant couple stepped outside to his gleaming black car and drove away to the opening night of a play at the Haynes Auditorium.

FROM HER PEEKING place in the sitting room Janna continued bouncing little Tonna on her hip to keep her quiet after the pair were gone. She was pregnant. She nodded in agreement with what she was silently saying to herself.

Later, upstairs in their room when Tom came in, as soon as he shut the door she told him about about the stylish couple and said to him, "I wish you could 'a seen 'em. Tom, someday you're going to buy me evening dresses like that, and high heeled shoes with just thin little straps around the ankle, and pay for me to have beauty shop hairdos, and little diamonds in my hair. And I'm going to be looking at you all handsome in a fancy black suit with a black bow tie and a sash around your middle like a king or a earl and little diamond buttons down your shirt and gold buttons on your cuffs. And you're going to drive us downtown to the theater in a big shiny car *all the time.*"

She watched his eyebrows rising and his mouth stretching into his grin, and she stopped him, tapping his chin with her forefinger. She said, "No, it's gonna happen. You're gonna to be a rich businessman. And the first thing we gotta do is learn you to read and write. Set down."

WA 168 65 GOVT=WUX WASHINGTON DC 8 1243P
MRS LINNET C LEWIS=
FOURTH STREET AT VICTORY STREET LC=

DEEPLY REGRET TO INFORM YOU THAT YOUR SON
LT PATRICK DANIEL LEWIS IS MISSING IN ACTION IN
THE PERFORMANCE OF HIS DUTY AND SERVICE OF
HIS COUNTRY. I REALIZE YOUR GREAT ANXIETY BUT
DETAILS NOT AVAILABLE AND DELAY IN RECEIPT
THEREOF MUST BE EXPECTED. LETTER FOLLOWS.

A man on a bicycle delivered this Washington, D.C. Army General's telegram on the afternoon of the first Sunday in August, 1943. Mama Linnet signed for it and as she did her hands began to shake and kept on shaking so that she couldn't read it. I held it for her and watched her tears come before she got to the bottom. Her body righted itself and then she took the paper with her own hands, and read it again.

"Tell me," I begged.

I could see her deciding. She sat down on the visitor's bench and patted it so that I would climb up there beside her. The yellow telegram in my hand glowed in a ray of the afternoon's bright slanted light.

"Your daddy might be missing. Right now we don't know for sure where he is."

"The Army lost him?" I said.

She said maybe they did.

I began to wail, "No. No. My poor Daddy is lost," and on.

She said, "But now listen, they might be mistaken about who it is. Lewis is one of the most common names, and the telegram says 'Lieutenant' but he is a Second Lieutenant. He was as last we knew, anyway."

WE LEARNED LATER that Daddy disappeared early in the Allied invasion of Sicily. He was with amphibious troops who left from Tunisia and found themselves in a pandemonium of horrible weather and military mix-ups.

IN A FEW MINUTES after the telegram Mama Linnet had pulled herself together. She told me to go wash my face and hands and put on the dress I had worn to Sunday School and church that morning. She said, "We need to go and see your mother. She probably got a telegram before I did."

But Mother didn't know about Daddy.

Mama Linnet gently told her and the first thing she said was, "Oh, my husband is dead. My daughter is fatherless." Next, "Why did they tell you and not me?"

"I don't know," Mama Linnet said. "But it's only that he's missing, and that's only if they're talking about the right man."

"Do they not know I'm his wife?" Mother said, with her voice rising.

Big Mimi said, "Child," and tried to take Mother's hand but she flapped the touch away.

"Am I not his wife? Has he gone off and divorced me and then died? What is happening?" Mother talked on higher and louder until soon she was screaming.

Big Papa eased over to me and led me out of the room by

the sleeve of my dress. He sat me at the kitchen table and got me a bottle of Pepsi from the refrigerator. He moved slowly, and I suddenly saw that he looked old and tired. He sat down across from me, tapping on the table while we listened to the three of them.

Finally Big Mimi's voice said, "Linnet, I guess you-all better go on. When she gets full-blown like this, she just has to wear herself out. I'm sorry this happened in front of The Little Child."

OUR CITY HAD a parade every October as the opening event of the State Fair. Good times and bad, Great Depression and World War or no, we had the parade. This year everyone especially welcomed it as a bright spot on the calendar, even though the planners had had to reach deep to the bottom of the barrel to make a real parade of it. A good turnout of watchers lined both sides of Main Street on the pretty fall afternoon. Mama Linnet and I stood with them and watched the handmade floats roll by, the first two on flatbed trucks and the other three pulled by horses and mules. The floats were decorated mostly with hay bales and crêpe paper, and carried pretty girls with lots of lipstick who were chilly in their evening dresses, and men who were this or that official, all waving at us. The band from the white high school had already drummed and honked its way by, and the black high school band, which everybody knew would have the best music plus a spectacular drum major, was still to come but we could hear them. After the floats there came about two dozen horses with riders. The horses passing by were big and loud-clomping, and I drew back unnecessarily. But then a horse and rider coming toward us caught my attention. They were different.

The horse was smaller and dappled gray, with a black mane braided into about twenty perfect knots spaced evenly down her neck. Her black tail was free and shining. Her pretty-prancing hooves were black and polished. She was full of herself, wanting to get on with it. Her rider was a straight-backed young woman in a black jacket, tan jodhpurs, and stove pipe black boots that came to her knees. She was smiling slightly. A simple braid of light brown hair hung down her back. The saddle was so little it seemed to disappear, leaving only the horse and rider who were pleased to show they were one being. I was wholly taken with wanting to be that. Do that. That horse-and-rider-unit. The desire was an epiphany that flooded me while the pair was in front of me. It washed away the confusions and fears of my early childhood and replaced them with a full clear Wanting. I was transformed from a child with a drifting soul to a girl on a quest.

The rest of the parade was vague through the filter of my longing.

When it was over, as Mama Linnet and I were walking home, she said, "You're quiet. Do you feel all right?"

"Would you get me a horse?" I said.

After a short time she said, "Yes. You can have a horse if you want one."

I threw my arms around her hips. "Oh Mama! Thank you. When? Tomorrow? What color can it be?"

She explained we'd need first to find a place for a horse to live, and we had a discussion about why that couldn't be the back yard. She said, "We can find somebody with some pasture and a barn just outside of town and pay them to board it. I can drive you there on weekends." And when I said I wanted to be with my horse every day, all the time, she added, "I can take you some weekday afternoons too. You have to go to school, remember."

Before we'd reached the house she'd learned it was the dappled horse and her rider who had inspired me. She said, "I noticed them too. I think I'll find out who that young lady is."

And she did, within a week. My heroine's name was Miss Georgia Teague and she was to become both my equestrian mistress and the caretaker of my horse.

THE NIGHT before Mama Linnet first drove me to Old Oaks to meet Miss Georgia Teague, a golden foal was born there.

That morning, as soon as we introduced ourselves, Miss Georgia said, "There's something you just have to see," and she led us to the barn to a mare and her newborn baby. Miss Georgia had had no sleep and was still in the state of spiritual joy that comes of having been part of a birth.

Inside the barn, in its shade, the mare was a deep bay color, and she looked us over intelligently and then accepted us. She was Miss Georgia's personal horse and had known nothing but good from humans. The baby was trying out her new legs, stepping and hopping around the stall. She noticed us and stopped in a spotlight of morning sun that came through a window. She stood shining, foursquare, surprised, nostrils wide. Her mane would later be black and fine and long, but now it was still charcoal and fuzzy above her face with its big eyes.

As I took in Fair Ellen—I hadn't yet named her then—

Miss Georgia's voice came to my ears as part of the living fairytale I was in. "We weren't expecting her to be a buckskin at all, much less a golden."

Mama Linnet said, "Do you think, a redder gold when she's older?"

"I do," Miss Georgia said.

"Would you buy her for me?" I said to Mama Linnet.

Miss Georgia saved Mama Linnet from having to struggle out an answer that would disappoint me. She said, "Baby horses have to stay with their mothers and belong just to them until they get bigger. But you could be her main person if you like. The one to take care of her and train her. I could show you how."

And so began my own newborn life in the spirit of the horse.

———

WE WERE VISITING Mother only about once a month now, and I was eager to tell her about Fair Ellen. In the past I had not had enough to talk to Mother about, and now I had been saving up the highlights, writing them down in my new equestrian journal that Miss Georgia suggested I keep, looking forward to sharing them. Also I had overheard Miss Georgia praising me to Mama Linnet, saying I was a born horsewoman. I thought Mother would join in the pleasure of all this and be cheered herself. But when I began to tell her, before I'd got out more than a little of it she said, "You can't do that anymore! It's too dangerous."

An icy fear numbed me. I didn't even start to cry, just sat staring at her.

"I won't have it," she said. "Don't you so much as go near

those horses one more time, any horse big or little, do you hear me?" she said, with her voice rising in pitch and loudness in that way I knew to dread.

Mama Linnet rose from where she had been sitting to chat with Big Mimi, and came and took me by the hand and led me to the front door. Big Mimi followed us, but so did Mother.

Mother said, "Linnet Lewis, don't you dare let my child ride horses. I forbid it. I will sue you and put you in jail if I have to, to keep her away from them. She's all I've got left. You swear on a Bible right now that you won't let her. Mother! Where is a Bible?"

Big Mimi put out an elbow and steadily pushed Mother back from the door, and opened it enough for Mama Linnet to slide herself and me out.

In the car, Mama Linnet concentrated on getting us away and on down the street before she looked over at me. I was staring into space. She said, "It's going to be all right, Mary Mavis." I hardly heard her. She reached over and patted me, and because she found my body was rigid she steered the car to the curb and leaned across and put both arms around me in a hug I was barely aware of and didn't respond to.

IN THE LAWYER CATO'S parlor that night he said, "Mrs. Lewis, could I caution you. A petition for guardianship of a child over the objections of a natural parent might not be granted. I don't have personal experience with such a case, but I would expect the process could be upsetting for all parties concerned. Including that it could be traumatic for the child herself."

"I understand," Mama Linnet said. "We need to go ahead. This child's mother is not in her right mind, and her father is missing and could be dead, and I am the only one she has left. She needs me to be able to make the right decisions, what is best for her."

"Cesarine has not been legally declared incompetent?" he said.

"That's right. But I'm sure her parents will back me."

"You haven't informed them yet what you plan to do?"

"I thought I'd talk to you first tonight, so we'll know more, and then share it with them tomorrow."

"Why do you think they would side with you against their daughter? Remember here, I have to be the devil's advocate."

"Yes. Well, Cesarine's mother, Gladys Lambert, and her father, Roy, are at their wits' end trying to hold Cesarine together. She's living with them, you knew that? Gladys and I have gotten to be friends."

He looked up from taking notes and said, "Does the child have an inheritance or income that her legal guardian would control?"

"That wouldn't matter. But if she has an inheritance from Cesarine's side, I wouldn't know. From her father's side of the family, you already know what's in my will. I guess that amounts to something. Hampton has nothing to speak of but I made him arrange for her to inherit half of anything he ever might have. He'll probably leave it that way. Pat has nothing unless there is some military benefit . . . if it should be he really doesn't come back. Mary Mavis does have a monthly service allotment from him that comes to me. . . . I don't know if they will keep sending it . . . I've been putting it in a bank account for her, and adding a little to it. I thought it would be nice for her to have when she turns twenty-one. That's all I can think of."

As he jotted those things down she said, "I hadn't realized: it does amount to some money. But this is not about money."

His eyes met hers over the top of his glasses and said, "We can hope Cesarine and her parents are of the same mind," and he finished on that note. He said, "Do you want me to explore what you can expect regarding her monthly service allotment and survivor benefit?"

"I'd rather not know for the time being," she said.

AT THE SAME time that evening, at the Lamberts' house, Mother was talking low and constantly to Mimi. She followed Mimi, who had left the house's sun room to wander without any purpose out into the fallen leaves of the back yard, around it, and into the house again.

"I want you to say you'll help me get my daughter away from that woman. If you don't say you will, I'll leave and take her and you'll never see either one of us again. I would do it. I have the money. I've already got a lawyer, and he'll go the police anytime I say. I could have him put Linnet Lewis in jail for kidnapping and child endangering. He said I could have you and Papa charged as accomplices if it comes to that."

Mimi had heard this several times already, and didn't repeat her rebuttals. But, same as ever since Mother was a child, there had come this time when she finally won.

"All right," Mimi said. "I'll talk to Linnet tomorrow. The Little Girl can stay with us for a while."

"Right now. Call her *now* and tell her to get Mary Mavis' things together *now*. Papa can drive over and get her."

"Leave me out of it," Pawpaw said from the kitchen.

MAMA LINNET SAID into her telephone, "No Gladys. I won't bring her over there to live, what can you be thinking?" And she said, "But you know it wouldn't be good for the child, with Cesarine in the state she's in, I thought we had an understanding about that." And after whatever else Mimi said, Mama Linnet went on, "You know it's no particular danger for a child to ride a horse if she's taught how and supervised. Your family had horses, we all did. This is not really about the horse, with you, what is it about? Why would you want to do this to your granddaughter, tear her up by the roots out of her home with no notice? Damage her just when she's beginning to recover from all the things that have happened to her? Just when she's getting her feet under her in life *because* of horses? Deprive her of the one thing that gives her joy and heals her spirit after all she's been through? Do you have no love or even pity in your heart for this child? Why would you want to help Cesarine do this?"

Mimi's response was short and cold, same as her earlier words.

As Mama Linnet listened her back straightened and her chin raised. Her eyes widened. When it was time to speak again she said, "That's what you'll have to do then. Come to my door with your court order and the police. I will not help you hurt Mary Mavis."

17

In the office of the state's Attorney General at the State Capitol Building, the one telephone that served the four staff lawyers rang loud enough to bother everyone's ears. The shared secretary answered, laid down the receiver, and tiptoed to whisper and fetch Willard Cato from his desk in a back corner of the big room. He came and spoke to his caller briefly. Then he returned to his station to get his leather briefcase. His expensive black wool overcoat hung near the door on a hanger on a coat tree with others not as fine that were just hung up by their necks, and he folded it over his arm. He went to the closed door of his boss' frosted glass cubicle and rapped.

When his boss finally said, "What is it?" Willard opened the door and said, "I need to go for the day. Family matter."

"This is not a good time," said Assistant Attorney General #2.

Until today Willard would have explained that actually it was a good time. He would not have added that his work was only clerical anyway. Nor that he had scads of unused leave.

Before today Willard would have kowtowed in the accepted folkway of the staff lawyers, stopping just short of pleading.

But today he just said again, "Family matter," and turned to go.

"Willard, you know," his boss said, "there's a waiting line for every one of y'alls' jobs. I talk to at least a dozen a week of legislators and Governor's friends and cousins, and county judges who have sons and nephews who passed the bar and would give up sleeping with their wives and sweethearts to work here."

"I can give you my resignation verbally now, and on paper tomorrow," Willard said.

He might as well have said, 'checkmate.' His boss did not actually have the authority to hire and fire his own staff, or even accept resignations, and they both knew it.

Both of them were shocked at what Willard said, but Willard didn't show it.

"Go on then, if it's that important. Be ready to hit it hard tomorrow," his boss said.

Willard looked as if he might say more, but then only left.

HE HAD MEANT to go directly to Fourth and Victory to counsel with Linnet, whose voice had been so tight and unsteady when she phoned him. Instead, after he got behind the wheel of his roadster in its reserved space at the State Capitol, he drove to the Women's City Club Tea Room and went in through the kitchen entrance to see his bride.

Lucy kissed him hello in front of her two assistants, and asked them in the nicest way—she paused to imagine how

Linnet would have said it—to continue without her temporarily. She led Willard by the hand into her tiny office and shut the door.

He said, standing straight and stiff, "Ah need to know if it would be agreeable to you if I quit my job."

She kissed him again, putting her thin arms around his big chest, and he went less rigid.

She said, "Does this mean you're ready to found your own your law firm? Tell me you're going to make our dream come true."

"I believe I'm ready if you are. But . . . it shames me, darlin', but according to my figures we'll need at least two years of your salary to make it while my practice is accumulating clients. That said, we wouldn't have to give up anything else. And after those two years . . . "

She stopped him with another kiss and then said, "Something we never talked about—and this is not the place to do that, and we can discuss it later, but you need to know: I don't want to stop working. I want a career too. I don't want to be a housewife. And that's no disrespect to you. It's that I like having a responsible job that I'm good at."

"I can understand that," he said.

"So unless something happens to me, we can count on my salary. Oh tell me what your office sign will say. The one that will hang outside. I want to see it in my mind," she said.

He grinned and with his arms and hands indicated a large rectangle in the air. "Classic and simple. White background with a black border. Chocolate brown letters outlined in black and gold. First line: '*Willard J. Cato, P.A.*' Under that: '*Attorney at Law.*' Later when I take in a junior partner, or two, or three, I'll make it '*Cato and Associates Law Firm*' and maybe indicate specialties."

"I am the proudest woman in the world," she said.

"I have to go," he said, "they're trying to take Mary Mavis away from Linnet."

MAMA LINNET HAD STATIONED herself in Fourth and Victory's sitting room at the writing table so as to keep an eye outside on the front walkway in case Mimi's threat should come to pass. And it did. Looking up from her distracted attempts to catch up on bookkeeping, she saw the enemies getting out of a parked car and walking toward the front door. Mother, Mimi, a man in a business suit. Following them, getting out of his own marked car, a uniformed policeman. Mama Linnet recognized him from the murder investigation. His name was Dwight Madrue.

She hurried to her apartment and telephoned The Lawyer Cato. "They're here. Can you come." Then she went back up the hall and answered the door and let them in. She said, "Please have a seat. My lawyer will be here in five minutes."

Officer Madrue's eyes and Mama Linnet's met briefly, and he lowered himself down to sit, but not in one of the hallway chairs; instead, he went away from the group and sat on the staircase. He perched there turning his visored hat around and around, staring straight ahead. The others sat on the hallway bench and the chairs, silently. But Mother could not stay still or quiet. She got up and paced in front of Mama Linnet. She said, "I don't have to wait for your lawyer. Where is Mary Mavis? She's had time to get home from school." When Mama Linnet said nothing she said, "You're hiding her, aren't you? I knew it."

Their lawyer had taken over Mimi's role of trying to soothe Mother. He was interrupting her with unwanted information when The Lawyer Cato came through the door. He introduced himself to the general group, but with his eyes on the other lawyer. When the man disentangled himself from Mother he introduced himself to The Lawyer Cato as Guy Keaton and said, "My clients have Judge Bratton's order to immediately place the child in the custody of her natural mother."

"This is a temporary order, I take it?" The Lawyer Cato said, "May I see it please."

Keaton handed him the papers and Willard scanned the pages and then said to Mama Linnet, "Under the law the judge had no option but to grant their petition. We can contest it, but in the meantime you must let Cesarine Lewis have her."

Mother said, "There, see."

Mama Linnet was turning pale and her voice broke as she said, "I'll go get her."

"And I'll go with you," Mother said. "I'm not about to let you sneak her out the back door."

"Somebody stop her for the good of us all," Mama Linnet said, leaving down the hall. Mimi and the opponent lawyer blocked Mother's way. Even the policeman came out of his state and stood between her and the hallway.

I was in Mama Linnet's bedroom. She had kept me home from school that day, out of prudence. And she had prepared me. Also I had been listening through the transom to the scene at the front door. I sat slumped on the side of Mama Linnet's bed.

She said to me, "Remember what we talked about might

happen? Well, it did. Your mother has come to take you to stay with her for a while."

"I know," I whispered.

"You don't need to worry about Fair Ellen. Miss Georgia will take good care of her and exercise her and keep her company. I don't think you'll be gone longer than a day or two, and if you are I'll go out there myself and tell her you'll be back. Here's your coat. Look, this is a twenty-dollar bill I'm pinning in the right-hand pocket in case you need it. But you'll be back before you have a chance to use it. You won't be gone long. I'll pack a few of your things in a suitcase and have somebody bring that to you later."

"I'm scared," I said.

"About Fair Ellen?"

"About me," I said, still looking down.

"Honey, you'll be with your own mother and grandparents. They'll watch out for you. You don't need to be scared."

"I'm scared of Mother," I said.

It had never occurred to Mama Linnet that Mother might harm me. That thought went through her like an electric shock. What if my fear was a premonition?

She stepped outside the doorway and called down the hall, "Mr. Cato, would you come here a minute please." He came into her apartment and there was no place to take him quickly so that the child would not hear. She told him, in such a way that he knew she was saying more than she was saying, "Mary Mavis is *afraid* of Cesarine. I hadn't thought of it that she would be *afraid her mother would harm her,* but she is."

He comprehended. He said, "Let me speak to Keaton," and left. While he was gone they could hear Cesarine's angry voice raised above the others. In about five minutes he returned and said, "He has a grasp of it that he's on the wrong side, but his hands are tied. He did go out on a limb and get Cesarine's mother to promise him in front of the police officer that Mary Mavis will be within her eyesight at all times when she's not at school." He paused and searched Linnet's face, and said, "Linnet, when we ask for permanent guardianship you must be able to present yourself as law-abiding. You can't do that if you defy their court order. Your options are to let her go now, which would likely be tempo-rary, versus running a high risk of losing custody permanently."

Mama Linnet's eyes went unreadable to him and she didn't speak her next thought. *"My real options are to turn her over to someone who might kill her, or else run away with her forever. Dear Jesus tell me what to do."*

If an answer came she could not recognize it. There was only a white fog in her mind. She proceeded blindly to do whatever it was she would do.

I left Fourth and Victory that afternoon crying silently, submitting to my victorious mother's painfully tight hold of my hand.

ON MY FIRST night at Mimi and Pawpaw Lamberts' house Mimi put me to bed on a little sofa in her bedroom, upstairs. Soon she put on her gown and took some pills and went to her own bed across the room. I don't know if she thought I might be already asleep, she didn't say anything to me. She turned off the only lamp and almost right away she was quietly snoring.

I lay there in the dark on sofa cushions that felt wrong

and smelled wrong. My ears noticed a wind outside through the tops of the trees near the house. My bed was near that wall. I knew the wind was blowing toward me: branches scratched at the side of the house, and then at the window which was nearby.

Let us in. We want to get you with our dry little fingers and our big arms. Whap. We can get in there if we really want to. Whap slide scree. Scree. We might be working our way between the screen and the window. We could break the glass, you know, and reach in there. We could get inside you with our fingers, you remember what it's like to have fingers inside you, now don't you. Or we could take you. Or strangle you right where you are. Or scratch you and whip you to death.

THE NEXT MORNING they found I was gone.

"She was never really here," Mother said to her parents, "You made that up, and made me believe it so I'd be quiet. Now you act like you believe it. Stop saying, 'Here's her little bed on the love seat,' that's a lie too. Stop asking me if I know where she is. She wasn't here to begin with, I tell you. Stop following me around!"

Mimi and Pawpaw took turns, one watching Mother and the other searching the house and yard for me. "Look in the trash barrel too," she whispered to him.

After an hour Mother was saying to the space in front of her eyes, "Maybe I killed her. I think she was here and I killed her and maybe I drove off in the night with her little body and put her some place where no one could ever find her. I should kill myself so we can be together in heaven with Pat. He's dead. We can be our own happy family again."

Mama Linnet opened Fourth and Victory's door to Officer Magrue and Chief Symmonds. Her hands shook as she let them in, and when she faced them they still didn't say anything. Magrue was leaving it up to his boss, and Symmonds was still thinking what to say.

"Why are you here?" she said.

"The little girl's missing," Symmonds said, "The Lamberts are hoping she might have come back here."

"She's not here. She wouldn't come here, she thinks I've betrayed her. But can you help me look, just in case?"

Officer Magrue said, "I'll go look where I found her before," and he turned to the stairs.

"What?" said Symmonds.

Magrue said, "Two years ago. The Anthony Bishop homicide. She's the one who found the body and it scared her half to death. She hid and I found her."

Symmonds shook his head. "She is one unlucky little girl."

Magrue started up the steps and said to the world, "Hardest thing I ever did was yesterday, enforcing that crazy woman's custody order. I shouldn't have."

"Magrue there's no need to get emotional," Symmonds said.

DURING THE VAIN search of Fourth and Victory Mama Linnet realized Symmonds had said *hoping*: the Lamberts were *hoping* Mary Mavis had come back to Fourth and Victory, not *assuming* it. Her fear rose higher, and she tried to get more information out of the Chief. He only asked for other possible places I might go.

"The Old Oaks Equestrian Farm, it's about seven miles out Old Highway 11. She might have headed there. She knows the way. She loves it there. I'll call Georgia Teague, she's the owner, and tell her someone's coming. She and Mary Mavis are fond of each other. Look in the horse barn first, the stalls and the hayloft . . . But you have to tell me the truth. I know there's something you're not telling me. Do you have reason to think she's not all right?"

Magrue had returned and was standing with them, staring into Symmonds' face. Symmonds told Linnet as gently as he could that Cesarine's parents had committed her to the State Mental Institution to protect her from suicide, and that she had said she might have killed me and hidden my body. He said, "But now that's probably a hallucination. She's lost so much of her mind she doesn't know what's real and what's not."

I WASN'T at Old Oaks, and Georgia Teague joined in being upset. She and Mama Linnet agreed to notify each other of any news.

The temperature dove to twelve degrees that afternoon, and behind that came an ice storm from the plains that would last for hours. By evening an inch of ice encased everything outdoors. No cars moved. No person, no animal, no bird, left its dwelling, and the outside world paused on hold, suspending all life except for the millions of drizzle drops of water that fell and fell, and froze as they hit anything. There was silence except for the background rattling of the tiny freezing droplets, a constant ghostly sound. Instead of darkness there came a fog that captured the faintest light from anywhere and absorbed it into an eerie glow.

But in Mama Linnet's bedroom it was pitch dark. She spent that night sitting in her rocking chair, still and upright, wrapped in a quilt, in blind determined vigil for me. She knew that pure evil does exist and she had recognized it for what it was, coming over them with the ice as its sign or disguise. She was not afraid of it. From time to time she heard the cracks like rifle shots as the neighborhood's huge old trees broke and then the crashing as they fell, one after another, glazed with more burden than they could bear. When this happened she winced in reflex and said, "Thank you Jesus for not letting it hit the house," and went back to keeping spiritual protection over her granddaughter.

Mother managed to try to hang herself during the deep of that night no matter the Suicide Watch sign on the door of her room at the State Hospital. An orderly looked in on her before she was dead. But she had deprived her brain of oxygen for an unknown length of time. The doctor on call said the level of damage could not yet be determined, and he left an order for her next-of-kin to be notified. However, by then the phone lines were down.

THE TRAINS in November 1943 were even more crowded than during the early part of the war, and somehow no one questioned it when I, a lone seven-year-old girl, stood on my tiptoes and bought a ticket, and boarded the right train, and rode awake all night so as not to miss the stop at New Orleans.

In the New Orleans station I wandered until I found

what I was looking for: a panel of four pay telephones like the ones in the station in Little Rock. I got in line behind a woman who was talking into a phone. When she finished her call I asked her to dial for me because I was not tall enough. I gave her a quarter, which was the only coin I had. I said, "Here's the number," and carefully unfolded my worn-to-pieces copy of the Menu from Cyrille's. I had treasured it since Mama Linnet gave it to me six months ago. The woman handed my quarter back to me and used her own nickel to dial the call. When Miss Savory answered she said, "Just a minute," and handed the phone on its long cord to me. Then she hesitated and instead of leaving she took a stand beside me, to listen to my conversation. At one point I looked around at her and said into the phone to Miss Savory, "Yes, a lady is here," and handed her the phone.

Miss Savory said to the woman, "Miss, I don't know who you are but if you could stay with that little girl just long enough for me to get there, I'll pay you however much you want. I can be there inside an hour."

When Miss Savory arrived and the woman wouldn't take any money Miss Savory pulled a card out of her purse and gave it to her. "This is my restaurant," she said. "You eat free for the rest of your life."

MISS SAVORY TOOK me to *Cyrille's* and fed me, and while she prepared the place for the day's business she listened to everything I wanted to say. It was a togetherness the two of us were used to.

Near the end of our talk, when Miss Savory was making a place for me to nap in the big pantry, she said, "You can stay with me long as you want. But think how worried Miz Lewis is bound to be about you. Will you let me tell her you're with me? I promise you, I promise you, your mother ain't gonna get you."

THE POLICE STATION desk officer who dealt with the public at the downtown station in New Orleans had met plenty of haughty women but he was not prepared for tiny Miss Savory. In five minutes she prevailed in her demand to be passed up to a superior who would put her in touch with the Little Rock Chief of Police about a missing person she wouldn't name.

Then to the superior officer she said, "He knows the missing person personally, and he knows me personally. He'll want to talk to me. Ask him. What have you got to lose? Your job, is all."

In Little Rock the phone lines for the public were still mostly lying fallen on the ground, buried in ice, but the priority lines had been patched. The call went through.

Chief Symmonds in Little Rock said to the New Orleans lieutenant, "Yes I know her. You're not bothering me. She's right, there is a missing person. Put her on the line."

The New Orleans detective said to himself, "Ya just never know."

When Savory was sure she was talking to Symmonds she said, "Tell this man here to go away and let me talk to you in private."

Symmonds did, and the detective left.

"Now," she said. "You know you can trust me, can I trust you?"

"Go on," he said.

"Can I trust you?"

"You can trust me," he said.

"The little girl, Mary Mavis Lewis, is with me. She needs me to protect her from her crazy mother, and I intend to do it. And I *can* do it. You got that?"

"Got it," he said.

"I need you to do two things. Tell Linnet Lewis—and only her, don't tell nobody else or you'll mess this up—tell her the child is with me, and she's fine. Miz Lewis can come fetch her when the time is right. And the other thing: help her get the legal say-so over the child. You help her."

"I'll do everything I can," he said.

"You know what? I believe you will."

He said, "Tell me one more thing. How did you manage to get the girl?"

It had not occurred to Savory that he would think she'd personally managed to come and get me away from Mother. She digested that and then her answer came out mixed with chuckles. "Keep your promises to me and someday I'll tell you, High Chief."

Miss Savory and Mama Linnet were of the same mind that I should stay in New Orleans until Mama Linnet was legally my guardian and the chance of further uproar had died down.

Mama Linnet mailed Miss Savory the papers necessary to enroll me in an elementary school. It was the middle of the school year but still I did well there in my new fresh start. The principal placed me in first grade, then in a week moved me up to second, and soon up again so that I was one of the smug third-graders. Third-graders were top of the heap, and just old enough to know how to let their underlings keep it in mind. I had never been a member of any group before, much less one accepted as superior. I picked up immediately how to act, and I liked it. It was a good school, and at last I had some friends and playmates who were real.

———

BACK WHEN MAMA LINNET and Miss Savory had made the decision for me to stay in New Orleans for an indefinite time, Mother was an invalid. She had stayed in a coma as the result of her suicide attempt. Mimi and Pawpaw were taking care of her at their house because they could not afford a nursing home.

Mother's spirit never came back, and in February her silent body drew its last breath.

Mimi and Pawpaw were exhausted and bankrupt.

The Lawyer Cato advised Mama Linnet to act fast, and she authorized him to put the papers in front of Mimi and Pawpaw to give up any claim to my guardianship without provision. They signed without a word.

———

MISS SAVORY SAID to Mama Linnet on the phone that I must be told that Mother had died. Mama Linnet said she worried that the news might cause me still another setback. But Miss Savory said, "It would be worse not to tell her. She already half-knows. I'm not about to keep it from her, she trusts me.

You would say the same if she was with you. Since I'm here and you're not, let me tell her." And so it was Miss Savory who told me.

Mama Linnet soon came to New Orleans on the train. She saw for herself how I was, where I lived with Miss Savory, where I went to school, what *Cyrille's* was like, and the city itself. She was satisfied about me, and couldn't get enough of New Orleans. She stayed a second day, keeping me out of school and taking me all over the city. It was the only big city she had ever been to except for Washington, D.C. where she had had no thought of sightseeing.

She and Miss Savory decided it would be best for me if I kept on where I was until school let out for summer. It was what I wanted too, after Mama Linnet assured me it wouldn't hurt her feelings.

She came on the train two more times to be with me for an afternoon and overnight in a hotel, and once she brought Janna McNee with her. Janna was pregnant. Mama Linnet said Janna shouldn't get any older before seeing New Orleans. Tom McNee had to stay home and babysit little Tonna.

When school ended in May of 1944 Mama Linnet came one more time, to take me home.

Saying goodbye to Miss Savory, I cried. But she said some things that made me feel better. One of them was that she would come get me next summer for a stay with her if I wanted to. And she said, "Ain't that right, Miz Lewis." And Mama Linnet said yes it was.

AFTERWORD

When I got back to Fourth and Victory in the late spring of 1944, the life there was different even though I had barely been gone six months.

The only boarders left that I knew were Tom and Janna McNee and little Tonna, who was now two-and-a-half. This family had added new twin baby boys. They now lived in what used to be my family's two-room apartment. Janna had taught Tom to read and was forbidding him to report that to the draft board.

Miss Claire and Roger/Tian were gone. She was now Mrs. Dr. Haynes Senior. Roger/Tian was now Roger Lee Haynes because he had consented to be adopted by Dr. Haynes Senior.

Mamma Linnet left Miss Claire's and Roger/Tian's room vacant in case Daddy came home.

There were two new boarders I didn't know. Both of them were nurses at the Catholic Hospital. (They weren't Catholic, Mama Linnet always felt it necessary to explain about them.) They left for work almost at dawn and came home early afternoons. Walking back and forth to work they wore identical outfits that impressed me: starched white caps and spotless white shoes, and white starched uniforms with starched bibs, and big navy blue wool capes.

I was comforted to know that Miss Lucy and The Lawyer Cato still lived across the street, at least that hadn't changed, and Miss Lucy was still in charge of the Tea Room. And now she also did the clerical work for *Willard J. Cato, P.A., Attorney at Law,* and she had run for and won a seat on the city council.

Mama Linnet had decided not to take in any more male boarders. She intended having Tom convert the men's floor into an apartment. She was savvy about the future, and figured soon there might be more demand for apartments than rooms-with-board. The future proved she was right. And she had her eye on another house that would probably come up for sale, the third and last in our same block. She said, "I think it would be nice to own a whole block in walking distance of Fifth and Main. Might be worth something someday."

What hadn't changed was Rationing, and the home effects of the war. New cars weren't being made anymore. Once or twice a week some man Mama Linnet didn't even know would ring the doorbell and try to get her to sell him her red truck or, second best, the Buick. There was a new product called Oleo that was supposed to replace butter. I would call Oleo a negative, I can't imagine anyone who wouldn't have. But as a positive there was Kraft Macaroni and Cheese, which not only tasted good but also was said to be a good substitute for meat. The new store-bought cottage cheese was also said to be a good substitute, but I couldn't understand why anyone would eat it.

I was eight years old and Fair Ellen was nine months old. On the morning of my second day home from New Orleans Mama Linnet drove us out to see her. When we arrived at Old Oaks in the Buick, Fair Ellen was far out in the pasture with her mother, and she turned to look hard at the car. She was still long-legged and gangly, but almost grown into a horse. She had fully shed her coarse winter coat, and her golden summer coat in the morning sun showed hints of the copper-red that would later be. Even while the car was still rolling she had galloped so hard to the fence between us she hardly stopped in time. She trotted alongside the car. When we came to a stop she stretched her head toward us, squealing and showing the whites of her eyes. As we got out of the car Miss Georgia was there to meet us, and she and Mama Linnet laughed and one of them said, "She's so nosey, always wanting to know everything." That's what they thought at first, but when I ran and climbed between the fence rails so that Fair Ellen and I could be together, plainly my horse was only interested in me.

The End

ABOUT THE AUTHOR

Ruth Byrn, 1938– , was born in the American south, where she still lives. She came to earth spang in the middle of the Silent Generation (Americans born mid-1920s to mid-1940s) and thinks it's accurate that these people are called both "the Lucky Few" and "grave and fatalistic." Her novel *Fourth and Victory* is not autobiographical; nevertheless, it draws from some of her first-hand childhood experiences of people, places, and events during the initial years of World War II.

Made in United States
Troutdale, OR
12/06/2024

25987216R00156